What People Are Sayi

M000098622

"As an educator, this is a book that I would highly recommend to my students in order for them to gain a better comprehension of history, a finer appreciation of other cultures, and an enhanced sense of how history impacts individuals. Personal accounts of history are always those that students remember most. They bring history itself vividly to life and allow students to keenly realize how politics, governments, and decisions made in "high places" can change, and even destroy, the lives of people we have come to care about." ~ *Patricia Silva, Educator*

"Poignantly illustrates the resilience of the human spirit and the unsung courage of the average person facing challenging life situations against the backdrop of dramatic historic events. "~ *Ross Donaldson, University Instructor*

"Stenholm weaves a beautiful story of the female spirit as her characters overcome tragedy and adversity that spans generations and continents. Crack evokes a myriad of emotions from jubilation and ecstasy to unspeakable emptiness and heartbreak. The one constant is the strength the women find deep in themselves to survive and better their circumstances and those of their family." ~ *Martine Marino, physical therapist, "MPT"*

"Carmen Stenholm's novel honors the spirit of women from all eras. The lives they led took strength to endure and courage to write about. It was truly a privilege to read their story." ~ *Amy Harakal, book club member / wife, mother*

"In thirty-five years of editing, I have seldom fallen in love with characters, seldom been brought to tears of joy and profound despair. This all changed with *A Crack Between the Worlds*. I love the women who came to life on these pages. They have become my family, my inspiration, too." ~ *Connie Donaldson, Editor of "A Crack Between the Worlds"*

Crack
Between the Worlds

Blessings & joy

Carmen Stenholm

by

Carmen Stenholm

ISBN: 978-0-9800064-7-6   Hard cover

ISBN: 978-0-9800064-6-9   Soft cover

LCCN: 2010921708

Coverart: Lesley M. Polinko

Dragon's Egg Press

Pittsburgh, PA

Printed in the USA

Dedication

This book is dedicated to the generations of men and women who came before me and without whom there would be no story.

It is a gift from the past to Gabriele, my granddaughter, who gives this work meaning. It began when she was born, when I felt the need to honor her past and give her a sense of herself through time. She lives because others chose to live even though, at times, life hardly seemed worth the struggle. She lives because, in each generation, there was someone who dared to dream and hope.

Acknowledgements

Karl, my husband, who believed in me and supported this work from its beginning to its end, has my everlasting gratitude.

No major undertaking is possible without the love and support of a host of friends and colleagues. It is my great fortune to have innumerable people in my life who gave selflessly of their time and talents. Three friends are at the top of the list of people who have my heartfelt gratitude: Connie Donaldson, superb editor and dream sharer, Lesley Polinko, the artist responsible for the magnificent cover of this book, and Joyce Faulkner, gifted author and publisher. The women of my book club who read and encouraged, then reread and encouraged some more, and friends of many years, like Martine Wattine and Patricia Silva, who believed this story was worth telling, deserve similar appreciation.

Perhaps most surprising are the many people who, without ever having met me, spent their time and energy to read the manuscript and support this effort. It will never be possible to put into words how grateful I am for your generosity.

Last, but decidedly not least, I am grateful to you, the reader. I hope you will find a part of your own story in this one.

CONTENTS

PART I

JOHANNA

Chapter 1

August 1871

Greta ran to the far side of the barn and stood on tip toe to get one last glimpse of the Gypsy wagon. She beamed as she saw the colorful wooden cart angle south. Even from this distance, she thought she could hear the clatter of its pans and ladles as it turned onto the road.

Then, to make sure the afternoon wasn't just a dream, she felt deep into her skirt pocket for the coins. She sighed out loud as she found them, and then clutched them in her fist. "They paid me! They paid me with real money! No pots, no twine, no bag of beans. They gave me money for my lace. For *my lace*."

As she turned to go back to the house, she moved slowly. She wasn't quite ready to go back there—to face cleaning up after the meal and Josef's sullen mood. She wanted to stay with this euphoric feeling a while longer.

She reviewed the best parts of the day as she made her way along the dusty path, trying to get the sensations back. She wanted to feel them again and again.

She remembered the old Gypsy's surprise when he first saw her pieces—how eagerly he reached for them, and the younger man's face, maybe his son or even grandson, with a smirk of her own as she recalled his initial condescending tone. His words said that they were adequate, but his eyes said something more. Despite his attempts to hide it, he was impressed with the quality of her work. Both of them knew it would fetch a pretty penny in the city.

Both treated her differently from other times. They even treated her children differently. They had given the girls gifts—two small carved tops, one painted with green stripes, one painted with blue.

Then, so much praise, so much admiration. The praise they wouldn't use for her lace, they heaped on the meal. They were so appreciative of the food she served them. They didn't just eat her bread. They inhaled its aroma each time they raised it to their mouths to take a bite. When she offered them more of her fresh butter, they forgot their manners and said yes immediately. And the beer. Unlike the men she knew, they didn't guzzle it down in three swallows. They drank it slowly. Old Gustav even closed his eyes as he swallowed. Not twice, but three times he commended Josef on the richness of his brew.

However, Josef acted like a dunce, like an ass. Did he really begrudge them the simple soup she served? Why wasn't he proud that his wife honored him by telling her guests of the wonderful crops he'd grown this season? Why couldn't he acknowledge that the seeds they traded for her lace last year made a difference?

Was he so grim simply to hurt her? Did he think she was flirting with the tinkers? Did he begrudge her when she refilled their glasses? If it had been one of his friends, or one of his brothers, he would have refilled them a hundred times! Why, now, was he being so tight-fisted?

When she offered to walk them to the barn, to show them the barrels of kraut, the bales of hay, the bags of feed stacked inside, he became even more miserable. He didn't say a word. He had just scowled at her and went to the side yard to continue cutting wood, with no farewell to anyone.

As she got closer to the front door, Greta's magical mood began to crumble. "Why did he have to be so..."

She was startled when Josef opened the door. He motioned her inside, and then carefully closed the door. When she turned to speak to him, he hit her, with the full force of his strength, across the face. The blow sent her reeling. There was a strange noise in her head. She felt the cold floor on her face—tasted the salty blood.

He clutched her by the shoulders and stood her up again. She cowered, waiting for another blow—but it didn't come. Instead he shook her and shouted, "You stupid fool! You stupid cow! What have you done to us? They are tinkers! They'll tell everyone about the harvest! They'll tell the others about our full granaries and barns!"

Then, as quickly as he'd begun, he let go of her shoulders and turned away. She fought to keep her balance and called out to him. "Josef, what..."

He turned for a second and looked at her before he went back outside. In that second, she saw the look in his eyes wasn't anger. It was fear.

With a swell of emotion that caused her stomach to burn, she remembered what his grandfather had told them each autumn as he warned them not to boast about their crops or good hunting in the forest. Grandpa had gone on and on about the murdering hordes who had attacked their village so many years ago. "In this valley," he had said, "we had no protection when they came. They took the best of what we had. They killed the strongest of us when we tried to defend ourselves."

Johanna

Until this moment, his words had just been the ramblings of a senile old man whose very reason for existence seemed to be simply to burden his family with fear and despair. Now, for the first time, she understood the possibility that his ranting contained some shred of truth.

She felt herself falling to her knees—this time not from the weight of a blow, but the weight of her newfound fear. "Dear God, dear Blessed Lord, don't let this be possible," she whispered. "Don't let me be the cause of such a horror."

October 1871

The only world Johanna knew was this valley. In her four short years of life there had been no reason to leave it, and certainly no reason to give thought to the rest of central Europe that lay beyond it. It was no concern of hers that independent kingdoms had recently united to form what eventually would become a new country.

It was an early autumn day as friends and family members rested following a noon meal of beer, bread and sausages. Food was cheerfully eaten in the middle of one of the fields being harvested that day. The potatoes and grain would feed the families of the village for another year. For untold centuries, the rituals of planting and harvesting had been shared by the people of this green, wrinkled valley nestled in the center of their ancient continent. The timeless rhythms of the land were reasons for celebrations and marked births and deaths, as well as seasons. Each family was responsible for planting and harvesting enough food to sustain itself for at least a year. Too many times, though, it was not enough and people went hungry, especially the children.

Hanni, as she was called, loved the undulating hills that rolled for mile after mile interrupted only by fields, woods, and the occasional cluster of stone huts topped with thatch. Few of the houses had been built by any of the men and women who now lived in them with their children. They were older than anyone remembered but still offered warmth and shelter to the families and animals of the valley when bitter cold gripped fragile lives. For more centuries than even the smartest among them could count, the people of the valley had been living and working in fields and homes passed down from generation to generation. As each home was built, wells were dug and, year after year, they provided sweet, clear water to families that struggled in ancient rhythms with the land.

They were good at working the land but their finest work was making lace woven so beautifully that it earned the admiration of traders from far-off communities. The peddlers came to the valley to bargain for it with meager goods and coins that seemed a fortune to people who needed little more than what they could produce themselves. The arrival of the merchants and the ensuing bargaining and exchanges added a pinch of spice to unhurried lives. The simple valley folk loved the news and gossip the traders brought. In hushed voices, they talked about Kings and armies. The tidings of births, deaths, and local scandals, along with the details of love affairs and marriages of peasants and royals alike became grist for the gossip mills. Reports of new conquests of land and maiden's hearts became the stories for many evenings' entertainment. Men smoking long-stemmed pipes huddled around open hearths while women knitted or sewed in failing light and children fought sleep on straw or feather pallets tucked into cramped corners.

Reports of capricious arrivals of local kings or their emissaries who raped and plundered their way across lives and holdings were also discussed. Those horrors became food for the nightmares of children. They were told to obey their parents or suffer at the hands of those evil men during their surprise visits.

Hanni was spared these horrifying accounts because her mother and father loved their little girl too much to frighten her. Of the five babies born to the couple, she was their only surviving child. Like so many others, Hanni's parents had lost their children to diseases that had no names. One, another girl born a year before Johanna, died when all her tiny teeth had pushed through swollen gums at the same time. It had been a nightmare of pain for the infant and an almost unbearable loss for the young couple who had lost too many already. Thus, they were forgiven for overindulging their fragile, little girl with big blue eyes as bright as cornflowers on a clear day.

The day was much like any other brilliant autumn day. The smell of newly-cut hay mingled with the odors of well-fed animals and wafted across the farmyards. Beds of flowers added their own scents to the profusion of smelly delights. The ground was hot under bare feet and a heaviness lay in the air, blanketing the slumbering village. Even the birds seemed to be napping, too sleepy to do more than chirp at the occasional warm breeze that ruffled a feather here and there.

The children were delighted with their parents' sleepy break since it meant a game of hide-and-seek without being told to get out of the way or do some unwelcome chore. In fact, it seemed to Hanni to be the perfect day. Well, almost perfect. One of her best friends, Sabine, and her older sister Mathilde, were still gone on a trip with their parents to a wedding—one of Josef or Greta's relatives. Piles of barrels filled with pickles and kraut were stacked everywhere and wooden crates holding vegetables ready for cleaning and canning leaned against the rock walls of houses and barns. Wagons with harvested wheat piled high above side railings were left willy-nilly along the communal path that led from house to house. Doors were thrown open to air out interiors.

Johanna

The children played in the last farmyard in a row of ancient houses. The yard was littered with tools that had seen hard use for many years. Baskets and barrels were thrown into corners or stacked into piles along rock walls built hundreds of years ago to form the foundations of buildings. The game had started and Kristel having drawn the short straw was "it." With her forehead leaning on the top layer of rocks marking the well near the center of the houses that could be seen from the top of Butter Hill, Kristel cupped her hands around her eyes to keep herself from cheating. She shouted her numbers from one to ten in a loud and confident voice. She was already seven years old so she was good at her numbers. Even though her hands muffled the sound, Hanni thought she was counting too fast. It didn't matter, though. Hanni had already found the perfect spot behind a barrel of yeasty beer shoved into a corner where the outside wall of her father's barn and the rock wall that went all the way around the main part of the village met. She had been told that this wall had been built by people called "Romans" many generations ago to keep the villagers in and their enemies out.

At the moment, Hanni couldn't remember who 'the enemy' was that the wall was meant to guard against, but it made a right angle that held a barrel and her own tiny body wedged into the crack between. She had even found an old straw broom that she leaned against the side of the barrel to hide the little bit of her legs that stuck out. Hanni hid undetected behind the beer barrel smelling of hops and clutched the handle of her frayed straw broom.

The attack came in early afternoon. Surging through a chasm in the mountains that skirted the eastern edge of her people's land, the barbarians brought steel deaths sheathed in fringed leather. Screaming, with dark hair flying about heaving shoulders, these warriors fell upon her slumbering family and neighbors.

No one saw the strangers coming. The children were too busy with their own game and the adults dozed under shade trees and against heaps of grain. None of the survivors could tell exactly when the slaughter began. Some claimed to have seen dark shapes stealing across fields at the foot of the eastern ridge of hills dotting the warm horizon. Others swear they saw men draped in dark clothing spring up from the ground like boulders suddenly animated with furious life.

No one had much time to shout a warning before blood flowed from gaping throats and twisted entrails slithered from cavities still twitching in mock life. The screams started as slumbering souls woke from pleasant dreams and felt their world and bodies sliced with knives and severed with axes. Lovers clutched in sweet embrace died in a tangle of limbs, as though arms and legs were intent on switching bodies. Babies, still nuzzled to ample breasts, now drank blood instead of milk between screams and gasps. These, too, were silenced as the butchering went on, but later, after the men and women who could fight back had been eliminated. Like a swarm of locusts, the men from the other side of the barrier of hills murdered and raped their way across fields and yards. No slaughterhouse operation was ever so efficient. Only the lucky or insignificant were left alive to remember the horror.

Josef felt the wrongness long before he saw the smoke. The forest was too quiet. There seemed to be something wrong with the very air.

Greta was in the back of the wagon, asleep with the girls. Two days of wedding preparations and celebrations had exhausted all three of them. He didn't wake her until he caught the first whiff of smoke.

"Greta, hold the girls tight," he shouted as he whipped the old mare into a gallop.

Something in his voice pulled Greta to attention. She grabbed her daughters as the cart jerked forward, and held them close as they bumped along the road. When they asked what was happening, she shushed them. She too could smell the smoke.

They were still a mile from the village when Joseph knew his worst fears had become reality. From the top of the hill, he could see the barns in flames.

Most of the screaming had stopped by the time he found Hanni, trembling behind the barrel. He hugged her close to his massive chest. The little girl sank into the crook of his arm. Her small, pale face, with eyes squeezed shut, thumped against the man's sweaty neck as he ran to the grove of trees that already sheltered other survivors. His voice, gruff with emotion, comforted her.

"It's alright now, sweetie. They're gone now. They can't hurt you. Hush. Hush. Don't cry. Don't cry."

Hanni muffled her sobs in his shirt, but could not stop the tears. The image of her dying mother's violated body, skirts crumpled about her waist and arm outstretched toward her dead husband, would not leave her mind. Through her sobs, she heard the anguished cries of others who had lost loved ones. Fear, rage, and despair filled the air.

Her village, "Werda," was surrounded by people who, like Hannis' own, insured their own survival in hungry years by killing and stealing. Raids, rapes, and murders had been committed and endured for untold centuries. It was impossible to say who was the first to kill but if anyone was asked, they would swear it was the other. They were sure that, for their part, they were only hoping to survive or seeking a just revenge.

The handful of survivors watched as the same bloodstained men who had altered their world forever carted away their precious harvest. The losses were heavy and not a single family was untouched by the atrocities. Hardest hit were children, like Hanni, who lost both mother and father. Although survival required sacrifice and few were in a position or frame of mind to share what little resources or good will that was left, Josef insisted that she become part of his household.

"We can't leave her. She'll die, too."

In all of their marriage, Joseph had struck Greta only once. She didn't want to even imagine what he would do to her if she denied this girl a home. Without daring to look into his face, she took the shivering bundle into her arms. She prayed that, if she took good care of this orphan, God might someday forgive her. She wasn't at all sure that Josef ever would.

The twenty first of October, 1875 marked Hanni's eighth birthday. Neither she nor her new family acknowledged it. If truth be told, no one even knew it was her birthday. It was like any of the other four years she had spent with her new family. Her real mother and father were a dim memory, remembered only as wisps of a dream long passed.

"Hanni, did you remember to get the wood for the fire? You'll need it to heat the water before noon. You have to get the washing done and hung out before lunch."

Hanni's mother's shrill voice interrupted her daydreams. How could Hanni forget a chore she alone had been doing weekly ever since she was big enough to reach the top of the scrub board? It was one of the many jobs Hanni was expected to do in order to "earn her keep." Because she was eight years old now, in addition to the chores she did at home, Hanni worked from morning to night at looms in the new industrial brick complex on the outskirts of the growing village. Her eyes were strained and reddened from long hours toiling in near darkness over looms stretched with colorful woolen threads. The monotonous work deadened many spirits, but Hanni had a dream that kept her hope alive. Someday, she would find a man who would love her and build her a house of her own. Someone who wouldn't care that she was an orphan with no dowry to mark her worth. Someone who would love her enough to work hard and provide for their family. She wanted children. Enough so she would feel as though she had a real family of her own, but not too many to feed. There would have to be some boys who could help their father farm the land and some girls who could help her with the house. Maybe four or five, but no more. She had seen other brides have a baby every year until, at 24 or 25, they looked old and tired enough to die.

She dreamed of a kitchen with a hearth big enough to heat the house and a swinging iron arm to hold a pot for the soups and stews she would make to warm cold bones during freezing nights. She dreamed of a parlor—well, maybe not a parlor exactly, but a room hung with tapestries to stop chills from creeping through cracks in mortared walls. A room where her husband and children would gather around her to eat and share their hopes and dreams. She imagined how it would be to smile at her own little ones and snatch a glimpse of her handsome man. He would be kind and gentle and his rough, work-worn hands would rest on small heads and shoulders as he encouraged this project or that. At night, in the dark, she imagined only tenderness and safety.

Chapter 2

Fourteen year old Hanni's eyes filled with tears as she stood in the tiny wooden church and faced the man, over twice her age, who would become her husband.

As the minister intoned prayers she'd heard a hundred times, Hanni struggled to remain upright. Walter stared at her with unflinching eyes. Suddenly, he was not the family friend she'd known all her life, not the worn-out widower she'd seen months before, red-eyed and trembling, as he walked beside his wife's casket to the cemetery. Now he was a stranger, a man with crooked yellow teeth and a scarred face who wished to take her into his home and make her his wife.

Her knees swayed. Breathing deeply, she glanced away from him to his four children all scrubbed and lined up in their neatly patched clothes. Hanni's head spun and she thought she might pass out. Lotte, a girl almost as old as Hanni, clutched her infant sister in her arms, her eyes daring Hanni's to take the baby away from her protective embrace.

"She doesn't even know me and already she hates me. She doesn't know that I don't want this any more than she does."

The thoughts of her soon-to-be husband, a lifelong friend of her father's, were difficult to fathom. He was a family friend—an adult she had pitied, someone she felt sad for the day she brought fresh bread to the house where his wife was dying. Elisabet had never recovered from the birth of her youngest daughter.

He had sat on the edge of his bed, eyes red from so many sleepless nights, and looked at the frail specter of his once robust wife. Dying, the woman had stared back at her distraught husband with eyes vacant from fatigue. In a shaky voice, he had promised to take care of their three daughters and son.

He needed a wife in order to keep that promise. So, Johanna now stood, small and trembling at his side. Her father, standing to her left, felt proudly content with the match he had made between his best friend and his adopted daughter. And his wife, who stood to his side and who had encouraged the marriage, indeed who had been the first to suggest it, smiled encouragingly. Would they make her go through with this wedding if she couldn't even stand up?

"I don't love him. I don't even know him. What about my dreams?" The beautiful valley, home for fourteen years, began to shrink around Hanni until it threatened to cut off her breath and life. She wanted to run away, to run to the city she had heard the Gypsies describe. In Dresden, she could perfect her weaving art, make new friends and fall in love. She pictured herself running, but she couldn't make her legs move.

So many futile thoughts ran through Hanni's mind as the preacher pronounced them, Walter Gustaf and Johanna Ilona, husband and wife, "Für Immer und Ewig", forever.

During the darkest hours of her wedding night, too tired to stay awake, Hanni imagined a dream lover, someone young and strong, someone she had chosen, holding her body in a tender embrace, kissing her face, still wet with joyful tears. His adoring smile softened the sharp angles of her body that had been curled into a tight ball, and she stretched to meet his eager touch. However, the force that met her responsive gesture was not what her wishful mind envisioned. She woke with a start as awareness of a hairy back was transmitted from the palms of her hands to her waking mind. A short, loud snore gave her the last motivation she needed to exit the warm bed. Perhaps if she got up and stoked the hearth with wood and started the preparations that marked the beginning of every day, "he" would leave her to her work and not insist she re-enter the bed and his embrace.

For Hanni, last night had been an endless torment of fear and repulsion. Uninformed about what she might expect on her wedding night, her husband's embrace had felt cruel. Driven by lust and a need too long unmet, Walter had unceremoniously taken what he was too impatient to coax from his child bride. His strong arms and calloused hands had moved across her body with hurried force to fit her into position for his heaving release. Unable to move beneath the bulk of the man to whom she now belonged, Hanni had barely enough space beneath the rock-hard chest to breathe. Her scream as he entered her was muffled by the nightgown—tenderly embroidered and smocked during evenings when she still held dreams of young love. It had been shoved up and bunched around her neck where it covered the lower part of her face and served as both a muzzle and veil behind which she pretended to hide. Her husband's body, as suddenly as it had energized itself into a frenzy, had just as quickly flung itself next to her and ceased all movement. Only the slight tremble of his chest as he breathed gave any indication that he was still alive.

As she slipped out of the bed and her bare feet touched the frigid dirt floor, Hanni began shaking with more than cold. She moved like a blind woman, tapping the ground with her toes before placing a tentative foot onto unfamiliar territory. Her tears began again as she realized it would not be unfamiliar for long. This was where she would now live. The ache in her chest grew stronger as she tried to recapture the feeling of the cozy warmth of her parent's house—but it would not come back.

Hanni had become an indispensable part of her adopted family. At times she imagined that she had more chores and scoldings from Mamma than the other girls, but Pappa more than made up for Mamma's crankiness. One of his prized possessions was a table loom, a gift from his parents. On quiet evenings when he was finished with his work and Hanni had done her chores, he taught Hanni the basic patterns for simple projects until he realized she was becoming a gifted weaver. The lessons then became much harder but, even at her young age, she could far outshine her sisters with her skills. He was especially proud of her when she started working in the weaver's factory when she was six years old and turned out to be very good at the large loom to which she was assigned. With scraps saved from her work at the factory, Hanni made a small but beautiful tapestry for one of the walls in the front room of their house. Pappa said he would treasure it forever. That was just two years ago but it now seemed like a lifetime.

Hanni knew that Pappa wanted her to marry Walter so that she would be taken care of and so his friend would have a wife to help with the household and children. Pappa hadn't known about Hanni's dreams. Maybe she should have told him of her dreams to go to Dresden, perfect her craft and find a husband. It was no use thinking about what she should have done. It was much too late to change the course her life had so suddenly taken. She knew she must find the courage to fulfill her part of the marriage vows even if she could find little joy in them. The familiar feelings of resignation and grim resolve that had crept into her heart during other difficult times were now back full force.

One memory seemed like yesterday. It was the first day she walked to work while it was still dark and entered the wooden gate of the largest brick building she had ever seen. The hall she was taken to was half the space of the building and housed dozens of looms of different sizes. There was not enough light from the row of small windows near the ceiling high above their heads. Weavers who had come even earlier were squinting to see threads of different sizes and colors they were preparing for the day's work. A stout woman wearing a grim face bustled toward Hanni and looked down at the small girl.

"I heard you're good. Think you can handle that one?" she asked pointing to a medium sized old-fashioned frame loom that was at least twice Hanni's height. It stood in a dark corner between a much larger loom and tables that held huge spools of colorful yarns and wooden tools for projects she could only imagine. As the woman pushed Hanni between rows of looms toward her new work station, Hanni kept her eyes to the ground, which began to tremble with the banging of shuttles and slamming of combs that kept warp and weft in their assigned orders. As she lowered herself onto the bench where she would spend the next ten hours, Hanni felt a desperate need to run. Then, too, her legs felt drained and she needed all her strength to listen to the instructions shouted into her ear.

Now, sensing her way forward in the dark, Hanni nearly cried out in pain when she stubbed her foot against a rock-hard corner of a chest and had to hobble on one leg to keep from falling down. Groping, she recalled the raised stone lip that marked the woodbin next to the hearth. Immersed in her thoughts, she had lost track of her bearings and didn't realize she had already crossed the small room that housed her nuptial bed. The same small room also contained the rough-hewn table and benches constructed of half logs that served her new family at mealtimes and any other time they needed a place to sit and work or just talk. In fact, all the living was done in that room with children bundled in quilts on shelves that were pulled down from the wall to serve as beds. Clusters of herbs, suspended with twine from wooden beams, completed the picture of domestic paraphernalia. Hanni tried to remember where different pieces of furniture stood so she would not bump into any more.

Caught in the shelter of darkness, amidst the smells and sounds of her new family, she felt suspended between the world of her childhood fantasies and the palpable reality of this dark room. A whimper tore through her reverie. The baby beginning to awaken. Hanni allowed herself another few moments to dream before going to her.

The night before, Walter had placed tinder and bits of scrap paper in the center of the hearth before stacking a few logs diagonally on top of the pile. Hanni made her way through the dim light to the alcove where hearth and wall met, careful not to stub her smarting toes again. Fumbling, she lifted a match and struck it against one of the rocks in the hearth. The flame sizzled into life and she bent to light her first morning fire in her new home. When it was lit and she was sure it would burn, she sank to her knees in front of the flames and hung her head in an attempt to pray. She had learned long ago to greet each new day with humility and gratitude. This day, she felt neither. This morning she was filled with so many thoughts and feelings that sorting them out into a prayer was beyond her. Instead, the only words she could remember were the ones to a nursery rhyme her birth mother had taught her long before she was killed. "Wach auf! Wach auf! Die liebe Sonne lacht dich aus!" "Wake up! Wake up! The sun is laughing at you!"

The squeaky, mewling sounds from the youngest of her new children increased. The fire burned bright and its light spread through the cabin in irregular swathes. The bundle, a seeming pile of rags, squirmed and emitted sounds more compelling than even a moment ago. Testing her foot against the dirt floor, Hanni winced again before making her way around the table and benches in the center of the room. Hurrying so none of the others would wake yet, Hanni snatched the baby and hugged her to her chest. The added weight of her burden put extra pressure on her swelling foot and made her retreat to the table and benches.

An inadvertent glance toward her bed in the corner revealed the watchful eyes of her new husband. She wanted to shrink into one of the shadowy nooks and escape the attention of the man still prone under a heap of quilts. The baby, Liesel, made escape impossible. She stepped into the brighter light at the center of the cluttered room and her eyes met his. The look Walter returned was more of amusement than criticism and she was grateful his quizzical grin did not become the laughter that would have humiliated her on their first morning together. In fact, the dimness of the room and warm tones of her small fire lent his face a softness and youth Hanni had not expected.

He slipped out of bed and pulled on his pants before crossing the room. With her back to him, Hanni felt his nearness before his hand stroked the top of her head and his arms reached around her to lift the baby from her embrace. He motioned with his head in the direction of a ledge to her left and she saw the pitcher of milk and small sack of grain for breakfast. Warming some of the milk and adding a sprinkle of grain, Hanni made a soupy liquid that she poured into a bottle she found within arm's reach. Taking the hungry child from her husband's arms, Hanni lowered herself and the squirming infant onto the stone ledge which ran around the hearth alcove. The stone bench was hard and still cold from the night air but offered a rest for her sore foot and a chance to focus her attention on the child in her arms. Hanni could no longer see Walter's face but his bare feet lingered beside her own far longer than she expected. Never one known for saying more than was necessary, Walter watched his new bride. Too shy to inquire about her husband's thoughts, Hanni held infant and bottle, absorbed in the sweetness of the other face that regarded her keenly.

Johanna

Greedy, sucking sounds interrupted the silence interspersed now and then by the pop of a burning log. At last, sated, Liesel's eyelids closed once more and the tiny mouth formed a slack circle around the nipple. Walter's hands reached under the bundle and lifted the tiny girl onto his chest. With one hand he cradled the child and with the other he helped his wife stand. Leading the way to their bed, his slight shove told Hanni he wanted her to get under the covers again. While she lowered herself onto the warm mattress, Walter took his youngest daughter to her own tiny bed, a box that had originally served as a repository for tools. The shadows his movements cast on uneven walls were exaggerated by the flickering fire.

Not anxious for this but no longer quite so afraid, Hanni did not cringe when Walter returned to their bed and removed his pants. Without a sound, his arm slid under her shoulders and he turned her to face him. Cupping her chin in his left hand, he tilted her face so she was forced to look up into his. When a sigh escaped her lips, he smiled and held her a little closer.

Chapter 3

Morning came heralded by the crows of a rooster that had been a wedding present from Hanni's father. Unrelenting, the cock's alarm became an endless series of shrieks. Soon, Hanni heard the twittering sounds of her two new daughters, Lotte and Minna, ages nine and seven. Baby Liesel and five year old Hans, were still fast asleep. It was time to start the tasks that would define mornings with Hanni's new family. It was odd to think of these people as her family, especially when the family she'd left behind was only a few houses—and a lifetime—away.

The giggles became louder when Lotte and Minna realized their new mother was awake. Hanni slipped her feet into the hand knitted house shoes she had left next to her side of the bed and pulled a robe over her thin nightshirt. The silvery dawn was just bright enough to guide her feet to the girls' bed tucked into the corner behind the front door of the cottage. A door on the opposite wall led to a second, even tinier room in the small house. Its floor was perhaps three feet below that of the front room, and a sloping path led to its interior. Supplies such as potatoes, coal, and tools were kept there, as well as animals when cold winters forced them indoors. Because the weather was not yet frigid, the two cows Walter owned stayed in the field adjacent to the village with the animals from other households.

Village families shared the pastures and gardens fed by a narrow river cutting the land into northern and southern parcels. Luckily,

Johanna

the river also ran close to Hanni's new home and had, on its banks, a perfect flat-topped rock on which Hanni could sit to wash clothes and linens—but not on that first morning of her new life. Neighbors had scrubbed the house and done the laundry to help her get a good start.

Today would be a day of new beginnings. Quietly, she made her way to the girls. A hush had fallen over the room as Lotte and Minna realized she was coming in their direction. They had decided to hate her when they saw their father regard her with that funny look on his face during the wedding yesterday. Lotte, especially, felt a need to torment her. In Lotte's opinion, Hanni had no right to be there in her mother's place.

Hanni peeled back the covers that hid the two little girls. Lotte was curled on her side facing her sister and the all-too-close new mother. Minna was on her back, holding two stiff arms at her side with her eyes scrunched shut. As Hanni slipped into bed beside the little girls, Minna's eyes flew open with alarm and Lotte's face became a mask of loathing as she squeezed against the wall. Hanni lay on her side facing the girls as she tucked the quilts around them. Her head rested on her right hand as she looked at Minna's startled face. With her left hand, she traced the outline of the tiny cheek. The upturned nose twitched as Hanni's finger drew a line from forehead to chin. Slowly, the child's eyes turned toward Hanni.

After a while, her little body relaxed. A few moments later, she moved enough to get nearer the kindness of the young woman. Snuggling into the neck and chest of her new mother, Minna felt strong arms reach around her shoulders and back. Hanni kissed the top of the head covered with untamed curls and felt hot tears soak the front of her nightgown.

A glance in the direction of Lotte's still cringing body revealed different feelings. Her eyes still blazed with hatred. The cock had finally stopped crowing. The silence held the promise of both joy and dread.

Minna clung to Hanni's neck as she turned and faced the sunlit window next to the hearth. Motes of dust danced onto a table littered with dishes from the night before. Hanni gave Minna a gentle hug, disentangled herself from the child's grip and planted her feet on the floor. As she passed the cradle on her way to the hearth, gleaming eyes spotted her approach and a furious squirming began. Scooping Liesel into her arms and onto her left hip, Hanni had almost reached the hearth when she became aware that Walter was not in the house. A glance through the window revealed her husband spraying the side yard with handfuls of grain. Frantic chickens jostled and pecked for a place near the man with their breakfast. The rooster was particularly insistent on getting his share of the meal. Walter, an apron tied around his middle, kept reaching into the pocket he had made by bunching the material in his other hand. With a graceful swoop he released grain in an arc around his feet. His expression was unreadable. Unhurried, he released the folds of his apron and brushed the remaining grain into the dirt around him. Several strides of his long legs brought him to the door of the barn. Hanni watched him disappear into its dim interior.

Hanni turned to her task of pouring water into the iron pot suspended on a rod which pivoted into and out of the hearth. Clutching Liesel, she took a piece of wood from the neat stack and nursed the dying flame. The baby squirmed against Hanni's hip. Unwilling to set her on the dirt floor, Hanni laid her in a box near the table she thought might have been used as a wood box in the past. Now empty, it made a reasonable place for the tiny girl. Hanni rushed to add a blanket and rag doll before Liesel could decide that this was not at all the proper place for her. Next, Hanni brushed crumbs and other debris from the table and found five bowls and spoons, which she placed along both sides of the tabletop.

A glance at the corner where Minna and Lotte slept revealed two pairs of eyes poking out above covers drawn as far up as they could be. Hanni smiled and told the girls to get dressed and make their bed. Minna scampered free of her bedding in one agile bound and landed on the floor giggling. Lotte chose to linger. Pulling a dress from a box at the foot of her bed, Minna wiggled into its folds before going outside to the outhouse with a half moon carved into its narrow door. She smiled as she skipped past, headed for the short, crooked path, with thistles and weed-infested patches of grass. Hanni smiled at the vision that reminded her of her own childhood. In a sack on a ledge above the small window at her side, Hanni discovered grain already ground into meal. A handful added to the boiling water with a pinch of salt was the beginning of breakfast.

Hans gave no indication yet of waking up. He was fast asleep in his bed, a drawer shoved against the far wall. A blanket, wadded up and pushed into one corner at the foot of the wooden box, left little room for the boy to stretch out. Hanni would have to talk to Walter about building Hans a bigger sleeping place. Hanni shook his tiny shoulders and was rewarded with a growl more like a bear cub than a little boy.

Lotte cautioned, "He doesn't like that."

"What do I have to do to wake him?" asked Hanni.

"Nothing," was the curt answer mumbled into bedding still pulled over half of Lotte's face.

Unable to think of what to say next, Hanni was spared a reply by Walter's voice calling from the doorway where he leaned against the frame.

"Lotte!"

Startled, the child scrambled from the blankets that had tangled themselves around her legs. Sullen, she slipped into a dress, slightly larger than Minna's, and tramped toward the door still blocked by her father's imposing frame. He stepped aside to make room for her, and then lifted his son from the tiny bed. As Hanni prepared a bottle for Liesel, Walter woke the boy by bouncing him up and down on his knee. The boy was still sleepy from yesterday's festivities. Minna and Lotte came into the house again and showed their father clean hands and faces scrubbed at the well in the middle of their yard.

"Look, Pappa. My hands are all clean," cried Minna.

"Good job, Liebchen. You are such a big girl. Lotte, how about helping your new mommy set the table?"

Lotte cast a resentful look in Hanni's direction. "She's not my mommy."

It was their first shared meal. Hanni had added a few flavorful herbs and a touch of honey to the gruel. The honey was a wedding present from one of the neighbors. Ladling generous portions into each of their bowls, she then filled mugs with water from the bucket and set them in front of each person. Minna smacked her lips while Lotte tried not to look too hungry. Hans squirmed on Walter's lap nearly upsetting his father's bowl. Liesel lay in her bed, sucking on the bottle of milk Hanni had given her earlier. After she sat down, Walter put Hans in Hanni's lap and took one of her hands while reaching with his other for Lotte's hand. Lotte reached for Minna's and Minna took the sleeve of Hanni's arm that held her brother. The prayer was as simple as the meal. Walter intoned, "Lord, we thank you for this food."

Later that afternoon, Hanni was surprised by a knock at the door. She opened it to find her parents smiling at her. Between them they were carrying the small table loom she had used since she was a little girl. It was a treasure that had been made by a great-grandfather long ago and had been handed down in her mother's family. She still remembered how her father's large hands had guided her own small ones as she had mastered the intricate patterns passed down from generation to generation.

"Hello. Come in. What an unexpected surprise." Hanni opened the door further to allow her parents and the loom to pass through.

The smiles on their faces widened as they saw the perplexed look on Hanni's.

"We've brought you something, Hanni," said her father as he held out the loom. "Actually, we always intended for you to have this."

Incredulous, Hanni looked from one parent to the other. Tears of joy welled up in her eyes and her voice trembled as she said, "Are you sure you want to part with it?"

"Yes, we're sure, Hanni. You're the one who always appreciated it, and you have such a talent. We know great-grandfather would want you to have it," replied her mother.

The loom was as unexpected as it was wonderful. It was true that her sisters were less skilled, but Hanni never dreamed that this treasure would one day be hers. She had expected it to go to one of their real daughters.

Tears welled up. It meant so much more than a loom. It meant that, perhaps, despite the mean things her sisters often said to her about being the runt, about not fitting in, her parents truly did consider her their daughter. Her father looked concerned. "You're not happy with the gift?"

"Oh Papa, so much more than happy." She couldn't bear to explain the deeper reason. Instead she added, "It means that I can now weave cloth for curtains, rugs, and bedding. With enough scraps of good thread I could even manage some clothes. I'm so grateful." She hugged him hard, and then hugged her mother too, despite her apparent discomfort at such a show of emotions.

With little else to offer her parents, she made tea from herbs she had found in the meadow below the peak of Butter Hill. Her parents seemed delighted, however, to sit and share this simple treat along with gossip Hanni had been too busy to hear.

"Hanni, guess what?" said her mother as she leaned closer and lowered her voice. "Ilse, the factory foreman's daughter, is pregnant! Can you believe that? You'll never guess who the father is! It's that boy from Helmsheim. His family owns the mill there. You know how he sometimes delivers sacks of grain around here. Well," and here her mother winked, "apparently, he delivered more than grain."

Hanni chuckled while her father shook his head and sighed. He was more interested in discussing the news about the conflict involving their king who claimed territory in a northern state that had been ceded to him by the church for some reason or other.

"It seems," explained her father, "that the people living there don't want to pay taxes to two kings. Their last lord continues to insist on payments from them and their new one wants even higher revenues. There's no way they can pay that much and I don't see any good reason for it either."

Hanni could see how worried her father was as he continued, "all this will do is lead to another war. We could have conscriptions as far south as this village. It wouldn't be the first time that our young men have had to die for no good reason."

Hanni's mother shrugged her shoulders and said with more than a little disdain in her voice, "Who can ever guess what's on the minds of lords and their like? They make their high and mighty decisions and we're the ones who end up paying for them."

"I don't want to see any more bloodshed or suffering," her father said. "We're just starting to recover from the famine and wars we had a decade ago."

As the afternoon wore on, they talked about this tidbit and that while Hanni poured tea, changed diapers, and prepared another bottle for Liesel.

After a time, Walter went outside to tend to his chores and returned with a frown on his face. "I have a bad feeling about your news, Josef. We've always had a hard time protecting our families in this valley. We're exposed and vulnerable. My Hanni knows that better than most. I don't want her to suffer any more losses."

Soon after Hanni put Liesel back into her cradle, Hans climbed up on her lap and, after playing with her hair, fell asleep in her arms, his fingers entwined in a lock that had slipped from her braid. Without thinking, Hanni began to stroke his boney little knees. Instinctively she brushed her lips across his tiny forehead. At that moment, something shifted deep inside her. Even though this was not the house she'd dreamed of and Walter was hardly the young man who had crept into her thoughts on so many lonely nights, Hanni felt as though she could perhaps find her place here. She was the woman of the house—of this house. She was the mother of this boy, of these girls. This was her place, a place of her own that was much more real than her dreams had ever been.

As the afternoon sun cast ever-lengthening shadows from the open door into the small house, Hanni's parents prepared to leave. Walter said his farewells and went out to milk his cows. Suddenly, the children's laughter outside was silenced by an angry shriek and accusations of cheating. Lotte, a furious flush on her face, burst into the house followed by a tearful Minna. Startled, Hans began to squirm and cry in Hanni's arms. Liesel added her wails to the turmoil and kicked at the blanket she'd been hugging. Walter, a frown on his face, turned to his oldest daughter. Before he had a chance to speak, Hanni stepped between them and asked, "What happened outside?".

"Nothing," replied Lotte and stalked out of the house.

Mumbling something under his breath, Walter left followed by Hanni's father. Their sudden exit left an emptiness filled only by the cries of small children.

It was hard for Hanni to know her own feelings at that moment. She had wanted to help Lotte. In fact, she had wanted to prove to her that she cared about her. Having been rebuffed, a pang of betrayal stabbed at her heart. Why had Lotte rejected her in front of the whole family, when all she wanted was to help? Hanni momentarily wished she could leave too. This was not, after all, her dream. It was as though she were an intruder in her own home. Eyes filling with tears, Hanni looked at her mother.

Not one to hold back her opinion, the older woman said, "You took her place, Hanni. When her mother died, she became the woman of the house. You came along and took it all away from her. She may never forgive you for that."

The truth and the harshness of her mother's words rang in Hanni's ears long after her parents left. That night, she decided to stay out of Lotte's way and speak to her only when necessary. It might not help the situation between them, but it would help Hanni in her struggle to maintain her newfound inner calm and keep her focus on the life she was beginning to build.

Chapter 4

The day was bitter cold, with a frosty wind blowing from the northeast. Hanni's hands nearly froze on the wires stretched between the rabbit hutch and shed where she hung wet laundry. The gusty wind whipped her fresh-washed sheets around her shoulders and head. It was almost no use to hang anything out today. There was only a small chance that the sun would begin to shine, but it was a chance she had to take.

Two years had passed since she married Walter. Two years and two babies, one of them dead. She had to hang these last bits of washing even if they didn't dry until tomorrow. There were two more tubs of washing waiting and most of her customers wanted their clothes and linens back by Friday. It was already Wednesday and she had at least two days of ironing to do with all the wash she had done this week.

The baby, Maria, lay bundled in blankets, dingy with age but warm and clean, in a carrying basket that Walter had bought last year before their little boy died. Hanni didn't want to think about that just now or the tears would start again. She looked at the tiny face peeking from the basket. Not for the first time, she wished this one were a boy, too. Boys had a better chance than girls to escape the drudgery and misery of their lives in this deadening valley. She dreamed that, somehow, at least one of her children would escape it.

Johanna

Pushing the last wooden clothespin onto the wire to hold the corner of a sheet, she glanced at the sky and hoped that she wouldn't have to bring all the washing inside and hang it throughout the family's tiny room. She prayed for a few hours of sunshine before nightfall.

The clotheslines had become a permanent fixture in their home. Walter, with the help of a neighbor, had strung the lines in criss-crosses under the eaves, where they would be out of the way, but handy when needed. When she was washing for her family, it had been a nuisance, but bearable. Now, though, whenever other families' sheets and long johns hung nearly to the top of their table and beds, the children complained and ridiculed.

Lotte grumbled between clenched teeth about the intrusion. "I don't see why I have to look at the crotch of Mrs. Gunther's bloomers while I'm eating. They're so big, they're all you can see in this house."

Hanni had to admit, it was sometimes funny to see the enormous bloomers of Mr. Gunther's new wife stretched across the entire width of the bench under the east window. Such comic relief was as welcome as it was rare in a house where too many people tried to find a bit of privacy.

Hanni, much as she wanted to, couldn't think of a different solution to their problem. She had started taking in the washing to help earn enough money for an occasional hunk of meat to feed her growing family. Walter did his best. He dragged himself home each evening exhausted from the farm work he now did for Mr. Ludwig after his twelve hours at the textile factory. The farm work gave them vegetables and the factory pay barely covered their housing. With no more emergencies or babies, they just might make it.

However, the queasiness in her stomach and the swelling in her ankles foretold the next little one. There was no mistaking it now.

Johanna

Her body was not getting ready for another of those protracted and painful periods she usually had. The time for that had passed and a new life was taking hold in her belly. An unbidden question of a God who would allow children to be born into so much misery and need was immediately followed by self chastisement for such heresy. She knew she should be both happy and grateful.

Hanni prayed every night—at least every night that she didn't fall into bed too exhausted to recite the words that now lacked conviction. Her mother would think she had failed in her duty to raise a good Christian daughter if she knew how much Hanni struggled to believe in a merciful or kind God after the death of her son. After Johann died—before he had even begun to live, before he said his first word or took his first step—Hanni felt only deadness inside too. When she remembered her old prayers—for a second room for the house, for Walter's pay at the factory to increase—she bristled with embarrassment at the child she had been. How could she have been so naïve, so foolish?

If she prayed for anything since that day, it was to keep the pregnancies at bay. Obviously she had failed in that too. She tried to think what life would be like without any more babies to feed and clothe. Guilty, she looked down at Maria and spent an extra moment patting the round cheeks reddened by cold winds. She was wasting time wondering about things over which she had no control and knew nothing about. God did what He did without hearing her prayers or for reasons she did not understand. Her task was to work and be grateful for whatever life He made for her.

Determined to keep going, Hanni bent over and lifted the basket that held Maria and swung her onto her left hip before making her way on the worn dirt path toward the house and the wash calling to her from next to the hearth.

Laughter and loud voices, interspersed with shrill shrieks, quickened her footsteps. Walter would not be home for hours yet. Another cry broke the air as Hanni flew into the house.

Nothing could have prepared her for the sight that met her eyes. Walter, with a grin as broad as his face, was twirling Lotte in frenzied circles between the table and the hearth while the other children sang frantic, off-key tunes to a rhythm that was anyone's guess. Her jaw slack with astonishment, Hanni stood in the doorway clutching the clothes basket and her baby.

"Sit and have a beer," said Walter as he pulled Hanni toward a stool opposite a stranger.

Amazement weakened her knees as she sank onto a bench. As her eyes adjusted to the dimness, she could see other people seated around the room. Even her parents and sisters were there. And among them someone she had never seen before. "What's going on here?" she shouted at the same time her eyes found the stranger sitting at her table. His head turned in her direction and a smile lit up a too-handsome face. Walter and Lotte danced toward her and Lotte grabbed the baby while Walter took Hanni in an unexpected embrace and swung her into the room.

One of her neighbors had come with his dog who lay curled under the bunk that usually served as Hans' bed. Now, it held not only her son, but two of her neighbor's children as well. A few people were standing or leaning against the wall at her back. How had they all managed to get there without her noticing? Too many trips to the river, a quarter of a mile from the house, for water and too many moments of idle musings had left her unaware of what was going on around her.

She noticed the score of beer bottles on the table and more on the mantle above the fire her husband had started. Amazement had taken her voice and shyness forced her eyes to the floor beneath her feet. As Walter lowered himself to a seat next to the one she had taken, he shoved a bottle of beer into Hanni's hand and ordered, "Drink!" Hanni raised the bottle to her lips and drank deeply. Not for the first time that day, her stomach began to lurch and she put the bottle back on the table. She looked wonderingly at her husband.

"It's a surprise party," he announced at last. "Your dad made all the arrangements."

"But what's it for?" Hanni whispered.

"Your husband was just made foreman at the factory," her father replied, his voice brimming with pride.

"Foreman?" she repeated.

"Yes," agreed Walter, gripping her hand and allowing himself one of his rare smiles. "I'll be making nearly half again as much and, if we're careful, we can build that house you've been dreaming of on the empty lot next to the mill pond."

Stunned, Hanni could only smile as she took another long draught of her beer. Finally, it seemed to quiet her nerves and settle her stomache. Her children's voices again became shrill with excitement as they speculated about all the ways their lives would change. Hanni barely noticed. As she sat sipping her beer, the sound of her guests' voices faded and she felt more than heard their presence. Her shoulders relaxed and she took another sip.

Almost of their own volition, her eyes strayed to the face of the stranger sitting across from her. A soft voice from Hanni's right said, "I'm Helga. This is my husband, Hans, We've just moved into the empty cottage near the vicar's place—the one at the edge of the forest going toward Butter Hill." A delicate hand pointed to the man across the table. Hanni could only think of her own swollen and chaffed hands still red from the cold. This Helga could not be much older than Hanni herself. There was a graceful air about her that was in sharp contrast to the old dress she wore. It was washed to a faded blue and, as a fold of it brushed Hanni's arm, she noticed that it was skillfully patched.

"Pleased to meet you," she murmured without taking her eyes off the bottle clutched in her lap where the folds of her skirt hid most of her hands' ugliness.

Helga got up and seated herself on the bench next to Hans. She picked up the full bottle next to the one her husband held in fingers stained with something Hanni could not even guess at. It was odd to have any guests at all, but to add strangers to the mix was almost too much for her.

"Hanni," gushed her mother as she took the seat Helga vacated, "isn't it wonderful that Hans and Helga have moved here? Hans is a shoemaker and the village needs one so badly. Helga has a weak constitution and needs a lot of rest. Our little village is an ideal place for both of them, don't you think?"

Without waiting for an answer, she rushed on, "Besides, Hans will work part-time for Walter at the factory when they need help during peak seasons. It turns out that Hans is a third cousin of my Uncle Arthur on my mother's side, so they're practically family."

Hans offered his stained hand, and Hanni blushed, startled by the strength of his grip.

The celebration lasted until the wee hours of the morning with more friends and relations dropping by to share congratulations, loaves of bread and other treats. Everyone who came brought as much as they could spare to help Walter and his family celebrate his success. The children stayed up much too late but, finally, curled into limp slumber in nooks and crannies left vacant by their now-drunk elders. Even the loud guffaws and occasional broken bottles throughout the night didn't wake them from their exhausted sleep.

Judging by the sunshine peeking through the small window next to the hearth, it was nearly noon when the patter of Liesel's bare feet near her bed woke Hanni. She couldn't remember when she went to bed or even when her guests left. Never one to drink so much beer, last night she had made up for a lifetime of near abstinence.

The thought of cleaning the wreckage from last night and finishing yesterday's laundry made Hanni sit up much too quickly. Her head was spinning and she sank back onto the bed. Was last night worth the sacrifice of this morning? Ah, but yes. Walter had gotten an unexpected promotion as well as a raise and she had hope again for a better future.

She forced her head off the pillow and her feet to the ground. It wasn't until after she had given Maria her bottle and Hans and Liesel their cereal that she discovered the basket of clean linens on the floor next to the table. Someone had washed her laundry! Every bit of it! All she had to do was hang it up and start ironing. As she looked around she had another realization. There were no empty or broken bottles to clean up. No dirty dishes to wash. No floor to sweep. Her whole house was spick-and-span from top to bottom and, for a moment, she wondered if she dreamed the party last night. Had Walter done her chores before he had gone to work? Had her mother and sisters stayed to help out? Her headache reminded her that last night had not been a dream and that she better hang the last clean batches of clothes and linens to dry. Still grateful and curious as to who might have done so much for her, Hanni stoked the fire, placed her two irons on the coals to heat, tied Maria to her chest and went outside with a basket of clean laundry under each arm.

Even the weather had turned bright and sunny and, if her head hadn't hurt so much, she would have been even more grateful for the wonderful turn life had taken. She would have to remember to say a special prayer of thanks that night. She smiled to herself as she acknowledged that she did still believe in prayer.

Lotte, carrying the now heavy Liesel squirming in her arms, and Minna tagging, as usual, behind her, hurried up to Hanni with unfamiliar speed. Wondering what the child was up to now, Hanni was unprepared for Lotte's question.

"What do you want me to do?"

"What do you mean?" Hanni immediately regretted her remark. She tried again. "You just never asked that before and I don't know exactly what you mean."

"I thought I could maybe help."

Surprise and delight fought for dominance on Hanni's face as she bent to lay Maria into Lotte's arms. The sisters stared into each other's eyes before Lotte turned to leave without ever getting a reply.

The unexpected remark had stunned Hanni into speechlessness. She roused herself to say to Lotte's retreating back, "Thanks for the offer. If you could just take care of Liesel and Hans and watch Maria for a while, it will help a lot".

"Sure."

Wondering at her daughter's uncharacteristic attitude, she turned to hang up a dripping shirt. As her hands held a corner over her clothesline and forced a man-shaped wooden pin over the wet fabric, Hanni remembered the stranger who made shoes and who would work for Walter now and then. His name was Hans, just like her little boy. That was where the resemblance ended. Her son, only a young boy, gave every indication of also becoming a strong and handsome man, but not for many years. His blonde hair and blue eyes promised a resemblance to most of the people in their village. Hanni had no doubt he would be tall and charming like many of the young men who were growing up much too fast.

This new Hans was different. His hair was the closest to black Hanni had ever seen. His green eyes looked out at the world from a face so startlingly handsome that it might have been beautiful if it weren't so rugged. Hanni had noticed broad shoulders that made him look strong even while sitting. It wasn't until he had gotten up to leave that she noticed how he towered above her and how he had to duck his head to get through the doorway.

Thinking of him gave Hanni a queasy feeling in her stomach that had nothing to do with her pregnancy. Even her cheeks felt flushed and she made herself think about Helga, his wife. Frail from whatever illness she suffered, she was nevertheless a kind soul. She had tried to talk to Hanni even when Hanni was too shy to do much more than offer an occasional short comment. In fact, it was Helga who had helped to bring in more beer and put more food onto platters. It was also Helga who had held Maria most of the evening when the baby fussed. Thinking about Helga, Hanni remembered the gentle arms that held her upright while her new friend helped her to her bed.

With that realization came another. Now Hanni remembered seeing Helga as she bustled about washing dishes, wiping the table and removing bottles to a wooden crate outside the door. She could see the movement of Helga's hands and hear the clatter of dishes as though from a great distance. She remembered how strange everything looked last night. It seemed she was looking through a tunnel, her peripheral vision a dark blur. As the evening progressed, the sounds she heard seemed to come from a great distance and Hanni was sure her head would never stop spinning.

The one constant was Helga. Helga at the sink, Helga next to the girl's bed covering them with blankets kicked to the floor, Helga

with a broom, everywhere. How could she have forgotten? Helga
had done it all.

Chapter 5

It was going to be the biggest wedding of the year. Hanni's sister, Sabine, was going to marry Peter Karr, the most eligible bachelor for miles around. It had seemed to everyone that Sabine, two years Hanni's senior, and their older sister, Mathilde, would never find husbands. However, Hanni knew very well, the two young women were simply unwilling to leave their comfortable home and doting parents. There had never been a good enough reason to exchange their undemanding lives for the hard work of managing their own families. That is, until Peter walked into Sabine's life carrying a huge sack of flour their dad had ordered. His hair and face were covered with a film of fine white dust. It did little to hide his handsome features and, from the moment Sabine laid eyes on him, it was apparent that her interest was not in his delivery. Hanni was happy for her sister.

Mathilde was not. The oldest of the three daughters had little to be happy about when it became apparent that she would be the only one without a husband. It had not been so much of a problem when Hanni had married a man twice her age with four children to take care of, but Sabine's was another story. Matti had envisioned the two of them getting old together, two spinsters with enough money and lots of freedom. Then, Sabine had spoiled it all by falling in love. Now, instead of being envied, Matti would be pitied.

She was nearly thirty years old and without the remotest chance of finding someone suitable for her to marry. Instead, she envisioned herself drying up and withering away as she cared for her parents in their old age, all by herself.

As Hanni prepared for the wedding, she wondered if Sabine and Peter would have children. Almost every couple wanted them. Not everyone could have them, though, and far too many of the young women died in childbirth. Helga had never had children and Hanni knew it was a terrible loss for her friend. They had talked about it once, shortly after they first met. Helga had come to help take care of Liesel when Hans had gotten chicken pox and Hanni was at her wits end with exhaustion. When Hanni insisted that Helga stay away, fearing that she too, might get sick, her friend had said that she loved every moment with the children and would not give up the chance to be with them for something as silly as chicken pox.

When Hanni replied that Helga might not feel the same way when she had a brood of her own, the pain on Helga's face stopped her in mid sentence. Turning away from one another, they busied themselves with the children. It was never mentioned again. Often, after that day, Hanni noticed the pain underlying the smiles Helga and the children shared.

Hanni swung the iron rod with the huge kettle of boiling water out of the cavity of her hearth, wrapped a rag around the hot handle, and strained to carry the heavy pot to the tub Walter had set up in the middle of the room. It was already nearly full of water and this last pot would get the temperature just right. She had hung sheets from her clotheslines strung around the tub to close off a private space for herself. Someone was always coming in or going out of the house and Hanni wanted a few minutes to relax and enjoy her bath.

Letting her dress drop around her feet, she stepped over the tall rim of her tub and lowered one foot slowly into the almost unbearably hot water. It took several minutes to get all the way in but once there, Hanni smiled and allowed her muscles to relax. Sinking deeper into the water, Hanni ran her hands over the loose folds of skin on her belly. She liked the smoothness of the soap on her skin as she worked it into a lather from a bar scented with lavender from one of her flower beds. Her mind drifted to a time when she had only as much skin as she needed, a time before her babies. She had married Walter nearly five years ago and in that time had given birth to as many babies. First Johann and then Maria, four years old now, followed by Trude then Otto and then Heinz. Last had come Olaf, just a few months old but already precocious and more than a handful. It was impossible to imagine life without them.

An image of Helga formed in her mind again and Hanni felt the strength of the friendship that had grown between them. Helga had sat with Hanni during each recent birth, her gentle words and touch soothing Hanni's agonized body until the next contraction gripped her in a vice of pain. It was Helga who bathed and dressed each child after the midwife had checked them, and it was Helga who placed each newborn in the crook of Hanni's arm.

By now the water had cooled and Hanni knew it was time to get out. She had stayed in the tub longer than she had intended and still had to bathe the children before they could get dressed and leave for church.

Lotte and Minna were next to bathe and then Liesel, Maria and Trude, who were small enough to fit into the tub together. Hans, now all of ten years old was the last to use the water which was barely warm anymore and had formed a soapy film on top. It made little difference to him as he slid down the sloping end. Hanni, who had wrapped a huge apron around the better of the two dresses she owned, was laughing with him as she rubbed a chunk of soap into his hair and scrubbed vigorously. Diving again to rinse the soap from his head, he emerged and stood more pink now than brown. Hanni flung a bath towel that was too wet to do much good around the boy and scooped him into her arms. It was a ritual they had enjoyed since she became his mother five years ago and was a perfect excuse to hold him close for a few minutes.

"You're getting to be such a big boy. I don't know how much longer I'll be able to pick you up".

"I can get out myself and sit on your lap".

"I'd like that, Hansi", said Hanni using the endearing version of his name.

Just then, an angry cry came from the girl's corner where Lotte and Minna were braiding each other's hair and Liesel and Maria were getting dressed. It was Liesel who was upset this time and the issue seemed to be about who would wear the larger, prettier dress.

"I'm older so I get to wear the bigger one!" shouted Liesel.

It was true. Maria, at four years old, was one year younger than Liesel. However, Maria was the bigger of the two, a fact that Liesel found nearly intolerable.

"This one is too tight for me." Maria held up the linen frock. She laid it carefully on the bed behind her and held out her hand for the one clutched in Liesel's grip.

Hanni set Hans on the floor and handed him his clean clothing before turning and walking to the girls. Before she had a chance to say anything, Maria picked up the small dress and slipped it over her head. "I think it will be alright one more time." Hanni, smiling, patted her on the shoulder. "My good girl," she whispered in Maria's ear, and then, a bit louder, "thank you."

She heard the familiar sounds of Walter splashing water from the barrel outside the door. As she glanced through the tiny window near the corner of the room, she could see him bending over the wooden barrel. He had taken his shirt off and suspenders hung at his sides down to his knees. His skin looked shiny where water ran down his back and sides. Another mighty handful shimmered in the air above his head and shoulders before it landed on his neck and back. His back still bent, Walter reached up on top of a wooden board for the large bar of yellow oatmeal soap that Helga and Hanni had made last fall. He had once told her that he liked the smell of it and the way it made his skin feel, so she made sure he always had some for his personal use. As soap suds began to cover his chest and arms and finally the hair on top of his head, Hanni admired again the taughtness of his muscles and the long back that tapered from wide shoulders to a narrow waist and hips. All things considered, Hanni knew she was a lucky woman.

There was not much time left and she reluctantly turned away from the window. Hans and Maria were now herding the smaller kids, Trude and Otto, around the flower beds on the side of the house. Hanni had told them they could each pick one flower for the wedding and they were making their selections. Little Heinz was napping so it was Olaf she needed to worry about. Just then, Helga's voice could be heard shouting a greeting toward the children in the garden. Hanni smiled in anticipation of her friend's appearance and shifted Olaf to her other hip before going to the open front door. Helga's smile greeted her as the small woman flung her arms around her friend and the baby.

"Here, let me have him. You go and get ready."

A mischievous smile accompanied these words but Hanni did not stop to ask the reason. She was grateful for the extra time to get ready and rushed into the house. Helga had Olaf pinned down on a bench and was tickling him to make him roll over so she could get the little cotton shirt over his head and arms. A cloth bundle had fallen near her feet but Hanni paid little attention as she finished her own hurried preparations. She draped a scarf over her shoulders depicting monks in brown robes baking bread in huge stone ovens. Walter had woven it for her birthday last year. He had made it from scraps of silk yarns left over at the factory. She was happy for such an occasion to wear it. Her hair, falling below her hips, was almost dry. Quickly, she parted it and began the daily braiding which no longer required a mirror or thought. All that was left was winding each braid on top of her head and pinning them into place. She was famous for her "crown" and took a secret pride in the abundance of shiny hair with golden highlights.

Walter entered, for a moment blocking the sun and putting the room into shadow. His cheerful voice and the returning bright rays dispelled the temporary shadows as he stepped around Helga and the baby to reach for his clean shirt ready for him on a hook next to the little window. Clean socks and his only pair of shoes, repaired regularly by Helga's husband, completed his toilet. His long brown hair, recently trimmed, was already tied at the back of his neck with a leather thong. Hanni noticed there was less of it now and a patch on top where, if she looked hard enough, a glimmer of skin showed through. Even so, he was a handsome man.

Although Walter was as old as her father, Hanni was acutely aware that she no longer looked so much younger than her husband. Giving birth to five children and breast feeding those who lived, had thickened her once slim waist and pulled her breasts closer to her stomach. Her legs were still slim and strong but that didn't count because no one could see them beneath the long, full skirt of her dress.

The little ones had now come in from the flower beds and were tugging at Walter to go outside with them and cut the flowers they chose. Even Lotte, usually distant and sullen, chatted non-stop as they all trooped out of the house after their father. Trude and Otto pulled at their father's trouser legs until he picked both up and carried them into the garden. That left Heinz, still sleeping, and Olaf, sucking on a bottle Helga had prepared for him, in the room that seemed suddenly too quiet.

Hanni bent down and reached under the bed for her shoes, failed to find them and looked puzzled. In the summer she always went barefoot, but she was careful to store her only pair of shoes under the head of her bed. The shoes were nearly as old as Lotte and were quite worn so she took care to protect them. On her hands and knees, Hanni reached under the bed as far as she could. Baffled, she got up and turned in the direction of her laughing friend.

Helga held out the paper-wrapped bundle as Hanni groaned her way to her feet. Still annoyed at not finding her shoes, she took the proffered bundle and untied the string that held the package together. Released, the paper opened as her old slippers, along with a beautiful pair of leather shoes of the same size, dropped on the table top. Stunned, Hanni sank onto the bench beside the table and stared at the beautiful gift. Outside, the voices of her children dimmed as she reached toward the soft brown leather, shoes more beautiful than any she had ever seen. There were even toe and heel reinforcements of a darker shade, and laces so thin and fine she hardly dared pull on them. Her eyes met those of her friend across the table and spoke of gratitude and love beyond words.

"I had to take your old ones so Hans could get the size exactly right," Helga apologized. She shoved the shoes closer to Hanni and bid her put them on.

Hanni lifted her left foot, laid it across her right knee, and slipped the soft leather folds of her new shoes over her foot. Then the right foot and still she could hardly believe Helga had made this gift possible. Hanni couldn't remember ever feeling so beautiful.

Shiny and bright from head to toe, she nearly floated across the floor and through the open doorway into brilliant sunshine. She couldn't stop smiling as she and Helga waited for Walter and the children to finish picking their flowers. Walter glanced up once in astonishment at his wife's glowing face before turning to the children again. Finally finished, he stole an appreciative glance along her body before reaching for her hand. Holding back, Hanni held out a newly-shod foot and waited for him to notice. When Walter's eyes finally rested on the end of her outstretched leg, his eyes snapped in Helga's direction. He murmured, "thank you" before returning his gaze to Hanni's shining eyes. Their brilliance was a sharp contrast to the dark circles underneath that never seemed to fade anymore. Walter, smiling, reached again for Hanni's hand.

Walter thought about their friends and how they helped out as much as they could with little shoes made from leftover scraps of leather, and clothes from family and friends whose children had outgrown them. However, there was seldom anything new for Hanni or Walter. Walter knew that Hans had made this new pair of shoes for Hanni at Helga's bidding. Helga would have liked to have done more for her friend but his pride and his wife's shyness would not let them take more. As it was, they would only accept the gifts she brought because they helped their children and they knew how much Helga loved them. Even the bright but taciturn Lotte had finally accepted Helga's gentle attentions and they often spent whole afternoons reading from books Helga brought. Both Lotte and Minna had become fine readers under her tutelage and knew how to write simple letters. Hans still resisted those opportunities, but Liesel and Maria had picked up considerable skills.

It was Maria, though, who had Helga's special regard. Helga had first met her three years ago when Maria had still been a toddler of one. Today, at four, the child was already reading well and starting to write. What was most surprising was Maria's facility with numbers. When she made little piles out of stones or grain, she already seemed to have a grasp of how they could be counted, divided, and multiplied. Walter would never forget the day when Maria stormed into the house and demanded that someone make Liesel give back eight of her clothespins.

In a voice choked with anger, Maria had cried, "We both had thirty and she stole eight of mine! I need them back because they're the people in my village. She doesn't need thirty-eight anyway".

From that moment on, Helga paid her more attention. Because she was just a girl, there was no telling how this talent would ever do Maria any good, but it was fun to see the child's excitement. Besides, it gave Helga another excuse to spend time with her.

Since Helga's first days at the little house, Trude, Otto, Heinz and Olaf had been added to the family. Another two were marked by tiny crosses in the garden.

Almost as one family, Hans and Helga, Walter and Johanna and, of course, all the children, made their way on the path that meandered across the meadow and between rows of family gardens. It was already filling with people on their way to the old church in the oak grove. Because it wound around the shoemaker's cottage, the path was one that Helga took each time she came into the village to shop or see Hanni.

It had been easy to sneak the old pair of shoes from under Hanni's bed and out of the house. Hanni wore shoes so seldom, she had not missed the old ones. It made her feel good to see the delight on Hanni's face and to know that her friend now had something new on this day of celebrating someone else's happiness.

As the three of them walked side by side along the road, Helga was filled with love for the young woman who gave so much and asked so little in return. She often envied her friend the love and companionship of her large family. However, Helga knew, too, that Hanni toiled from morning till late at night and lived a life not of her own choosing. She cared for her own household and worked endless hours washing and ironing for others. Somehow, even with Walter's promotion a few years ago, there never seemed to be quite enough money or time to take care of everyone's needs. One of the children was always sick while others needed clothing or the house required repairs—along with the yearly addition of another crib.

The path was now winding between gardens divided into roughly one acre plots. Each family grew vegetables and fruit trees that met their personal needs. In addition, one family tended bees and sold or traded that precious sweetener.

"Do you want me to carry Olaf for a while?" asked Hanni. "He can get heavy even though he's still small".

"No, he's fine and I love having him in my arms", replied Helga. They walked slowly on, side by side. The going was slow and a warm breeze stirred flowers on either side of the path. Sunshine bathed their skin and Helga glanced again at Hanni's smiling face. "I've never had a friend like you", she finally said. "You're like a sister, except better. There aren't any bad memories of growing up—just understanding and sharing."

Hanni stopped. When Helga stopped and turned to her friend, she saw tears in Hanni's eyes. Neither spoke. No words were needed. Instead, the two women embraced.

Later, while Olaf slept in the crook of Helga's arm, Hanni picked Heinz up and Walter swung Otto onto his shoulders. Maria, dragging Trude through the weeds at the side of the path, insisted on telling her younger sister the names of each of the flowers they trampled beneath their already dirty feet.

"That's not a flower, Trude, that's a nettle. Don't touch it! It'll sting. Mommy uses it to make tea when she has a headache, but she always puts on her gloves before she picks it."

"I want to give some to Mommy," insisted little Trude.

Johanna

"Why don't you pick some of those little yellow ones? They're called buttercups. They're pretty and there are so many of them. See? They're growing all over the hill. That's why it's called Butter Hill. I think."

"There he is," shouted ten-year-old Hans as he ran in the direction of the older man with the same name. Helga, her reverie interrupted, smiled as she spotted her husband striding through the trees from their cottage in their direction. Walter waved his greeting and Hanni, shy as always, lowered her head to gaze discreetly in the direction of her friend's handsome husband. Even after nearly four years, she flushed and was struck dumb whenever he was near. Today, though, she would have to speak to him and thank him for the wonderful shoes he had made for her. In her thoughts, she practiced again what she would say but was not satisfied with any of the words that came to mind.

"Thank you, Hans. You're the most thoughtful man in the world. No. That sounds like I don't think Walter is thoughtful. How about, I've never owned anything so beautiful in my life. No, that doesn't sound right either."

They met in the clearing in front of the little church where most of the neighbors, and some of the groom's family from the next town, were already gathered. Walter, after lowering Otto to the ground between them, shook Hans' hand and thanked him for Hanni's shoes before walking toward Josef, Hanni's father. He was standing in the midst of a growing crowd of men and greeted his best friend with an embrace and a slap on his back. "Yes, yes," he said as each new friend approached, "it will be hard to see her go. But Peter is a good man. And, at least, married to a miller, she will never be hungry."

As Hans drew near, Helga slipped her arm through his and both of them faced Hanni. They didn't really face her as much as stand in front of her lowered head. At last, Hanni managed a, "They're beautiful. Thank you," without ever raising her eyes above Hans' knees. Smiling, he bent down to touch the shoes and feel their fit. Hanni nearly jumped out of them at his touch. No one could guess how the pressure of his fingers on her ankles and feet made her feel. All she could do was hold still while he explored the seam that ran across her arch. As he kneeled on the ground at Hanni's feet, images raced through her mind that made her stomach lurch and her knees weak. Overwhelmed with desire, Hanni blushed and turned her head to hide her guilt and embarrassment."They seem alright," he pronounced as he stood. Hanni repeated, "They're beautiful."

She felt stupid, but Hans seemed pleased and smiled as he turned with Helga in the direction of the church. The little group made its way to the door of the church that had served their village for countless generations. It was a place of worship and much more. Everyone Hanni knew had been baptized there and married couples each had been wed in its dim interior. Those who died were honored here and laid to rest in the graveyard next to the stone wall that surrounded the yard on three sides. Behind the tiny altar, a trap door opened to stone steps that were older than the church itself. No one knew who had built them or why.

Entering to the sounds of a violin playing a traditional wedding hymn, Hanni felt a sense of peace settle over her. She made her way with Walter and the children to seats near the back, where she could easily reach the door if the baby became disruptive. Even sitting on each other's laps, they took up all of one pew.

Chapter 6

Hanni loved the tapestry. It hung over the bed she and Walter had shared for eleven years—the bed in which all of her children had been conceived and born. For perhaps the hundredth time, she sat on the edge of that bed and looked lovingly at Walter's gift to her for their anniversary a few months ago. Like every time before, she was struck by its beauty.

"Mommy, I'm hot", mumbled Maria rolling her head and shoulders toward the wall, and kicking off her covers. Hanni had put the nine year old girl into her bed so she could sleep without disturbing her sister. Usually, she shared a cot with eleven year old Liesel but her heated body and tossing and turning made it impossible for Liesel to get any rest. In fact, Maria sometimes kicked so violently in her delirium that Hanni and Walter had considered tying her to the bed posts. However, neither of them had done more than suggest it.

Hanni fetched another cool, wet washcloth from the bucket next to the sink. Wringing it out before she returned to her bed, she placed the cloth on Maria's burning forehead. "The fever will break soon and you'll feel much better, Liebchen." Hanni called all her children "little love" but it was especially true of this one. Maria had always delighted and seldom caused concern. That's what made it so hard to see this gentle, bright girl so miserable. She looked so small in the big bed holding one of Hanni's hands as Hanni stroked her wet hair with the other.

Johanna

Again, Hanni stole a glance at the tapestry Walter had woven just for her. Two friends, dressed in flowing robes, strolled through a garden surrounded by angelic children at play. It was easy to imagine who had served as the inspiration for Walter's idealized theme. Hanni and Helga often walked arm-in-arm in front of their little house while the children played around them. However, there the resemblance ended. In the real world, there were no flowing robes and their garden grew cabbages instead of flowers. The children showed a slight resemblance of features but, more often than not, Hanni's children played in dirt rather than on green grass under shadowed oak trees.

She loved the tapestry. She could feel her husband's love through every weft and warp. He was kinder and gentler than she ever thought possible in those distant days when she first came to know him. She had no doubt that the life he had wished for her and their children was closer to that in the tapestry than what he had been able to provide. All the love and wishful thinking could not give them the extra room they needed so badly or even the food that was so often absent from their table. Neither could it buy the medicine Maria needed right now to break the fever.

"Here, Liebchen, try to drink a little more water," Hanni urged— but Maria was asleep again and Hanni's head hung low with fatigue and desperation.

Three more children had been born since Sabine had married Peter six years ago. Karin, now four years old, was a quiet girl who preferred her own company to that of others. Werner was now two and as precocious as any of Hanni's other boys. There had also been "little Helga", named in honor of Hanni's friend. The baby girl was a fragile, sickly child who had lived only a few months. Helga had helped deliver the infant and had taken care of her while Hanni recovered from the difficult birth. Baby Helga's death had devastated both women and often when Hanni went to put flowers on her children's' graves, she would find some already placed there.

Johanna

The door opened, letting sunlight brighten the dark interior of the house as Helga stepped inside. She set a basket of vegetables on the table before turning to Hanni and Maria on the bed. "Hanni, you look tired. Lie down next to Maria and I'll take care of the rest for a while." Hanni, too tired to argue, climbed around her daughter and laid down beside her. Their heads lay on the same sweat-soaked pillow, and Hanni flung an arm around the girl's waist. She was instantly asleep. Helga looked lovingly at both before taking the vegetables she had brought to the sink for a scrub.

The pot of vegetable soup was boiling when Walter came home for lunch. He had found most of the children in the yard and called to them to come inside with him when he entered through the open door. The scene he found at first put a smile on his face. Hanni was asleep with Maria. Helga sat with her head resting on the table where she'd been cutting vegetables, snoring softly. As some of his children trooped in, he turned and walked to the bed.

His smile turned into a puzzled frown when he shook Hanni's shoulder and stroked Maria's cool brow. He sat on the edge of the bed as his wife stirred and slowly sat up. Behind him he could hear children scraping chairs and putting bowls and spoons on the table. Helga groaned before getting up and moving the soup pot to where they could all reach it more easily.

"Something isn't right" he said with an edge to his voice. Hanni was instantly alert and looked at Walter. Their eyes met a moment before Hanni recognized the horror in his. She turned and flung her arms around Maria, shaking her first-born. The child's head wobbled loosely until Hanni clutched it to her chest. Keening wails escaped her throat as she tried to form words. Strangled cries from Helga and the children were added to the heartbreaking din. Walter, still sitting on the edge of the bed, turned away from the two people he loved most dearly and, slumping, let his head fall into his large, calloused hands.

Johanna

Three days later Hanni and Walter stood side by side next to Maria's grave. The service was over and their first daughter together had been laid into the ground in a simple pine box Walter and Joseph and Hans had made. He reached for Hanni's hand. She turned to face him, dry-eyed and calm. Too calm, he thought. "I don't understand," she said turning back to the grave with its fresh dirt and flowers. "Why did God take her from us? Why Maria, why not this one?" she said rubbing her hand across her swollen belly.

Walter looked at her and, for the first time in their life together, saw grimness on Hanni's face at war with her gentle nature. "I don't know, Hanni. He gives life and He takes life. It doesn't make any sense to me how or why".

The following week, a cry rang out from the street where it forked toward the town square in one direction and toward the factory in another. "There's been an accident at the factory!"

Hanni's heart sank as she heard those words shouted by one of her neighbors. In another minute he was running up the walk to her house. Her knees instantly weakened and she felt as if she would collapse. "Please, God, don't let it be true," she prayed. "Please, God, don't let it be Walter."

But it was. It was Walter doing what he always did, helping others. He had tried to pull a weaver from under a collapsed shuttle when the whole loom crashed onto the stone floor pinning them both under its weight. Walter had fallen across a floor strut and broken his back, dying instantly. The other man had died more slowly after an agonizing hour of failed attempts to free his broken legs and chest.

Hanni leaned against the door frame listening to her neighbor explain how it happened. She kept missing the details as her mind shut out his words. "There was nothing anyone could do. By the time we got there it was already too late. We tried Mrs. Meinhardt, we did our best. I'm really sorry".

Johanna

His voice kept on making sounds she could no longer understand as others gathered to hear the news. A few of them were women, neighbors and cousins, who drew close to her immediately.

Hanni could feel her legs lose their solidity, like ice melting into water. She felt hands gripping her arms, then felt herself evade their grasp as she started to black out. The pain, as she landed hard on the window sill, brought her back to consciousness momentarily. Then stronger, rougher arms wrapped themselves around her and lifted her as she lost consciousness again.

Sometime later, Hanni woke up in bed—their bed. It took a few moments for her mind to focus and remember he would never share it again. She turned her head at the sound of dishes clattering. Helga was pouring hot water from the kettle into a mug. Before long, the smell of chamomile with a hint of mint reached Hanni's nose and her stomach growled with anticipation.

Helga walked to the bed carrying a steaming mug, a wan smile directed toward Hanni. "Here, dear heart, drink this."

Hanni pushed herself to a sitting position and leaned against the headboard beneath Walter's tapestry. She took the mug of tea from her friend's hands and set it on top of her rounded belly. The baby growing inside her stirred and the mug swayed spilling drops of hot tea. Hanni sighed and smiled gratefully into the worried eyes of her friend. "Helga, I don't know what I'm going to do now. How can I manage without Walter?"

"Lotte and Minna are old enough to find work and little Hans is already sixteen so he can hire out. If the girls work in the factory and little Hans can trade work for food on one of the farms, you should be able to make ends meet. Liesel is already eleven and Trude nine, they can help with the wash you take in. And you know Hans and I will help as much as we can."

Johanna

"I know you mean well, Helga, but that still leaves Otto, Olaf, Karin and Werner and this new baby. I don't think I can farm and take in washing too. The landlord won't let me stay if I don't produce at least as much profit for him as Walter used to".

"Hanni, you have to take first things first. First of all, we must lay Walter to rest." At this moment Hanni's face contorted with grief and something else. Helga took the mug of hot tea out of Hanni's hands and placed it on the floor. Worriedly, she leaned closer to her friend and said, "I know this is painful but it must be done. Now, you don't have the burden all on yourself. Everyone in the village has agreed to take care of the funeral and you know I'll help with the children".

Another shudder swept though Hanni's body and Helga realized it was not just Walter's death that tore at Hanni but the birth of his last child.

Willi was born the next morning, nearly two months early.

For a few weeks, Hanni moved through one day after the other in a mental shroud that would not lift. The baby bound to her chest in a cloth sling slept peacefully, his fists pressed into his mouth. Her breasts refused to produce more than the smallest bit of milk. It was just enough for the tiny infant. Every day she walked to Walter's grave while Lotte and Minna took care of the younger children and Hans walked from one farm to the next looking for work. "Help me Walter. Please, if you can hear me, help me".

Then the day she had been dreading came in the form of a black coach drawn by a matched pair of the blackest horses Hanni had ever seen. The man who stepped out of the vehicle and crossed her yard to stand in her doorway looked into the small home crowded with children and asked, "I'm here to speak with Johanna Meinhardt. Would that be you, Ma'am?" looking at Hanni sorting wash next to a tub of steaming water.

"Yes sir, that's me," said Hanni in a tired voice.

When she went outside and stood with her arms folded over the squirming bundle on her chest, the stranger looked at her and sighed. "I'm sorry, Ma'am, I've been instructed to inform you that this farm has been rented. You will have to vacate within the week." Without a word, Hanni looked past him toward the fields Walter had tended every day for as long as she could remember. The silence stretched before them like a soft cloth stretching more and more tightly in opposite directions. Minutes later just before it ripped, the stranger tipped his hat, said "Ma'am" once more and turned to leave.

"Where should we go?" Hanni called before he could step into the coach. He turned around long enough to shrug his shoulders before climbing into his black vehicle and signaling the driver to proceed. Much more quickly than they had come, the horses left in a cloud of dust.

When it was time to move, Hanni and her ten children moved from the small house they had lived in for over twelve years and into one of the "charity homes" provided for the needy. It was an apartment with a kitchen and three other rooms that could be used as living or bedrooms. With Hans' help, Hanni, Lotte, Minna, sixteen year old Hans, and even some of the younger children, Hanni moved their lives in one day. There was not much furniture. Her bed and table with chairs, wooden wash tubs, their zinc bathtub, a few dishes and pots and their linens were all the family owned.

Helga was not feeling well and had to be left behind, fuming. Now more than ever, Hanni needed her help, but she hardly had the strength to get out of bed. Hans insisted she stay home. "Don't let her lift the heavy stuff. She hasn't had a chance to recover from the last birth and she's still nursing. Promise me you'll take care of her," she shouted as he left.

Johanna

There was actually more space than they'd had in the cottage, which they desperately needed, but it was on the fourth floor which meant Hanni had to carry heavy baskets of dirty or wet laundry up and down three flights of stairs. She believed it would not take long for her body to be as broken as her spirit.

As they were finding places for their belongings, Lotte and Minna took Hanni aside. Lotte, now twenty years old and Minna, two years younger, had something important to share. We know how hard it is for you right now and we're old enough to work. It's just that there's no work for us around here so we've decided to go to Dresden." Hanni looked at her two oldest girls to see if they were playing a bad joke on her. Their eager faces told her how serious they were. "We talked it over after father died and Uncle Peter talked to a relative who lives in Dresden, and it's all arranged. Minna and I can work in the porcelain factory and live with his cousin and his wife. Besides, Peter and Sabine's mill is doing so well that they deliver grain and flour every month in Dresden. They can check on us regularly."

Hanni only stared. There was nothing to say. It had all been arranged without her. Dresden was less than an hour's train ride away but it might as well have been another country. All the stories she had ever heard spoke of miles of cobbled streets, buildings larger than her entire village and shops with more things to buy than she would ever be able to imagine. It was hard to think about her girls lost in such a crowd of people and buildings. However, Hanni knew there was no future for Lotte and Minna in their small village and their chances of finding a husband were even less than before their father died. She would not, could not, stop them. She did the only thing left to her, she hugged both girls and told them, "I'll miss you terribly".

Hans and Liesel soon joined their older sisters. Dresden had not only factories to work in but an unquenchable need for healthy, obedient servants in the fancy houses of the rich and royal. Hans found work in the stables of an estate owned by a distant cousin of the queen. It was a summer residence and the work was no more demanding than what Hans was used to at home. Eleven year old Liesel was taken in by a family near the main market place in downtown Dresden that made its money in trade. They were wealthier than anyone Liesel knew or could imagine and, because she had cared for so many younger siblings, she was hired to assist the nanny for the three youngest children.

People were kind and gave Hanni almost more washing than she could manage, but the money was never enough to feed the remaining children, much less to properly clothe them. For that she had to depend on the charity of her neighbors and her parents. Even with their help and the four oldest children gone, Hanni had barely enough money for rent or food. Sabine, when she came, brought flour. "Here, Hanni, there's a turnip, some carrots and a sausage we had left over from yesterday. You can chop them up and have a little meat and vegetables in your soup. A little flour and water aren't enough to fill up all these bellies."

"I'm doing the best I can, Sabine. There just aren't enough hours in the day".

There was one final heartache that was almost more than Hanni could bear. She hesitated at the door, gathering her courage before knocking and entering her friend's home. Helga was asleep on the sofa, covered with heavy quilts. The dark circles under her eyes stood out in stark contrast to her otherwise pale, drawn face. Her disheveled hair was matted to her forehead. Hanni walked quietly across the room, trying not to awaken her. Helga, seemed to sense her presence, though, and opened her tired eyes. She managed a weak smile and faint, "Hello."

Hanni dampened a washcloth in the bowl of water that sat on the table near the sofa. Sitting at Helga's side, she reached over and wiped her forehead with the cool cloth. "How are you feeling?" she asked softly.

Johanna

"As well as can be expected, I guess. I'm glad you're here because I need to talk to you. Hans made some juice from the strawberries Mrs. Brenner brought a few days ago. It's there on the table. Pour us both a glass, would you please? No, don't argue with me. I don't have the strength for it." Hanni stopped shaking her head and did what Helga asked. When they were both settled comfortably again, Helga on the couch and Hanni in a stuffed chair next to her, Helga said, "I think it won't be long now, Hanni, and I want you to know that you're the best friend I've ever had."

"Shush. You don't need to say anything," Hanni said, smiling. "Besides, I know you'll get better. You just have to. You're the only friend I've ever had. What would I do without you? I'd be all alone."

"No you won't. You'll never be alone. You have your children and you have Hans. He's your friend too. He loves the children in his own way. He'll take care of you as best he can." Helga was losing strength and gasping for air but the intensity of her gaze kept Hanni from speaking. After a minute or two, she continued, "Hanni, promise me that you'll look after him, too. You'll need each other."

"Of course, I'll do anything I can for him. But don't talk like that. Save your strength." She turned her head so her friend could not see the tears flowing down her cheeks.

Hanni cared for Helga every day between chores, until the consumption she had battled for so many years finally won. She was buried on October 5, Hanni's birthday, next to the infant who bore her name. Hanni was 26 years old.

Now the days, even when the sun was shining, seemed grim and dark to Hanni. A depression had settled around her heart like a shroud. She tried to believe the priest when he told her that everyone gets their due, and suffered even more from guilt when she could not believe him. Praying harder and longer didn't work and at night she fell into exhausted sleep. Now there was no one to ease the burdens or even talk to. What she needed most was companionship. The kind Walter and Helga had given her those many years. Although she had never taken it for granted, she never imagined that one day she would have to live without it. The loneliness, when it surfaced, seemed to shred her heart until her chest burned.

Trude had taken charge of her younger siblings now that her older brothers and sisters were gone. Otto, Heinz, Olaf, and Karin could always be seen tagging along after her. That left three-year-old Werner and Willi, still a toddler, for Hanni. Especially at night, Willi would often wake her with his wheezing. Sometimes, already past the point of exhaustion, Hanni woke up to an unnatural silence and found him not breathing at all. For the next thirty minutes or so, she would cuddle, shake and force a bit of mint tea into the tiny mouth. Hanni was too tired to think about what might happen if she failed to wake up one night. It was one night at a time and each night she tried harder to spend a little more time in prayer before going to sleep. The best she could do was ask God to give her a bit more strength.

Chapter 7

"Mommy," came the urgent call from somewhere down the street. It was Trude. "Mommy, I got something for us."

Hanni was hanging freshly washed clothing on lines in the enclosed courtyard near their apartment. She stopped her work when Trude, now eleven years old, rushed down the back steps carrying a large box. The girl's chin helped to balance the cumbersome burden and her bright eyes shone above her smiling mouth.

For the most part, Trude was a quick-witted and practical child. Only last month she had shown Hanni blood soaked panties. There was no alarm in the girl's voice when she said, "I was hoping this wouldn't happen for a while but I guess it doesn't really matter. I don't want kids – ever. Being a woman is a lot of hard work and kids just make it worse." Hanni had a moment of parental pride before concern tugged at the corners of her mouth.

"What could she possibly have in that box she proudly dropped at my feet?"

"They're shoes!" the girl squealed and, indeed, they were. There were seven or eight pairs of shoes in the box, and they looked to be new. Astonishment and concern fought on her face as Hanni picked up one pair after another before dropping them back into the box.

"Where did you get these?" she asked, though she recognized the style and workmanship.

Proudly, Trude told her mother that she had spoken to Uncle Hans weeks ago and told him they all needed shoes and that, since he was a shoemaker, he should get to work. Hanni was aghast. How would she pay for these treasures they needed so badly but could never afford? The only pair of shoes she'd even recently owned was the one Hans had made her so many years ago and she had given that pair to Lotte and Minna when they left.

Walter's shoes had been too torn up to be of use to anyone and she had cleaned them and buried him with them on his feet. The gift of shoes was more than she had ever imagined. The look of pride and delight on Trude's face had been replaced by a look of concern when the expected enthusiasm was not forthcoming from her mother. Hanni looked at her pretty, green-eyed daughter and asked what these wonderful shoes cost.

"Oh, that's the best part, Mommy. Uncle Hans said that he should have thought about doing this a long time ago and that it's his pleasure to make them for us. He also said that it would be real nice of you if you would cook the rabbit or something he'll bring next Sunday so we can all have something good to eat."

Hanni, too stunned to reply, said nothing. After a few moments, with no further response coming from her mother, Trude turned to retreat to the end of the yard where the other children were waiting. Hanni lowered herself carefully to the ground so as not to wake Willi who was sleeping strapped to her left hip. She picked up and examined each pair of shoes. All similar in shape, they were of varying sizes so that each child, as they grew, could have a new pair to fit into. At the bottom were two shoes slightly different from the rest. The leather was just a bit softer and a delicate design had been stitched from the toes to where the laces started. Each shoe seemed to have a wing of some kind stitched on the top and when she put the two shoes together, she could see the form of a butterfly. They were the most beautiful shoes Hanni had ever seen.

It was still three days to Sunday; plenty of time to finish everyone's washing, clean the house, gather the herbs and wild mushrooms she would need for a delicious meal, and bathe herself and all the children. Yet, a sense of urgency gripped Hanni. She wondered what she really looked like since Walter died more than a year ago. When he was alive, she could always tell when he thought she was pretty. After his death, until this moment, she had been too depressed and too busy to care about her looks and had done only what was necessary to get by. She didn't have a full-length mirror, so a large window pane had to do. She opened the window to an angle that allowed her the best reflection and studied the threadbare black dress she'd worn all year and that now hung more like a dark blanket in shapeless folds around her body. Suspended on bony shoulders, it dropped to the floor like a rag. Making sure no one was outside to watch her, Hanni twisted and turned to glimpse her image. Her posturing revealed only cotton bloomers and pale skin stretched over a small frame of delicate bones. Grief and hunger had robbed her of fat long ago. What remained was a slim and remarkably youthful figure left firm and subtle by hard work. Her belly had been stretched too often by pregnancies to be flat, but the crisscrossing of stretch marks, like a road map across her stomach, were faded. Her breasts, flattened by babies and sagging with the weight of time, were small now, with nipples even darker than she remembered. In spite of these changes, Hanni saw a reflection that was graceful and pleasing overall. Her thick hair was still luxurious and her eyes still a brilliant blue. All that was needed was a sparkle of hope and joy to make them beautiful.

Friday and Saturday were a blur of activities. Each of those nights Hanni fell into bed late. Both days she seemed to float on a cloud that lifted her heart and made her feet want to dance. The chores seemed easier somehow and even the children were less demanding as her happy mood spilled over into theirs.

On Sunday morning, they enjoyed a meal of bread and plum jam, jealously hoarded since the previous winter. After church, scrubbed from head to toe, and proudly wearing their new shoes, they headed for the forest skirting the southern edge of the meadow next to their vegetable garden. Each of them carried either a sack made of old cloth or a basket for the bounty they expected to find in the shadows of giant birch, pine, oak, and maple trees. It was a beautiful day with sunshine filtering through thick foliage. Mosses, and fallen needles and grass, littered the ground making a soft, almost spongy carpet.

Over the course of the next few hours, in spite of frequent stops to admire crawling things and colorful wild flowers, they managed to fill their baskets and sacks with an assortment of mushrooms, tubers, and herbs.

Triumphantly, the family marched home, exhausted by their work and play. Dirty hands and faces were washed before Hanni put a loaf of bread and a pitcher of milk on the table. Everyone was enjoying this day so much that even the youngest two did not complain when it was time to lie down for a nap. As the older children ran outside to play with their friends, Hanni called after them, "Don't get your clothes dirty!"

After another thirty minutes of sorting and washing their forest finds, Hanni filled the largest wooden tub with water that had been heating on the pot-bellied stove for the past couple of hours. She then allowed herself to sink into its luxurious warmth. Her thoughts, as the warm water loosened tense muscles, wandered to the evening ahead. Hans had let her know they could expect him around five o'clock so they would have time to prepare the meal and feed all the children before the smaller ones had to go to bed. That meant she had a couple of hours to finish her bath and pre-cook some of the greens that were drying on a folded towel on the wooden board next to her stove. Each time she imagined herself and Hans working together in the small confines of her kitchen, a warmth, totally unrelated to the heat of her bathwater, coursed through her limbs and chest. Just the thought of his nearness unnerved her and she lost track of the mental list of things still left to do before he arrived. With a will of its own, her mind recalled in vivid detail the slope of his broad shoulders and the way his long legs strode rather than walked like ordinary men's. Unbidden, an image of the gentler stride of her dead husband crept into her mind and, with a jerk, Hanni sat up in her tub, almost frightened.

What was she thinking? Worse, what was she doing by allowing her secret longings to take over this way? Only a few days ago she was a tired, young woman growing old far too quickly. She had more children than she could feed and she was letting herself think of and long for a man too recently widowed. Yet, what was done was done, and it was too late to cancel the dinner she had dreamed of for days.

Despite her attempts to pretend that this day was little different from all the rest, she rose from the now lukewarm water and dried her body with the large cotton bath sheet she had woven when she first married Walter. He always admired it and would have liked the fact she had taken care of it for so long. Her skin, pink and glowing, felt soft to her touch as she slipped the nicer of her two dresses over her head. Required to wear widow's black, she found it suited her. Although her dress hung in loose folds across shoulders and narrow hips, a small, white lace collar not only provided stark contrast but drew attention to her luminous eyes. She toyed for a moment with the thought of leaving her long hair loose about her shoulders and back before braiding the still-wet strands and coiling them about her head as always. Anything else would be unseemly.

As she set about the task of slicing mushrooms and wild onions, the children stirred from their naps and assembled in the kitchen waiting for scraps to still their hunger. Dinner was still two hours away. As she worked, the boys played with the toy soldiers and animals Walter had carved from scraps of wood, and built imaginary forts and battlefields. The girls kept to themselves and whispered conversations imitating older girls in the neighborhood. Feigned exasperation at imagined slights gave rise to tossed hair and too-loud sighs. They were an almost-perfect picture of what was to come when they reached puberty and Hanni, glancing in their direction, felt both pride and foreboding.

Pushing thoughts of future concerns aside, she continued her preparations. The mushrooms and onions were done and waiting in a bowl to be quickly reheated and poured over whatever meat Hans might bring. Hanni was finished peeling the potatoes, and she cleaned and saved the skins to be used for the base of a vegetable soup she would cook tomorrow. After adding a bit of precious salt to the pot, she placed a few more small logs on the hearth and guessed the potatoes would be ready in about half an hour. That would be just about right if Hans was on time. He should arrive at any moment. Hanni's heart skipped a beat.

It was more than two hours later before they heard a knock on the door. The children had been playing quietly between snacking on pieces of bread and the soup Hanni had made an hour ago. Upon hearing the knock, everyone was still and looked at their mother. Softly, Trude whispered, "Don't let him in." Hanni looked at her daughter with eyes both pained and puzzled. Slowly, recognition of the child's wisdom began to register on her face but her feet seemed to move of their own volition toward the door. Another knock.

Johanna

He was leaning unsteadily against her door frame. His flushed face betrayed the amount of liquor he had drunk and his slurred apology when he said, "Sorry I'm late," did little to convey any real concern. Hanni opened the door wider and Hans lurched inside, swinging a crumpled sheet of newspaper dripping with blood. Lowering himself heavily onto the bench next to the kitchen table, he pushed the bundle at Hanni with the words, "Brought this for you."

Hanni mumbled a "thanks," as she scooped the mess from the table and dumped it into a large bowl in the sink behind her. A chicken's head rolled out of the bundle and blind eyes stared at her. Once-white feathers, now red with blood, were plastered to the tiny face. It was the first meat in the house in months and Hanni looked at the gruesome sight with mixed feelings. Her shy "thanks" was followed seconds later by, "It's alright. I mean, that you're late." Her glance fell on her children, huddled in a pile on her bed. Countless eyes, all shades of blue and green, met her own.

The sound of bench legs scraping against the floor yanked her head in Hans' direction. She faced his unsteady form moving in jerky motions toward the door. "Where are you going?" she asked much too loudly.

"Home," was his curt reply.

"But I thought we were going to have dinner together."

"Not tonight."

It was the night that even more of Hanni's innocence died. Throughout the dark hours after Han's departure, her dreams were replaced by a pragmatism that extinguished any residue of childish hope. Hour after hour, Hanni sat at the table while a candle burned fitfully in front of her tearful, swollen eyes. She imagined the many people she had loved. Her real parents, although she couldn't remember them well anymore, her adopted parents and sisters, her husband

and children, and friends. So many of them had died, including too many of her babies. More shattered dreams and lost love than anyone should bear.

But not until tonight had anyone left willingly. When the others left, they left completely and forever. The pain of their loss had been nearly impossible to bear. Tonight had taught her that there was an even greater loss. She now understood that love, when not fully and equally shared, could tear at the fabric of her heart and destroy, bit by tiny bit, all hope and dreams. With all the other losses, all she had to do was survive. The loss of hope, however, demanded that she not only survive, but also harden her heart.

Dawn was breaking when she finally blew out what little remained of the candle. In the silence, the corners of Hanni's mouth twitched in the beginning of a smile as she surveyed the living treasures whose muffled breathing was interrupted by an occasional soft snort or cough. All that was most important to her was right in this room and she vowed to never forget that everyone and everything else was insignificant.

She filled the kettle with enough water for coffee and the coffee grinder with enough precious beans for one good cup. Turning the metal crank on top of the wooden box, she began to hum an old folk song:

Kommt ein Vogel geflogen
Sezt sich nieder auf mein Fuss
Hat ein Zettel im Schnabel
Von der Mutti einen Gruss

A bird settles at my feet
In his beak he carries a letter for me
Greetings from my mother

Chapter 8

"4 October 1909. Dear Mommy," Hanni's neighbor read aloud, "I'm sorry not to have written sooner. I hope you are fine and that all the kids are healthy. Everyone here is doing well. Lotte, Minna, and Liesel are busy working. They all have handsome suitors. You would like them. Hans stays busy with his two jobs and I hardly ever see him. Otto is working with Hans making deliveries every morning and he is looking for another job, too. I am enclosing some money from all of us. Of course, I don't earn as much as the others, but I did contribute. We miss you and love you. Please give everyone a kiss for me. I will try to write again soon. Love, your daughter, Trude."

Hanni smiled as she listened to the account of her children's lives. The letter had arrived yesterday and she had eagerly waited for Mrs. Kohl to have time to read it to her. She was so proud of the fact that all her older children could read and write. They would never have to rely on someone else to read letters or newspapers for them. She would have loved to have been able to write Liesel and tell her all about their lives in Werda. Not that there was a lot to tell. Life had not changed much at all. Still, it would have been nice to write about the little things like Liesel's friend, Heidi, finally having her baby baptized or the new blue dress Mrs. Kerne had worn to church on Sunday.

However, writing was a distant dream now. Hanni didn't dream much anymore. Her life had become almost predictable in its routines and only rarely was she reminded of dreams she once had. The two years without Walter had been lonely ones. They had been years of labor, washing clothes for townspeople who had grown wealthy on inheritances and risks she would never have dared to take. It was no use thinking about that. She had never had more than the bare necessities and often not even those.

There was a small sack of precious sugar behind her on the counter that someone had given her in payment for laundry she had finished ahead of schedule. It was worth much more than the money she would normally have been given and tears filled her eyes as she thought of the kindness of the woman who had pressed the treasure into her hands. She was using a little of it now to bake a surprise sweetbread for the children. She herself couldn't eat sugar. There was a wound on her leg that refused to heal and the doctor who looked at it had clucked his tongue and shook his head before telling her she had the sugar disease. "Diabetes," he had said it was called, according to his medical dictionary. It caused all kinds of problems, he warned, and he had made her promise not to eat sweets, even fruit. She had no problem making the promise. There was rarely fruit she could afford to buy and never any sugar. Every once in a while, she couldn't resist dipping a wet finger into the sack and sucking it till all the sweet granules had melted in her mouth.

Maybe she should make another, smaller sweetbread for Hans who, since his drunken appearance with the chicken, had started dropping in at her house unannounced. He liked sweetbread. She could always give it to one of the neighbors if he didn't show. Her face lost some of its softness at these thoughts and she hurried to fetch more flour from the bin on the corner shelf. She knew she shouldn't do the many little things that made his life easier or more pleasant. She did his laundry even though he had stopped making her shoes long ago. He was still welcome in her home at any time, although he had told her years before not to drop in at his house unannounced or uninvited.

Her children thought she was silly and wrong to be so obliging to a man who did so little for her in return. They did not understand the joy he brought into her life, along with the pain.

It hadn't always hurt so much. In the beginning, after the first dinner he had missed, when all the children were still at home and he had come late and too drunk to stay and eat, he had been the most attentive friend she could have hoped for. Smiling at the memory, Hanni rolled out the dough and sprinkled sugar over the paper-thin surface. He had been so sorry two days later when he dropped by unannounced and brought her flowers and a dressed chicken. The flowers were a first in her life and the chicken more meat than they had had in a year or more. Even the memory of it made her mouth water as she recalled the oooohs and aaaahs when the children saw her treasures. Only Trude kept silent. Her cold stare unnerved Hanni.

For Hanni, it had been the beginning of a magical year. Much as she had been hurt, Hanni could not stay angry with the only man who had ever tweaked her imagination and roused her body. At first, they met after church on Sundays. Usually, he brought a bit of fruit or even candy for all of them to share as they walked across the meadow and into the forest. The children usually ran ahead and gathered flowers as well as small creatures with too many legs. Hans walked beside Hanni. Sometimes they discussed village issues or problems with one of the children. Often they didn't talk at all.

Eventually, Hanni became less shy and proved to be a charming conversationalist. It was the first time in her life that she expressed opinions and had someone listen. In her father's home, she had been too young to engage in adult conversation. With Walter, it had been a different matter. Her husband had rarely expressed opinions himself and limited his conversations to the absolutely necessary. So, for Hanni to have the opportunity to develop ideas and share them with an animated companion was like discovering a new world.

Johanna

"What did you think of the sermon this morning?" Hanni asked Hans as they walked along the river bank.

Hans looked quizzically at Hanni before responding. "No, Hanni. I want you to tell me what you thought of it first. I want to hear your opinion."

"Well, I thought he was right about God wanting us to forgive others, but do we have to keep forgiving over and over again, even when someone keeps hurting us? I don't know if I agree with that."

"Of course we do, Hanni. That's what it means to be a Christian. No one is perfect. We just have to accept each other as we are and learn to forgive each other's faults."

Hanni wanted to disagree but something inside her would not allow her to contradict Hans. She nodded her head, as if in agreement, and continued walking.

With time, as Hanni came to recognize her own values and prejudices, she also learned to be observant when dealing with her customers. She discovered there was much more going on in the lives around her than she had ever suspected. When she met with customers to pick up or deliver laundry, she now talked to them and listened to their problems. Often what she heard was only gossip and contradicted itself from one person to the next. Eventually, though, patterns seemed to appear. She would hear about a neighbor cheating on her husband or someone beating his wife. She heard about the good and the bad relationships in her own village and neighboring towns. Everyone seemed to be involved in some way with everyone else and she wondered what she had missed all those years when she kept only to herself. Sunday afternoons she shared village news with Hans, who sometimes had his own information to contribute, and they would compare their treasure trove of tidbits.

Johanna

Slowly they had grown closer as they discovered common bonds. Shared interests and shared proximity led, inevitably, to closer physical interest as well. One day Hans took Hanni's hand as they walked on a trail in the forest next to the river. On the tiny bridge, they stopped and turned to each other. He took her into his arms and held her head to his chest. Through his shirt, Hanni could feel the thump of his wildly beating heart against her cheek. His bare skin where the shirt opened in the front revealed dark hair and a sweet but powerful scent. Everything about him seemed strong, from the softly curling hair to the ripple of hard muscles under darkly tanned skin. Hanni had not felt safe like this since she was a child in her father's arms. It was glorious.

Then came the invitation to visit him for a fitting of a new pair of shoes. During that fitting, Hans explored more than the shape of her foot. As his hands swept over her ankles and calves, she gasped. He immediately stopped and drew away. Afraid she had offended him yet fearful he would stop forever, Hanni had said, "No, it's alright. Please don't stop."

He reached for her thighs and she moaned and slid further down into the chair. Before she could change her mind, Hans picked her up and carried her to his bed. She did not protest.

From then on, it became their routine to spend Sundays together. It was always the same except that she began to bring his laundry home and had it ready for him the next Sunday. Sunday evenings in the little cottage in the forest became the focus of Hanni's life and she longed for them like a girl longs for the touch of her first love. She even dared to dream of marriage. It was not so uncommon for widows to remarry and she felt young enough to hope again.

She knew the moment she conceived. Like the petals of a flower, her body had opened itself to receive his gift of new life. Perhaps for the first time in her long stream of pregnancies, Hanni felt elation.

Johanna

This is what her life had been destined for from the very beginning. Combining her body and spirit with Hans was her reward for all the years of dutiful living.

She planned how she would tell Hans that he was about to become a father. They had planned a dinner for just the two of them in his cottage following Sunday's service. Hanni mentally rehearsed how they would walk hand-in-hand along the winding trail through the forest and into the clearing where his cottage nestled between giant oak trees. She imagined how they would prepare their meal together and how they would build a fire in the hearth even though the evenings were still warm. They would sit in the glow of flames as she told Hans of the event that would cement their relationship forever.

"Hans, we're going to have a baby," Hanni murmured as Hans was kissing the nape of her neck.

The moment he heard the news, everything about him changed. Instead of joy softening his features, they became hard and distant as he pushed her from him. Rising stiffly, he walked away from her and stopped in the middle of the room. Still facing away from her, he asked in a voice dripping with rage and expelled in one-syllable bursts through clenched teeth, "How could you let this happen?"

Shock rendered her speechless. As the silence between them drew on, Hanni finally crumpled into a tearful heap and between sobs cried, "I thought you would be happy!"

"Happy!" he shouted. "You've ruined everything!"

Chapter 9

In retrospect, Hanni understood what Hans meant. His life was just how he wanted it. He had no responsibilities except to go where he wanted and to do what pleased him. She was a diversion that cost him little. With the birth of his child he might have to become more involved than he had ever intended. So he pulled away. They saw each other infrequently during the months of her pregnancy. When the tiny pink girl was born, Hanni called her Maria, after her first daughter. It was a good name, and maybe this Maria was destined to have a life much longer and luckier than the Maria who had come before.

Once she was born, however, Hans couldn't resist her huge green eyes and gentle temperament. He began to stop in more frequently, often bringing little sweets or an occasional piece of meat, to keep up Hanni's strength as she nursed his little princess. Again, Hanni began to hope.

Then came the war. It was 1914 and Hanni, who now could rely on the children to read her the news, became increasingly afraid. The leadership of the various empires of Europe, monarchies waging their endless battles for dominance and control, were doing what they had always done. However, there was a new threat in the air. Rebellion was brewing once again. The rumblings of disenfranchised and starving masses were heard and felt throughout Europe. The note of desperation, fear, and rage had set the tone for the times to come and those times were almost upon them. Hanni felt it in her bones.

There had been talk for many years about the unrest in the eastern German states. Now it had become critical. There were rumors about uprisings and a persistent resistance to the monarchy that controlled vast holdings and a multiplicity of ethnic tribes. There had always been trouble, but this time it threatened to engulf them all.

It was called a "World War." Hanni couldn't imagine anything that huge. All she knew was that this war involved all of her world.

Treaties had been signed that insured that her family would be a part of the changes that were certain to take place. All of her sons— Hans, Otto, Heinz, Olaf, even Werner—were involved. At first it seemed impossible that all of them would have to go and fight. Some of them were barely men. Surely the younger ones would stay behind and keep the farms and factories going. However, soon each one had taken up arms and marched off along with the rest. Only the really old men stayed behind to help with the crops and guard their town, though there wasn't much they could do if the enemy surged over the hills and swept through their streets and homes.

Hans and Hanni said their good-byes in his cottage after dinner on the last Sunday before he left. They made love like they had before Maria was born. Afterwards, he held her hand across the top of the table and told her he would leave the next morning. She held her breath as tears gathered in her eyes, hoping he would use this poignant moment to ask her to be his wife. When the words she longed to hear failed to come, her tears flowed even more freely down her burning cheeks.

Hans returned three years later. She also received Otto and Werner safely into her arms. For Hans, Olaf, and Heinz she received three separate letters, each one a blow that brought her to her knees. "Dear

Johanna

Mrs. Meinhardt, We regret to inform you that your son..." No one knew exactly where they had been killed. "Somewhere in the east" was all they could tell her. She had lost three more children and did not even have their bodies to bury. They were somewhere on foreign soil and she would never be able to take flowers to their graves.

The two sons who returned were not the same sons who had left. Werner came home first. When he first appeared at her door, she hadn't recognized him. He had aged at least a decade. After experiencing so much destruction, he was anxious to build a life for himself. He refused to accept that his and others' sacrifices had been in vain.

Otto, came home wounded and even quieter and more withdrawn than before. He never talked about his experiences on the front, but some nights Hanni awakened to the sounds of his sobbing. He returned to Dresden and when he was able to find work, he always sent her what he earned. He kept only enough for his basic expenses and the whiskey he seemed to need now more than food or friends.

Hans had changed, too. He no longer wanted to talk when they saw each other on Sunday afternoons. They seldom went to his cottage, he came to her apartment for lunch instead. She did not give up hope of a future with him until the evening she dropped by his cottage unexpectedly. Hanni knocked repeatedly and when he finally opened the door, she knew something was very wrong. His hair was disheveled and his shirt had been hastily tucked into unbuttoned trousers with suspenders pulled awkwardly over his broad shoulders. Reluctantly, he held the door open for her as she entered the small room she knew so well and loved so dearly. The smell was wrong. A musty smell of passion hung in the air. She sank into a familiar chair as he offered her a drink. When she declined, he sat across the table from her and finally met her eyes.

Johanna

"Why, Hans?" was all she could manage.

"I'm a man and I needed someone. She was willing. I never made any promises," he finally replied.

No, she admitted to herself, he had not. Still, he had once done all the wonderful things that made her believe he felt for her as she did for him. Obviously, she was wrong. She needed time to sort out her feelings before she said more. Getting up from the table, she looked at the familiar surroundings before letting herself out the front door.

A few months after her surprise visit he came by one Sunday to apologize and to ask if he could see her again. She had, of course, accepted his offer because life without him remained unbearable.

Now, several years later, they spent time together irregularly but without malice. They had even begun again to discuss current events and politics in Europe. It was always a good time without expectations or guilt. They were now too old for either and had made up their minds to be friends and just a little more.

There were only two things that still upset Hanni. One was the tension increasing once more in Europe and the other was Maria. The rest of the children and grandchildren were doing fine. Some better than others, but no one was of too much concern. Lotte and Minna had opened their own porcelain business and were building quite a reputation. Liesel had married a police officer and had two children. Trude was married to a butcher who already had three children and she was expecting her first baby any day.

Karin was also a mother but had never married. Hanni didn't understand why Karin had refused the father of her son. However, since she was doing well and was supporting herself and her child on her teacher's salary, Hanni did not complain. In fact, she was quite proud of her daughter who had studied so hard to become a professional, independent woman and who had been able to keep her position even when some of the people in town had petitioned the school board to remove her after the birth of her son. The school board voted in favor of Karin because she did an excellent job and, after all, there were many single mothers after the war.

Neither Werner nor Willi had married yet. Willi was working at odd jobs and showed little interest in settling down with anyone permanently. Werner was apprenticed to Hans, learning to craft leather into useful and, sometimes, beautiful shoes and boots. He wasn't home much, preferring to spend his time in the shoemakers' cottage workshop instead of his mother's apartment. In fact, Hans had added a small bedroom to the back of the cottage where Werner often slept. He loved the woods and solitude so it seemed a perfect place for him. To some extent, Hans had replaced Walter as the boy's father, and Werner was the son Hans never had.

Maria was the only one of her children who troubled Hanni. It wasen't that the girl misbehaved or even had bad intentions.

However, her last child had a spirit unlike any of the others. Her gentle baby had become bright, inquisitive, adventuresome, and even rebellious. Hanni worried where that independent spirit would take her. One thing Hanni had learned was that an unquenchable spirit — especially in a woman—was seldom rewarded.

PART II

MARIA

Chapter 1

"Don't call me that! My name is Mia!" screamed the little girl, throwing her mother an angry look. She hated being called by her dead sister's name; and hated even more that her mother refused to change it. Nearly five years old, Maria was absolutely certain about some things. Like what she liked to eat, the uselessness of naps, her love of the pretty jewelry some women wore, and, most important of all, she was obstinately certain about what she wanted to be called.

What Mia couldn't figure out was why she had to live in a shabby place with too many stairs and why she couldn't have the same kinds of things some other kids had. At the moment, her special concern was her shoes. They were dark, sturdy, and ugly. It was true her mother's friend, Hans, made them especially for her and they were comfortable—but the dark leather went all the way up past her ankles and the laces were leather, too. They didn't look anything like the pretty loafers tied with colorful ribbons that the other girls had. Reluctantly, she pulled the ugly shoes over knitted socks. The socks were held in place by clasps that hooked into the top of the fabric with small metal loops. These, in turn, were tied onto strips of cloth which attached to a band around her waist. The whole affair did its job but was uncomfortable, especially when the band around her waist slid to one side or the other and the strips of cloth were stretched too tightly at awkward angles around the top of her legs. Mia made a promise to herself never to wear the things again once she was grown up and could do what she wanted.

Her musings were interrupted as Willi, her favorite brother, burst with a crash through the kitchen door. He was a tall seventeen-year-old who always had a ready smile for his baby sister. Mia raised adoring eyes in welcome. She gave him her most captivating pout as she stretched both legs in his direction and pointed to the untied laces on her shoes. Charmed in spite of himself, Willi knelt in front of the child and leaned forward to tie the laces. His fine blonde hair fell over his forehead and Mia couldn't resist rubbing her hands through its soft strands. They laughed together as Willi whisked her off the chair and onto his shoulders. Shrieking with delight, Mia bounced as Willi hopped from one foot to the other reciting her favourite nursery rhyme.

When their mother entered the room, they stopped and Mia slid from her brother's shoulders to his chest, resting her head in the crook of his left arm. Mia closed her eyes and endured her mother's probing fingers that checked that her garter was on straight for their outing. Willi had promised her a visit with his friend who lived on a farm a few miles outside of Werda. He assured her she would get to see and pet cows, horses, chickens, and rabbits. Rabbits were her favorites. She loved touching their soft, silky coats and watching their little noses twitch.

And they were being picked up in a horse-drawn cart!

Chapter 2

Two years later, the loom thumped its familiar rhythm as Mia shuttled back and forth, weaving a pattern as ancient as the wind that whipped the trees into a frenzy outside her window. Her 24 year old big sister, Karin, sat cramped in a tiny corner of the room mending underwear, taking time off from her six day a week teaching job. Near her, Henrich, who at the age of six was more like a brother than a nephew, sat reading on the ragged, overstuffed thing that used to be a sofa. Hanni, her mother, stood in her accustomed place at the pot-bellied stove, stirring the contents of a soup pot. On a clothesline strung between the top of the door frame and the top of the window frame behind Mia, hung someone's clothes to dry. From the size of the cotton panties, they looked to belong to their downstairs neighbor. At the thought of the old, rotund figure, Mia chuckled.

Disturbed by Mia's laughter, Henrich looked up from his book with a frown. She laughed louder, satisfied that she had managed to interrupt his concentration. She had to do something to end the unbearable quiet of this apartment.

Since the war ended, there had been no excitement. Not that she missed the frantic running and hiding every time the siren sounded. The lack of anything to eat had been a problem, too. However, that was all over with and all she wanted now was some fun. She knew that every day couldn't be filled with music and dancing—but would it be so hard to have an occasional funny story, or just a normal conversation to dispel the somber memories? Instead, everyone in her life seemed bent on burying their noses in books. Even Willi couldn't be coaxed into playing anymore. He now spent endless hours studying, going to classes, and taking exams. Mia hated it all. Because she was only seven, no one listened to her! The best she could do was find what she needed in her own imagination. So, while her hands wove woolen threads into intricate patterns, her mind wove fantasy worlds in which she danced in light-filled halls and walked through gardens of sweet-smelling roses, lilacs, and lilies.

A knock on the door startled everyone. The habits of fear and sudden flight were still too recent to dismiss. Everyone held their breaths in anticipation as Willi opened it. It was only Hans, come for a bit of warmth and company. Mia glanced at her mother and noticed the slight smile spreading across her still-pretty face.

"Come in, "she said, "have a seat by the stove."

After Hans removed his coat and sat down, Mia, eyes downturned, sat on a stool near his booted feet. She didn't know how to feel about Hans. He was always kind to her and to mother, but there was something about him that made her uneasy. She liked being close to him, but she wasn't sure if he felt the same way about her. Nearly always smiling, he seemed to like her company and never gave even the slightest indication that he didn't want to be near her. Even at this moment, he pulled her onto his lap and wrapped warm arms around her shoulders. The bristles on his chin tickled the back of her neck and she giggled and squirmed before finally bursting into outright laughter.

For a few minutes, no one said a word. The only sounds were of Hanni stirring the contents of the pot and the crackling of firewood in the oven. The quiet was different now. Warmth and light with a golden sheen and a sense of contentment filled the air. Mia had noticed before that Hans had an almost magical ability to put people at ease, especially her mother.

Hanni set a cup of tea and some bread on the table for him. A look from her mother told Mia that they wanted to speak privately and she reluctantly slid down from the wool-clad lap. Rough fibers scratched the back of her bare legs where the top of her stockings ended and the garters met the bottom of her underpants. Hans patted her head and smiled as she moved to the other side of the room.

Mia decided to join Henrich on the sofa. Kneeling, facing the wall, she looked, for the thousandth time, at her mother's tapestry, the one she got from Walter before he died. The scene of two young women strolling in a garden, surrounded by angelic children at play, made Mia wonder again what her father had been like. He must have been, like Mia herself, a dreamer. She wondered what their lives would have been like if he had lived. The descriptions she'd heard were of a loving, hard-working man who adored his family.

She had always assumed that Walter was her father. Why would she think otherwise? Mama was mama. Papa was papa. However, a few months ago, Trina, who was two years older than Mia, and a bossy mean girl, had whispered something to her that she couldn't forget. "How could he be your father, you dumb goose? He died 10 years ago! You're only 7 years old." Now, she was confused.

She shot a quick glance over her shoulder at Hans, sitting at their table with his back to her. He was the only man Mama ever invited into their home. Glances into the tiny mirror hanging above the sink didn't give a clear answer. The green eyes that peered back at her were like his—but they were set in a face that was almost a duplicate of her mother's. It was hard to know for sure. However, since Trina's revelation, Mia had noticed how people looked at her when they saw her with the handsome, charming shoemaker.

María

If he was her father, why didn't he claim her as his own? Wasn't she pretty enough? Wasn't she nice enough? She knew she was smart enough—she'd already passed up much older children in school, including that Trina.

It was impossible to ask Mama, or even Willi, about it. No one talked about Mama's relationship with Hans and it was understood that questions were not allowed. Everyone knew that private things were kept private.

Henrich stirred and put down his book as Mia scooted her way into the corner of the sofa. Henrich wasn't bad, just boring.

"What are you reading?" asked Mia.

"Nothing you'd like," came the terse answer. Feeling his own rudeness, Henrich grinned sheepishly before adding, "It's just some stuff about sailing ships."

He seemed surprised that Mia was interested. "How far do they go? How long would it take to go to a totally different part of the world? What does it cost?"

With such prompting, Henrich launched into a discussion of the technical specifications and merits of clipper ships. She let him ramble on, but all Mia wanted to know was where she could board the nearest one and where it could take her. Their conversation wove in and out of various themes including some of the possible destinations for the world travelers they both dreamed of becoming. Neither had known about the passion they shared for unknown places and people. Talking together was like dreaming out loud and they hardly noticed when Hans took his leave and Hanni resumed her chores. Her mother's shoulders now drooped slightly and some of the sparkle was gone from her eyes. Mia noticed, but said nothing.

Maria

She'd been working on the report for weeks already and it still wasn't what she wanted. Her fifth-grade teacher had asked the whole class to write about, "What I will do after I finish school." To make matters worse, she would have to present the highlights of her report orally in front of all her classmates. Mia knew very well what she would do but she was not sure she wanted to share that information with anyone.

Mia and most of her friends were expected to do the same things their parents had done for generations. One or two might be an exception but it was rare in the ancient town. That is, until this last war. The war had made some difference in some people's options and expectations. Her own family was a good example of that. Most of her older brothers and sisters had moved away to find work. Karin, although she had come back to Werda, had returned with a college degree and was a teacher. However, it was Willi who had become the pride of the family when he received his law degree and started his own practice in Werda.

One thing was certain, Mia would never wash someone else's dirty clothes or work in a factory weaving cloth for sale in foreign ports. She wouldn't work on any of the local farms either, even though some girls seemed to like that kind of life. In fact, none of the domestic chores held much appeal for Mia. She had seen the old women on their park benches across the street and had noticed how they carried old regrets in the pouches under their eyes. Their lives, for all the years they had lived, had uncertain value. She would never sit on those benches and look back on a youth spent serving her "betters." Never! Well, then, perhaps it was best to tell them of her dream—that she, too, would become a teacher and work in a city, almost any city, as long as it was far from here.

"Who's ready to give the next report?" a high-pitched voice asked. Not a sound could be heard as eyes focused on the top of desks or the back of heads. Finally, the silence was broken by the same voice. "Mia," it announced. The sound was more like a shriek to her ears than an invitation and Mia shrunk deeper into the space between her chair and desk top. Audible sighs of relief released from the other students did little to dispel her anxiety. She could hear her heart pounding in her chest. She had been preparing so long but now that the moment to deliver had arrived, she couldn't seem to breathe, much less speak. Her throat tightened and blood rushed into her cheeks. It was unbearable. All eyes fell on her. She heard giggling. Could she dare again to be so different?

Almost of their own volition, Mia felt her legs move and lift her body out of her seat. Heart pounding, she ran past the rows of desks toward the front of her classroom. Instead of stopping, her legs carried her past the astonished teacher and out the door that slammed shut behind her. Down the stairs and through the front gates, her legs didn't stop until she was in a forest clearing well away from the ancient school building and laughing children. Slowly, Mia sank onto a mossy stump and hung her head on a chest heaving for breath, and constricting around her heart like a vise. She cried, but not for long.

"All right, all right," she said as she wiped at her tears with the back of her hand. "I'm different. I can never be like them, I could never be satisfied with their lives. It's stupid to try to keep it a secret. This is who I am. She vowed to never run away from who she really was.

Returning to face the crowd of jeering classmates was the hardest thing she'd ever done. Explaining her fear of exposure and criticism to an enraged teacher was nearly impossible—but, somehow she

Maria

managed both. With her strong voice belying her inward fears, she read the paper to her classmates. When she finished, her classmates' faces were expressionless. Her teacher remained scowling. She sent Mia home with a reprimand and a note for her mother to sign.

News travelled fast in the small town, and Hanni had already heard about Mia's embarrassment when her humbled but defiant daughter stepped into the living room and nearly disappeared amid the day's washing.

"It's alright, sweetie." Hanni smiled and put her arms around her daughter's frail shoulders—but for Mia it would never be alright. Fighting tears and her mother's arms, she shoved her teacher's note into Hanni's hand.

Chapter 3

It was May 15th, 1929. Mia's 18th birthday. Slender, with softly curling light brown hair, her green eyes sparkled at the thought of her rendezvous with Kurt.

Earlier that morning, Hanni had handed her a package wrapped in sacking, the kind used to hold potatoes or other bulk foods. With a gentle smile, she waited for the young, nimble fingers to untie the knot. The twine-wrapped sacking promised little at first sight. However, as Mia pulled the string free, the sacking opened to reveal an exquisite fabric the hue of a summer sky, dappled with tiny flowers in yellow and dark blue. A gasp escaped her mouth as she unfolded the dress. Hanni's smile broadened. Saving a few pennies each week, it had taken her most of that year to finally buy the cloth. She had sewn laboriously during dark nights while Mia lay sleeping, exhausted from studying from morning to late night. The look on her daughter's face was well worth the effort. Mia glowed as she danced around the room with her new dress held tightly against her body.

Hans stopped by for a bit of soup around noon and brought biscuits and a new pair of shoes for Mia. They were more stylish than any he had made her before, with tapered heels raised at least two inches higher than the others he'd made. He had blushed when she kissed his cheeks and hugged his stooped shoulders. His best gift, though, was when he told her, "You are a woman now, my little Mia." Her heart flooded with happiness at his words.

Maria

The dress felt wonderful against her skin. It was the first new garment she could remember. She was glad to be alone on the walk through the woods to their favorite rendezvous. She couldn't help but stroke the curves it made around her hips, to feel how it stretched tightly across her full breasts and accentuated her narrow waist. The dress's simple elegance and the stature her new shoes gave her added an air of sophistication she relished beyond words.

That was exactly what she needed for her meeting with Kurt. He was, without a doubt, the most handsome young man she had ever known. As if that weren't enough, he was the son of a family that had built a business trading fine, local porcelain all over Europe. They even had their own factory, and artists competed to work for the well-known and generous merchants.

Although Kurt was a partner in the family business, in actuality he worked for his father. Being the only child of his doting parents, he would eventually inherit the entire family fortune, but in the meantime, he depended on their generosity.

Mia knew that Kurt's parents liked her well enough. They admired her tenacity with her studies, her willingness to work hard helping her mother and anyone else who needed an extra hand. They also approved of her ambition to improve her lot in life. Mia also knew they secretly hoped Kurt would outgrow his infatuation with her and chose someone they considered more appropriate for someone of his social standing. Thus, she was never comfortable in their tolerant, but distant, presence.

With Kurt, however, there was never a hint of condescension or arrogance. He was forever encouraging her to talk about her opinions and dreams. He adored her quick wit and curious mind almost as much as her sumptuous young body.

He loved the way she challenged him—to think more, to stretch his vision of the world. They often spent hours discussing local politics, the fate of post-war Germany, the lack of food and jobs, and Mia's plans to change not only her own fate, but the fate of her country. She had never told him about her dearest wish, though; to raise a family with him. For that, she would give up her career and most of her idealistic dreams.

Of course, she would continue to work hard helping those less fortunate than herself. That was only right. Even her mother, who had less than most, shared a bit of food or an extra penny whenever she could. Of course, they always put something in the basket that was passed around in church after Sunday sermons. It was part of her family's tradition. However, if truth be told, even though she said a prayer for her future with Kurt every week and hoped her mother's donation would be enough to get God's attention, she was not convinced that it was money well spent. Except for giving her a place to sit every Sunday, the church had never done anything for Mia or any of the other people in her congregation who desperately needed the few pennies they put in the basket. Besides, her priest was the fattest man in town and she couldn't imagine that he ever felt the hunger pangs that everyone else endured regularly.

Kurt didn't agree. In fact, he was the most devout Christian Mia knew. So far, it hadn't affected their love for each other but she knew they'd have to discuss that difference again if their relationship were to become permanent.

For now though, it was enough just to be together. The thought lent speed to her footsteps. Finally, she neared the clearing next to a thick grove of oak trees. A small brook tripped over boulders creating a gentle waterfall. It had become her favorite sound.

Lunch with her mother and Hans had made her a bit late. At first, treading softly on spongy ground, she was afraid that he had gone. Or, maybe, her imagination warned, he never came. "But that's ridiculous," reminded her reason. He knew very well it was her birthday and he would never miss the opportunity to wish her well on such a special occasion. Kurt was the most dependable man she knew.

Finally, walking around the trunk of a huge ancient pine, Mia spotted the corner of a bright red-and white checked cloth. Walking nearer, she saw Kurt sitting on its edge. As he looked up, the corners of his eyes seemed to soften and his gaze filled with love. For just a moment, his intensity stopped her in mid breath, and it was a few seconds before she could return his smile.

The matching napkins in silver napkin rings and the fine china plates on the tablecloth could only have come from Kurt's factory. Delicate crystal flutes and a bottle of champagne were propped against a piece of slate stone. At least she thought it was champagne. She'd never had any before and had only heard about it from friends who claimed to have tasted the fine beverage. In an open basket in the middle of the improvised table was an apple torte. A burning candle drew her eyes to a small package at its base.

Tears filled her eyes and love flooded her chest. Her pounding heart threatened to burst through the fabric of her new dress.

Kurt reached for the glasses and handed one to her.

As if in a dream, the summer haze blurred the contours of Mia's surroundings. Only the bright tablecloth had a sharpness that defined this moment. Mia's gaze rested on the bottle now in Kurt's left hand. Condensation had formed and beads of water ran in rivulets along its tapering sides while Kurt's right hand twisted the cork back and forth. His eyes returned again to the rivulets of perspiration that flowed from Mia's neck and disappeared into the cleavage between her breasts. The sudden, explosive pop of the cork startled them both. Froth spilled from the bottle neck and over Kurt's knuckles as nervous laughter escaped the lips leaning toward each other.

Maria

Drawing back a little, Kurt filled their glasses before reaching for the package leaning against the candle. "Happy birthday, my love" he said as his glass clinked against hers and they took their first sip. Handing her the package, Kurt took Mia's glass and set it next to his own on a flat surface of slate while he waited for her to unwrap the tiny parcel. With trembling hands she unfolded the paper and opened the black velvet box. The brilliant ring nestled in its soft crevice was a stark contrast to the midnight darkness of the box. The hard, shiny gold band was dotted with gems that sparkled as rays of sunshine bounced from their chiseled edges. A gasp escaped Mia's throat and prompted a satisfied sigh from Kurt. As their eyes locked, he said the words he'd been rehearsing for weeks.

"Mia, will you marry me, please?"

He hadn't meant to say, "Please," but her brilliant smile made him forget his mistake. Tiny tears gathered at the corners of her eyes as she softly exhaled, "Yes."

Taking the box from her outstretched hand, Kurt removed the ring and slipped it onto Mia's finger. Handing her one of the glasses, he raised his own and said, "To us."

The bubbles had finally stopped tickling the inside of her nose and Mia was able to eat her dessert. Either the champagne or her happiness was making her feel as if she were floating. In fact, she wasn't sure if she had even tasted the food she had just eaten. Kurt was equally joyful. They loved each other deeply and had known almost from the first time they met that they would spend their lives together. He was positive that no man had ever loved a woman as much as he loved Mia. Her radiant face confirmed that she loved him just as much.

However, it wasn't her face that kept attracting his attention. The breasts that had stirred his passion when she had first arrived were now even more inviting. The heat of the day, and perhaps the champagne, had made Mia perspire and the flimsy fabric of her dress was now moist and clinging to her body. Nipples, hard and erect, pushed against it and kept Kurt's stare fixed on them. Almost of its own accord, his hand reached across the space that separated him from Mia. Her giggles died abruptly as his fingers closed over her breast. Leaning forward, she met his embrace. Their mouths touched even as he drew her body more firmly into his arms and, losing their balance, they rolled in a tangle next to their makeshift table. Although he had been absolutely sure she would say yes, he was still relieved at her reaction.

He was everything she'd ever wanted, ever dreamed of. The hot mouth and urgent body crushing hers consumed her with passion. However, that was only the beginning. Handsome as he was, his best quality was the way he loved her and Mia felt engulfed by more than his arms. The chest crushing her own held a heart as strong and compelling as the legs that were now prying her thighs open. Until now, his love had always been gentle and kind, filling her life with tender moments and a dreamlike quality. Until now. Now, the passion could no longer be denied as they clutched each other with an almost frantic lust. Mia had only hinted at her passionate nature and Kurt had never asked for more than a kiss. Everything was different now. They were engaged. Like magnets, they were inexorably drawn into each other's embrace as pleasure sought more and more of itself.

When the sun had lost some of its intensity, Mia lay in Kurt's arms resting her head on his chest. "Tell me again about the house we'll live in," she begged. Breathing in the perfume of her hair, Kurt started from the beginning.

"There's a clearing on the east side of my mom and dad's property. It's separated from the main house by a grove of trees. The place is perfect for starting our life together and my dad said I can build a small house of my own there. It's far enough from my parents for privacy, but close enough to be convenient. It means I can still walk to the plant with my dad in the morning and come home for lunch most days."

Mia listened in rapturous silence, imagining the two-story house that would someday be her home.

"Tell me more about the house itself," she urged him on.

"Well, it will only be one story to begin with. Not as grand as my parents', but we can add on someday if we want. Of course, we'll buy stone from the same quarry that my dad used when he built their house. It'll have a formal entrance, with at least eight steps leading up to it and beautiful, carved oak doors. The entrance hall will go all the way from the front door to the back. If you walk all the way down the hall and go out the back door you'll go out onto the patio that overlooks the garden. We'll have a formal sitting room with a big fireplace for when we entertain guests. And, across the hall from it, there'll be a family room with another fireplace. It'll be much cozier and I think that's where we'll spend most of our time. Down the hall will be the bedrooms. Ours will have a large, private bath. A bathroom for everyone else will be between the second bedroom and the dining room. The kitchen will be in the back with a servants' entrance."

"Servants!" Mia gasped.

She hadn't thought about having help—but, of course, it made perfect sense. She would be expected to entertain friends and receive business associates in addition to running a larger house than she had ever imagined. She had only seen the outside of the few grand homes in Werda like the one he was describing and her eyes gleamed at the thought of having her own big house to manage. His parents had never invited her to join them in their stately home. Mia knew that the vegetable garden in back of their house was tended by at least one gardener and that the three floors of endless space were kept in pristine condition by several local women who took pride in working in such a prestigious manor.

"It sounds wonderful," she said.

Kurt was puzzled by the sudden wistful quality of Mia's voice. "What's wrong, sweetheart?"

"It's just that your parents have always been polite to me but they've never even invited me to visit them. Have you talked to your parents about this? Do they approve of our getting married? Would they really let us build a house right next to theirs?"

"To tell you the truth, Mia, they approve because they want me to be happy. They know I love you and will marry you no matter what anyone thinks or says and they want my family to have a good start. For now, that's the best they can do. Besides, they really like you and they intend to get to know you much better once you are a member of the family."

The happiness and confidence in his voice helped to allay Mia's fears somewhat and she allowed her imagination to dwell on what her new home and new life would be like. For longer than they both realized, they remained silently in each other's arms while billows of white clouds scuttled across a deeply blue sky. Finally, the chill in the evening air brought them back to reality. They realized it was time to pack up the remains of their memorable picnic and smooth the wrinkles in their clothing as best they could.

As they rewrapped the crystal and china in cloth napkins and towels, Mia tried to imagine how she would tell her mother the wonderful news of her engagement. She also couldn't wait to tell their friends.

"Will we meet anyone at the pub tonight and tell them the news?" Mia asked as Kurt picked up the bike he had left leaning against a tree at the head of the trail.

Maria

The past few months they been meeting various friends and colleagues at the "Dragon's Lair" on Saturday evenings. Almost everyone they knew had gotten in the habit of stopping for a glass or two of the locally brewed beer that was becoming quite popular, even in far-flung regions of the lowlands.

"Why don't we? I know everyone is going to be there. We can really celebrate!"

Smiles lit both faces as the lovers walked through familiar countryside and onto the cobbled streets at the edge of town. Here they stopped to embrace one more time before going their separate ways.

As Mia neared the drab building in which she lived, the tenement loomed above her and she was struck by the contrast it made to the images that were dancing in her mind of her new home. She felt especially bad comparing the worn woman who would greet her in the apartment to the polished woman of means who would soon become her mother-in-law. Still, she couldn't help but juxtapose the two realities that occupied so many of her thoughts. Her own mom was much prettier than Kurt's elegant but distant and severe mother. Even in her threadbare but clean raggedy dresses, Hanni gave the impression of a once-beautiful woman. The high cheekbones and sparkling blue eyes allowed a glimpse of intelligence and sensitivity no amount of poverty could dim. The arms, so frail looking in faded sleeves, hid a strength won by hard work and a long history of holding countless children in their able embrace.

Kurt's mother resembled more a drudge dressed in finery. The sparkles came from jewels instead of her spirit. Nevertheless, she cut a striking figure in her silks and furs. However, when Mia was honest with herself, she would much rather have those assets and a similar social position than bear the fatigue and grim relentlessness of poverty.

Maria

Keenly aware at that moment that she would have both beauty and the means to dress it well, Mia threw open the door to the small, aging flat she shared with her family. Hanni was hanging up the last of the wash she had finished for a customer a few blocks away. Clotheslines were strung from beams and sills and most of the room was hidden behind sheets, shirts, and bloomers. The pungent odor of strong soaps assailed her nostrils; the small radio on a shelf above the sink bleated a tinny song into an otherwise quiet room.

Hanni, bent over a woven basket containing a few more soggy articles and a handful of wooden clothespins, straightened her back painfully and smiled at her youngest daughter. Mia had burst into the solitude of her home with an energy that Hanni both enjoyed and resented. Mia was always eager about something and bustling about as though she were the natural centre of the world. So unlike Hanni's other, quieter children, Mia was always on the move and making plans. Even when she studied, she seemed restless. Life was always somewhere else for Mia and, like a breath of fresh air that was sometimes a little too crisp; she seemed to unbalance the room just a bit by her presence.

Today, the flush on her cheeks looked even deeper than normally and she seemed about to explode. Hanni's eyes shifted from Mia's face to glide down to the top of her new dress. Slowly, the smile on her face disappeared and Mia realized, too late, that the buttons didn't match the right holes. She had dressed too quickly and without enough thought after the picnic and her passionate lovemaking. Hanni took in more details and Mia felt her flush deepening to a furious crimson under the quiet inspection of her mother's gaze. Sadness was now the only visible emotion on her mother's face and Mia felt somehow cheated of her moment and the impact she expected her announcement to have.

"You don't understand," she wailed, anger drawing the fine muscles around her eyes and mouth into a grim mask.

Maria

"I think I do, Maria." It was not an accusation or a question. Having said it, Hanni turned back to the washing that was still in the basket at her feet.

"No you don't! You don't understand at all!" shouted Mia with a force that stopped her mother in the middle of picking up a wet pillowcase.

"What don't I understand?"

"I'm engaged! I have a ring! He asked me to marry him and live in a beautiful, big house and it's the most wonderful day of my life! Or, at least, it was! And now you've ruined everything! And I've told you a thousand times not to call me Maria! My name is Mia!"

With each word, Mia's voice became louder until it broke on the last syllable of her name and she flung herself across the room and onto the battered couch. She hit it with such force that the old, framed tapestry hanging on the wall behind it shook from the impact and the frame slid into an awkward angle. Hanni raised her eyes from her still-stooped position and looked at her angry daughter for a moment before continuing her task.

Hanni had made a tea with the dried chamomile she kept on the shelf above the stove. It helped calm her on those nights when she had trouble falling asleep. This evening, the brew was in Mia's hands, half finished and almost cold. Both women were grateful that a local soccer game had kept the other members of the family busy outside the house. It gave them a chance to recover from the earlier scene and calm the angry feelings that filled both their hearts.

A knock on the door startled them. No one ever knocked, except strangers, and few of them had reason to climb the many flights of stairs to the fourth floor apartment. The knock came again before Hanni could get up from her chair where she'd been reading about one of the local politicians. She had learned to read a few years ago when Mia began her teacher's training. Now, she read the local newspaper at the end of each day.

Mia was slumped into one corner of the sofa but had at least dried her tears by the time Hanni reached the door.

"Good evening, Ma'am."

The uniformed officer standing with his hat in his hands in her doorway was no older than her youngest son and, for a moment, Hanni thought he had come to visit Willi or Werner. However, he had trouble meeting her eyes and kept twisting his hat in hands that had begun to shake.

"There's been an accident, Ma'am."

Hanni's heart skipped a beat.

Twisting the hat into an unrecognizable chunk of fabric, the young man cleared his throat. He forced himself to look at her and said, "I've been told to report to you that the young Mr. Meier, Kurt Meier, was thrown by the horse he was exercising and the fall broke his neck. I'm sorry, Ma'am."

There was a muffled sound on the other side of the room. As Hanni closed the door and turned to look across the room, she saw Mia sliding from the edge of the sofa onto the floor into an unconscious heap.

Chapter 4

M ia, slouched into a corner of her mother's sofa with a pillow supporting her back, clutched another pillow to her extended belly. Her uncle, Otto, was sitting in Hanni's rocking chair,
rubbing the stump that was once his leg. A bottle of whiskey dangled
from his extended hand between two fingers. Every few minutes, he
swung his arm in a backwards arc and lifted the bottle with the back
of his elbow while aiming the stream of liquor into his mouth. The
only sounds in the room were his gulps and finishing sighs. Enemy
fire had shattered his leg and torn apart his belly in 1916. His only
comfort for the past 13 years had been the numbing liquid. Otto drank
another sip and stared at the tapestry above Mia's head. The women
and children playing in idyllic bliss were his father's vision when he
wove the tapestry for Hanni. It bore little resemblance to the mother
who was, even all these years later, still washing other people's dirty
linen. However, that, and even his constant pain, was not his concern
at the moment. Today was December 22nd and it promised to be an
unusually cold day for the baby who was about to be born.

Hanni had told him to take care of his sister during the time she
would be away delivering the clean linens she had ironed that morning. Not that he could do much for Mia except sympathize. His own
pain kept him from being able to do much for himself let alone for
anyone else. His sister's occasional moans and gasps held his atten-

tion even though, unlike his pain, hers would stop after the delivery of her baby. Still, the girl was miserable and frightened and the labor, which had started last night, had grown intense. It was a difficult labor, even considering it was the first for Mia. After a cup of coffee early this morning, half of which she had thrown up, Mia had sat or lain on the sofa all day. Shortly before Hanni went to deliver her work, the midwife had left with the words, "She's not dilating. It'll be a while before you need me."

Otto knew Mia would just as soon give up her own life rather than deliver and be responsible for a new one. All she had ever wanted was a loving husband, respectability, and enough money to be comfortable. Kurt had been her promise of that kind of future and his death had been the death of her dreams. Otto could sympathize with how someone's dreams could be blown away in a moment, leaving behind only the shell of a life. However, Mia had more than her own misery to contend with. She would have a child to care for in just a few hours, if she was lucky. He had nothing but his bottle and his mother's occasional left over dinner to sustain him.

Another, this time more-urgent groan escaped Mia's lips. She hugged her belly as if trying to hold the baby inside. She wanted Kurt and a house with a warm fireplace and a soft bed on which to deliver their first child. Instead, she didn't even have enough food for herself much less for another mouth to feed. Her mom had been accepting of the pregnancy and, at least in the last month or so, even a little excited by the prospect of a new baby in the house. Hanni was always optimistic. Silly really, under the circumstances, Mia thought.

For Mia, this was the continuation of a life that had lost all meaning. Her hopes and dreams had been broken under the hooves of a wild horse that would not be tamed and her future would be crushed by the life trying to break free of her body. Her pregnancy and impending motherhood had robbed her of the possibility of finishing her education. Each painful contraction, while helping to bring forth a new life, was squeezing to death Mia's dream of becoming a teacher.

Without an education, the only work she was qualified to do was sewing men's suits at the clothing factory. The pennies she earned would never be enough to raise a child properly. Kurt's parents would be no help, either. Although they expressed regret for what the loss of their son's life meant for Mia, they had not shown any interest in their son's child. The one time they came to visit Mia, they even hinted at a doubtful paternity of the unborn baby.

Devastated, Mia refused to seek their help, even when food got so scarce that Hanni finally went to the fat man who had once been their priest to ask for assistance. Little could be done, she was told, for sinners like her and that she and her family must now suffer the wrath of God for their transgressions.

The pains were coming faster and even stronger now. She couldn't hold the birth back much longer and only hoped that her baby would be a boy. Someone who could make his own fortune in this cruel and unfair world. As another wave of unbearable pressure bore down on her abdomen, the door flew open and Hanni rushed into the room followed by the midwife. The two older women glanced in Otto's direction and, by force of their will, seemed to elevate him onto his crutches and toward the door. The scrape of his wooden supports and the clink of his bottle against his right crutch sounded shrilly in Mia's ears as she gasped for another breath. With one last glance into what had become a decidedly female domain, the crippled veteran closed the door behind him.

Now the hard work began. Mia's body arched in pain. She couldn't imagine this going on any longer. Wave after wave of searing pain continued. Hour after hour of unforgiving torment tore her body apart. Even the midwife, Mrs. Hoffman, who had seen the most terrible suffering, eventually had no more words of comfort and her encouraging smile vanished sometime during the night. It was morning of the second day and Mia still hadn't dilated enough to make birth possible. It looked as though her body wouldn't give any more. Hanni left to get another batch of herbs for the tea that her daughter needed every hour or so to give her strength and help the contractions.

Exhausted, Mia was caught in a nightmare of endless suffering in which she saw her body twist in the throes of birth and heard her voice scream as if from an impossible distance. Something had to be done if mother or child were to survive. It was unlikely both would. Mrs. Hoffman was 180 pounds of robust gentleness, but even her formidable strength was faltering. She dabbed at the sweat of her own brow almost as often as that of Mia. The minutes and hours took with them what little strength and life remained in Mia's body.

In a last desperate effort, as Mia released another anguished scream, Anna Hoffman threw her considerable weight with as much force as she could muster onto the mound of Mia's belly. It was a matter of pushing the baby out and risking its death or losing the young mother. A gamble, at best.

At that moment, it was hard to tell who screamed the loudest, Mia or Mrs. Hoffman. A second later, the only sound was Mia's weakening breath. Her torment was almost over but she was beyond caring. Mrs. Hoffman moved from Mia's side and in front of her outspread legs. There, between the bloodied thighs, was the slippery lump that had been so reluctant to leave its mother. Grabbing the tiny legs and turning the infant upside down with a shake, the tired midwife was rewarded by a weak mewling sound that, once started, grew louder and stronger with each moment. A quick rubdown with a soft cloth and a check of the infant's body confirmed the apparent health of the little girl that had caused so much grief for her young mother. A few minutes later Mia, too, was relatively clean and comfortable in a new gown and fresh sheets.

Maria

Hanni rushed breathlessly into the room as Mrs. Hoffman covered Mia with a down and feather duvet. Hanni questioned the woman with her eyes and was reassured by a comforting smile.

"They're both exhausted, as you can imagine, but they seem fine," said the midwife.

"Where is the baby?" Hanni asked, and Anna Hoffman pointed to the bundle in the basket at the foot of Mia's bed.

Hanni lifted the tiny child into her arms and smiled at the wrinkled, puffy face resting in the crook of her arm.

"Has Mia seen it?" she asked the midwife in hushed tones.

"It's a girl. And, no, she was too exhausted to take a look. Let her sleep. She's had a terrible time of it."

At that moment, Mia's eyes, bloodshot and weary, opened and met her mother's. Feebly, she reached her arms out and said, "Let me hold my son."

"Here, darling. But it's not a boy. You have a beautiful little daughter."

Her face expressionless, Mia became rigid as Hanni laid the newborn in her arms. Looking at her daughter, Mia's eyes now registered something akin to revulsion. She had counted on this baby to be a small version of Kurt. Someone who would fill the void that his death had left in her life.

"But it was supposed to be a boy," Mia said in a voice deadened by pain and disappointment.

"It is what it is and she is a blessing regardless of what you hoped for. Now, let's take a look at her and give thanks to God for her life. What will you call her?"

Maria

Mia looked at the tiny girl in her arms and wondered about a name that might suit. She had never considered having anything but a boy and had decided long ago to name him Roland. The paper-thin eyelids fluttered open and Mia was startled to look into vivid blue depths so like Kurt's. She glanced over at the novel she had been reading right before her labour began. Its heroine, Ella, had grown up an orphan, never knowing her mother who had died in childbirth or her father who had left her on the orphanage steps.

"Ella. Her name is Ella."

Chapter 5

Snowflakes fell thick and heavy due to the easterly blowing in from Poland. The living room, a roaring fire in its hearth, was warm and cozy with delicious smells coming from an iron pot heating spiced bread and raisins. Mia could not remember any time other than Christmas when Hanni made this delicacy, a family favorite. She had to save most of the year to afford the ingredients. Raisins were particularly expensive and Mia knew that Hanni had been hoarding them since last summer.

Mia was tucked between cushions in her favorite corner of the familiar old sofa. Little Ella was in a basket between the window and fireplace. Gurgling noises coming from her daughter as well as the occasional gong of the church bells calling worshippers to various services broke the silence. Mia relished this quiet time. It was her time, nearly alone, before her family would appear, each member with some dish or other, to celebrate the holiday. After the meal, she would be expected to go to church with them and pretend to care about the message of peace and hope she had heard every Christmas since she was as small as Ella.

She wished she could be the one to stay behind to bring in a small tree and add candles, also hoarded all year, then carefully place underneath it all the gifts everyone had made. There would be at least one present for each child. The adults didn't exchange gifts. There was not enough to go around as it was. Since she was a mother herself now, this would be Mia's first Christmas in which she would not be getting a gift either.

It was all too depressing, especially when she thought about the wonderful holidays she and Kurt had planned. Unconsciously, shoving her thumbnail between the grooves that separated each of the small gems, she turned the ring he gave her and pushed it around her finger. Neither the pop of burning logs nor the still soft but needful sounds coming from the basket captured her attention. When she was in this kind of mood, her own thoughts seemed to wrap around Mia like a shroud, making her oblivious to anything but her own musings.

Since Kurt's death, she thought about their imagined future time and time again. She knew most people thought she wanted him for his wealth—but she truly had loved him and would have married him regardless of how much money he had.

When the front door flew open and slammed the wall, Mia startled out of her reverie. With a jerk, she sat up and gaped at Hans. He struggled with a large box which she assumed was filled with shoes. He kicked the door shut behind himself.

"It's dark in here," he said, walking toward the hearth and dropping the box on the far side of the stove.

"And the baby is crying," he added, surprised that she didn't seem to hear the wailing.

"Why don't you light a candle or, better yet, I'll light one and you take care of your daughter."

Wordlessly, Mia rose from the couch and picked up the infant whose diapers were soaked and dripping. The clothes used for sheets, as well as the bunting tied around Ella, were equally wet and the distinctive odor of ammonia reached Mia's nose.

Maria

"How long have you been sitting there in the dark?" asked Hans, not unkindly.

"I don't know, maybe an hour or so."

"Most likely more, from the smell of that baby. When did she eat last?"

"I don't know, Hans, but she's just wet, not hungry."

"I wouldn't be so sure about that. Look at the way she's gnawing on her fist. When you're finished cleaning her up, I'll hold her while you fix a bottle. I guess your milk still hasn't come in, right?"

"You know it hasn't and I don't need to be reminded of it."

"Sorry, Mia. I know this is a hard time for you. Christmas is a hell of a time for anyone who's grieving for someone. But, it's been nearly a year since Kurt got killed and you have his little one to take care of. You're going to have to face that responsibility eventually. The sooner the better. Hanni can't do it for you forever."

It was probably the longest speech he ever made to Mia and she sat with Ella on her lap in stunned silence. The candle sputtered on the table and the glow of burning embers in the hearth vied with the last glimmer of light coming in from the window. Mia didn't know what to say. Maybe there was nothing to say to the words that were only now coming into focus in her mind. He was right, of course. The past months, since Kurt's death on that early spring afternoon, had been a blur of pain and emptiness. Even the birth of her daughter was just one more episode in a series of unspeakable agonies that were strung together like pearls between vast expanses of emptiness.

"You're right, Hans. I haven't been of much use to anyone lately."

Her stricken face and the hollow sound of her voice brought Hans to his feet and, with two strides, to Mia's side. Uncharacteristically, he closed the distance between them even further when he took a seat next to her and put his left arm around her shoulders while wrapping the other around the bundle on her lap.

"We'll manage, Mia. You take as long as you need. There just isn't any easy way to stop hurting."

Stunned by his display of affection and support, Mia lowered her head and allowed the tears to roll down her cheeks, past her chin and onto the chest still swollen but empty of milk.

Hanni's steps created a familiar echo in the hall outside the front door. However, they were not alone. Other noises intruded into the silence following Hans' speech. There were strange voices whispering in hushed tones and Mia wondered who might have been invited to share this evening with her family. Nothing could have surprised her more than the faces of Kurt's parents framed by the doorway's peeling paint. Mia noted little lights dancing off the tiny beads of water left by melting snow on their matching coats. For a very long moment, everyone on both sides of the door stared silently at each other. Finally, Mr. and Mrs. Meier moved aside enough to let Hanni pass them. Facing one and then the other in turn, she began to introduce them to Hans. "That won't be necessary. We just came to drop some things off," said Mr. Meier in a voice colder than the weather storming outside.

"We'll just leave them here on the table," he said, as he walked into the apartment and with an abrupt motion of his arm scattered tiny shirts, socks, a woolen coat with matching cap, and a knitted blanket across the table. Mia suspected that at least some of the items were made by Mrs. Meier's own hands and she raised herself from the couch extending the baby in her arms in their direction. A brief smile crossed Mrs. Meier's face as she stepped through the door. However, it was wiped away by her husband's next words.

"We'll be going now."

Maria

That was all. Just a turn of his wife's shoulder and a shove through the door and they were gone. Stunned, Mia sat back down cradling the child tightly. She stared at her mother across the room without seeing her.

Scooping Ella's presents into her arms, Hanni dumped them on the couch next to Mia and turned toward her stove to begin preparing a small duck she had bought for Christmas dinner. It was the only time they ate meat all year except for the rare occasions when one of her children traded something for a sausage or two on the black market. She wanted it to be good. She needed it to be good. She needed something to lift the spirits that had sunken so low in her house.

Chapter 6

Dresden sparkled under the brilliant rays of an August sun high over the Elbe River. The spires of the Zwinger, a gothic architectural beauty of massive granite lace, stretched into a deeply blue sky. The buildings of Dresden that dated from the middle ages were grey with age but splendid nonetheless. Even the lampposts were intricate, gnarled ironworks of exquisite craftsmanship that towered over the gardens and walkways of ancient buildings. Once home to kings and their families, the opulent edifices now hosted fabulous concerts and artistic exhibitions. Now seeing it herself, Mia understood perfectly why people called it, "The Pearl of Europe."

Sitting on the steps of the Museum of Art, she had a view of the river only a few yards away. Boats of all sizes carrying everything from well-dressed sightseers to mountains of coal criss-crossed the dazzling water. It was hard to say whether the city on the other side of the shore was a green landscape dotted with buildings or a city of stone overgrown with trees and shrubs of all sizes. Either way, every-thing looked clean and fresh, except for the black clouds of smoke rising from river traffic.

Ten-year-old Ella played with children among the trees lining the riverfront of the museum. Mia looked on as her daughter ran and hid behind a column of masonry that supported a statue of an ancient hero. She should know who it was but lacked interest in such things as history. She'd been far too busy making a living to worry about things she couldn't change. Not that the past ten years were all that bad. In fact, a few things worked out pretty well. Mia was better off than many single mothers her age."

First and foremost, she was a hard worker. She'd sought employment in one of the town's small family businesses that produced fine men's garments, and was soon promoted to manager of four girls assigned to sewing vests for suits that would be sold in some of the most expensive outlets in the city. This was in spite of her young age and concerns that she would not be able to earn the respect and cooperation of employees who were years older than she was. However, the owner's gamble had paid off and within the last year she was given responsibility for the finished product—entire suits—with only two superiors to answer to.

Her first goal had once been to run the shop entirely but that had proven impossible. There was no way she could transform herself into a man. Then she dreamed of someday having a shop of her own in which she could design the clothing and pick the fabric for her creations. She had so many good ideas about what might sell well. Over the years, she had come to accept the fact that no one would give her the chance to prove herself. Although the owner of the business and his two managers appreciated her work, as far as they were concerned, women were useful—in their place.

Screeching children's voices drew her attention to the scene on the pavement below the museum steps. They were happily at play, including Ella, who was surprisingly athletic.

"Maybe I shouldn't be so surprised. After all, Kurt had been strong and agile. It was one of the reasons he loved horses so much. He loved the feeling of being in control while racing his horse at full speed and making nearly impossible jumps—but that's exactly what killed him."

Maria

Thoughts of Kurt's untimely death made Mia's anxious eyes sweep the scene before her for a glimpse of Ella. She found her running along the path next to the immense, undulating river. She was farther away from Mia than she was supposed to be, but Mia chose to allow this small infraction of the rules. The sight of her running daughter filled her with pride.

Long and slender, with hair flying wildly behind her head and shoulders, the girl moved with grace and strength. Mia could see the first glimpses of the woman Ella would someday become. Her agile, darting moves and light brown hair, combined with a strange shyness so like her grandmother's, had earned her the nickname, "Mouse." Of course, she hated it just like Mia used to hate her given name. No one meant any harm. If the truth be told, the name fit Mia's scampering, furtive child—happy only when she could twist and tumble in her sleek, exuberant way.

Mia wondered what Kurt would think of her if he had lived to see his daughter now. His parents had never returned to visit her or the child after that first Christmas and she had given up hope long ago that they ever would. Neither had anyone taken Kurt's place as Ella's father. Oh, there had been a few short affairs but no one had even come close to meeting her expectations. Mia had made up her mind shortly after Ella's birth that unless she met someone who could offer her and her little girl a good home and a respectable position in the community, she herself would care for them both the best way she could. No way would she become a drudge to some working-class nobody who came home at night with dirt under his nails, smelling of beer and smoke from the pub. Never in her life would she give up her independence just for the sake of "having a man." Somehow they would survive and she would make sure Ella had better opportunities than she herself had been given.

"Ella!" her voice went trailing after the child still running in the shimmer of fading light. "Time to go back!"

Maria

They had plenty of time to get to the station to catch the late afternoon train back home, but Ella could be surprisingly slow to respond to her mother's demands. It might be half an hour before she would stop her chasing around and meet Mia at the bottom of the museum steps.

Mia gathered the sacks of edibles she had traded for some of the garments she made long after she stopped sewing for her supervisor. Preparing for today's early morning bartering, she had sewn shirts at home until late into many nights and had managed to get six sausages, a pad of butter, a whole smoked ham hock, and a sack of sugar for them. Her brother-in-law, a butcher, had contacts in the countryside who were sometimes willing to trade extra meat for Mia's shirts. The butter and sugar were unexpected treats pried from the farmer's reluctant wife by shrewd haggling that Mia had to admit she actually enjoyed. She had everything in two cloth bags and wished Ella would come to help her carry one of them. It was just like the girl not to pay attention and, as her impatience grew, Mia felt the heat of rising anger creep into her neck and face along with it.

"Ella!" she called again and saw her daughter's head turn in the direction of her voice. "I'm leaving!"

With that, Mia turned and walked at a leisurely pace toward the corner where she would have to turn left toward the station. Ella had not moved. At the corner, Mia stopped and deposited her burden on the pavement at her feet and leaned against the stone building in which royalty had once lived. It now housed offices for a sprawling bureaucracy. As Mia's eyes searched for her daughter, they found instead an old organ grinder turning a lever that animated a box on wheels that produced sounds approximating a familiar tune. He even had the requisite monkey dressed in garish clothes to complete the picture of poverty earning its keep. People, strolling arm in arm or holding hands, passed by and dropped coins into the green velvety hat lying on the sidewalk in front of the organ. With each clink, the man would nod his head in thanks and the monkey would make a pleased fuss. It depressed Mia to think this man and his animal might be sleeping on the same street corner tonight while she had a soft bed at home. There were too many people out of work and too few resources.

Ella still hadn't come and Mia was contemplating going on ahead and hoping the girl would remember the way to the train station. It would serve her right for making her mother wait again. Yet the streets were hardly safe, and she would never forgive herself if something dreadful happened to Ella. Still, her aggravation grew until it threatened to overwhelm caution.

It was not a surprise then for Mia to feel both anger and relief when Ella finally ran up next to her, panting. At least 30 minutes had passed since she first called her daughter and Mia wanted to slap the child. Instead, she took her arm and shook her hard until the look of exuberance on Ella's face turned to resentment and pain.

"When I call you, I expect you to come!" she shouted as she gave her daughter one last shove in the direction of their goal. She had meant to simply whisper, but her anger had created a contorted sort of loud stage whisper. A few people had turned around to look at them, including the organ grinder, and Mia increased her pace to a near run. She had shoved the smaller of the two bundles into Ella's arms and now refused to turn and look to see if the child was keeping up.

"It serves her right," she thought. "She needs to learn a lesson."

At the station, they still had to wait a few minutes for their train to arrive. Mia had set her own bundle on the floor between her feet and Ella was squatting beside her, still clutching her burden and panting. A young man, maybe even younger than Mia, glanced in her direction and then stared in open admiration. It sent a flood of warmth through Mia's chest that did a lot to restore her good mood of the afternoon. Sometimes, she was amazed at how little it took to make her happy. Glancing away from his handsome face, she lowered herself to look at the daughter who would not meet her eyes.

"Let's get some chocolate while we're waiting," she offered.

It would be ridiculously expensive, but the smile that spread across Ella's downturned face was reward enough, even though the long lashes still hid eyes that refused to meet Mia's own.

Chapter 7

Mia was one of the last people to get out of Dresden alive at the end of the war. The Allied attack on the city that had been declared "safe" by the International Red Cross would someday become another example that atrocities are not limited to certain nations or ethnicities. Once again, the world was reminded that children and women died as readily as soldiers. In fact, more easily, since their ability to defend themselves was limited to hiding in ineffective shelters where the intensity of bombs and fires left bones melted into sludge.

Although Ella had turned sixteen, she was still a tomboy. Her lingering infatuation with one of the pilots in the Luftwaffe, Germany's air force, was Mia's chief worry. Four years earlier, Karl had paid little attention to the child so obviously obsessed with him, but Mia suspected that he was paying closer attention now that Ella had become a pretty teenager. Other than that, Ella gave Mia little to worry about. She did well in school and passed all her exams with flying colors. No one doubted that she would someday become the teacher she and Mia desperately wanted her to be.

On the fateful day of the attack on Dresden, Mia had taken the day to spend peacefully, gloriously alone. It was her intention to visit at least one of the museums and art galleries and have lunch in her favorite restaurant overlooking the quay near the Zwinger, a collection of baroque buildings dedicated to the arts. She was in one of her much loved exhibits when the bombing started. At first it was like every other time. The sirens began to wail their warning as usual. After several minutes, it became apparent that the noise would go on and on.

Visitors inside the museum were trying, like Mia, to ignore the warning. They were mostly women and men too old to serve in the military machinery honed to fine misery by Hitler's agents. They had experience with the sirens. They knew the mechanical shrieks, while alerting people to imminent danger, could not predict where the bombs would fall. Few of those unlucky enough to be near a point of attack survived the experience. Few of the veterans of the past four years bothered to hide.

However, restlessness began to replace the resignation of the museum's patrons when the shrieking wails didn't stop. This was no ordinary day, and no ordinary strike. When explosions rocked the very foundation of the building, people mobilized in frenzied fear and stampeded toward the exits. Still the sirens wailed and still the shattering of rock and bones and lives continued.

When the lights failed and she was alone in the huge hall, Mia determined she must escape. She thought of Ella, safe in Hanni's kitchen, and how much she wanted to see and hold her daughter in her arms again. Another explosion rocked the museum. As the wall in front of her began to tremble, she caught sight of the magnificent tapestry it held. About five feet wide and three feet tall, it was a fifteenth-century scene of five people cavorting in what was clearly a wine cellar and bar. The laughter and exuberance of the finely executed cloth figures reminded her of the tapestry Walter had made for her mother before she was born. This tapestry showed the same sense of wonder at the joy simple pleasures could bring and Mia knew she did not want to leave it to almost certain destruction by the flames that would no doubt spread throughout the city.

Maria

Quickly, she removed the tapestry and twisted it into a loose, tube-like roll, wrapped it around her body and held it in place with her belt. She needed her arms and legs free to run. Once she was in the main hall, the bodies darting in disarray around her slowed her only a little. Mia had wandered these halls often and she knew every exit. To her left and down the stairs was a side entrance that would bring her close to the street where she could cross to get to safety. Not to a city shelter but to the relative safety beyond the bridge that spanned the river in front of her. All seven bridges surrounding Dresden led to farms dotting the countryside around the city. The east bridge was close enough to provide her with the best route to safety.

As she ran, the screams of burning women and children vied with the pounding of her heart and the relentless whine of sirens. Several people shouted and pointed through holes that had, only a short time before, held stained glass windows now blown into bits. She would not allow them to register in her brain. Her world contained only the pain of pumping legs, a chest about to burst from exertion and the will to keep going.

Still, the bombs fell. The city was on fire.

Sometimes jostled by other running souls, sometimes in a vacuum created by the needfulness of her mind to disengage from the horror around her, Mia reached the bridge. Others had arrived before her and a human jam had developed near the center. However, the mass of bodies was not an immovable force and with each new blast and shudder of the earth beneath her feet, she pressed her way to the center of the human throng.

The bridge swayed furiously. The girders holding the immense structure above the roiling waters began to twist and crack. The bodies of escaping humanity mirrored the whirlpool of liquid below their feet. Coming apart only to come together again, the human flood made its painful way across the expanse of bridge and onto the other shore.

Maria

Just as Mia set foot on solid ground, an explosion hit the bridge dead center. Glancing quickly behind her, she saw it crumble as women and children fell to their deaths. For just this moment, she could not block out the sight. Her eyes filled with tears. Almost instantly, she regained control and began to move on. She ran until she collapsed in blind, terrified exhaustion on a patch of grass out of reach of the bombs that were still aimed for whatever life was left in Dresden.

Sometime the next day she woke up in a strange bed in a room she did not recognize. Her first thoughts were of Ella and her mother. Were they frantic about her safety? She must get to them!

Near the far wall of the room, an old man and woman were sitting at a simple table hunched near a radio tuned too low for her to hear. When they noticed she was awake, the old woman came to her bedside and stroked her cheeks.

"You were lying by the front gate yesterday. We thought you were hurt and brought you in but there seems to be nothing wrong with you." The woman had a gentle smile and kindness filled her voice.

Mia would have argued that point but was grateful for their generosity. She managed to struggle into a sitting position while swinging her legs over the side of the bed. The woman rejoined her husband at the table and motioned for Mia to join them for a cup of a steaming drink.

No one had been able to get coffee for years so Mia assumed it was one of the various brews made of grains that, if you had a good imagination, might substitute for coffee. At her approach, the old man turned up the volume and motioned for her to sit on the chair next to him. The woman pushed the steaming cup in her direction.

A reporter was describing the inferno that Dresden had become. Few of those who had been unable to get across one of the bridges were expected to survive. The death count was as yet unknown. He then went on to describe the political repercussions of the attack. The Americans had occupied most of the territory west of Dresden. Germany would be divided up into regions governed by various allied partners. Not all of the countryside around Dresden was destroyed and, toward the east, Russians had taken up residence.

The war was over. Germany had lost.

The Russians, in Werda! Everything she had heard about Russian soldiers evoked images of brutality and horror. She determined to go home only long enough to get her mother and daughter and a few of her remaining essentials before leaving the home that now belonged to their enemy. She desperately hoped Ella and her mother had survived.

After thanking the old couple for their hospitality, Mia began her anxious journey home. With the train station and the rails destroyed, a normally relaxing one hour ride turned into a fear-driven two day walk.

Her hands searched each pocket as she made her way from the house taking a mental inventory of her possessions. There were at least three farms between Dresden and Werda where farmers sold food for the right price. Aside from the tapestry tucked under her coat, Mia had several pieces of jewelry and some coins hidden inside the lining of her coat that she had been saving for desperate times. If she was lucky, she'd be able to barter for some basic staples.

Maria

At the first farm she came to, the owner and his wife gave her a bowl of soup and hunk of bread but had nothing to sell. No one else she met could spare any food until she met Roland Brandt digging up root vegetables near a fence bordering the gravel path leading to Werda. He sold her a handful of carrots and turnips for at least three times what they were worth but, after considering a moment, pushed a hamhock and two potatoes he withdrew from a nearby cart into her trembling hands. When Mia started to thank him, he turned away without a word and gruffly waved her away.

As Mia turned the last corner onto Hanni's street, she could not stop the tears when she saw her mother's building still standing. She ran toward it with renewed energy and began calling Ella's name. Hanni met her in the stairwell and crushed her in a tearful embrace.

"I have not stopped praying since the bombing started. I knew God would bring you home safely," sobbed Hanni. "Ella will be home soon."

Slowly, they unfolded from each other's arms and climbed the steps to their apartment. As they sat at the kitchen table, Mia told her about the incredible destruction in Dresden, about saving the tapestry, the kind people who had taken her in and cared for her, and her renewed determination to leave the area and make a new start —someplace where the war had not destroyed so many homes and lives. Quietly, with hope filling each word, she added, "I hope you'll come with me."

Hanni shook her head. "I cannot imagine ever leaving my valley."

Hanni began to tell Mia what had happened in the days since the bombing. Russians had swarmed into the town and into every home. Many of the young girls and women had been beaten or raped or both. The boys and old men who tried to protect them were either hurt or killed. Hanni and Ella had escaped that fate by hiding in the tool shed near their vegetable garden next to the river outside of town. Mia listened as her mother recounted the events of the past few days. There was nothing to say that didn't feel like death, except that she knew she was alive to feel it.

Hanni concluded by pounding her fist on the table. She would not leave the place of her birth, the place where, now, so many of her children and loved ones were buried. For a moment she looked wistful. Then, answering the unspoken question in Mia's eyes, she said in a cracked whisper, "They haven't found Hans yet. I suspect he's been killed somewhere in the forest and simply left there." And then she began to recount the horrors all over again. On and on her hollow voice droned. On and on the tears flowed from an endless well of sorrow.

Later, after Hanni had collapsed onto her bed, Mia wondered why Ella hadn't come home yet. She had assumed her daughter was running an errand or visiting one of her girlfriends. However, she should have been home by now. As the minutes ticked by, Mia, already anxious, paced across her mother's creaky floor. When Ella returned, Mia would tell her of the plans she had made on her journey home. She would head west and find work, if that were possible. As soon as she was settled somewhere, she would return for Ella.

Ella would want to go with her immediately, but that wouldn't be possible. She would have to find a place to live first and Ella would have to finish school before she could leave. That was the most important thing. School. As soon as she was settled and Ella finished her classes, she would send for her. "I promise," Mia thought. "I promise."

On the street below, Mia heard Ella's laughter. A moment later, she heard a man's voice, more urgent, more intense. She drew one of the dark curtains aside and saw their shadows twisted on the cobbles of the street below. Ella, her back leaning against the alcove wall, had turned her face upward while Karl rested his weight against her stomache and chest with one forearm supported by the wall above her head.

Mia reached for her heart and grasped the fabric of her dress under her breast. Quickly, she turned around to see if Hanni had heard her gasp. Her mother stared at her, waiting for an explanation. Instead, Mia turned back to the night. When she found her voice, she shouted, "Who are you with, Ella? And, what are you doing?"

"A friend," the girl answered. "He brought me home from the dance."

"Who gave you permission to go to a dance?" Mia didn't trust Ella—especially when it came to Karl. Fear for her daughter mixed with anger gave Mia's questions a startling edge.

"Quiet out there!" Mrs. Klaus the neighbor living in the apartment below them yelled.

"I didn't expect you to be home." Ella yelled back. "So I decided to go."

Furious at the defiant tone in Ella's voice, Mia turned to the sink and filled her mother's bucket with cold water. She hardly felt its weight as she carried it to the open window and threw the water on Ella and Karl standing on the sidewalk below.

Karl grunted and stormed off into the night.

Ella screamed and stamped her foot.

"Enough!" Mrs. Klaus shouted.

Ella, dripping and furious, ran up the stairs, screaming. "How could you?"

Maria

As soon as she was in reach, Mia grabbed Ella's hair and pulled her into the room.

"I wish you were dead!" Ella's face distorted with embarrassment and rage.

Taken aback, Mia's fury drained away. She hung her head and watched droplets of water splash from Ella's hair onto the old floor.

Chapter 8

Standing on the ship's upper deck, tightening the scarf around her neck, while her hair was whipped by an early spring wind, Mia leaned as far over the bow as her torso would reach. Bracing her feet to a bottom rail, she spread her arms wide and let her body sway with the undulations of the hulking metal beneath her. Thoughts, like the wisps of cloud above her head, flew in and out of her mind. It seemed so long ago that this journey had begun. Was it the day Dresden was bombed when she knew she would have to leave for good? Or was it long before that when she had first heard about America, the land where streets glittered with gold and gems and opportunities waited to be discovered? Perhaps it had begun as far back as the day Kurt had died, more than twenty-seven years ago.

Her thoughts drifting, she remembered her forty-fifth birthday last month and the party her best friend, Marina, had organized. More friends than she knew she had, came to drink beer and eat the "wurst" sausages and potato salad that Marina had prepared. Some brought more food and a few had managed presents, in spite of wages barely sufficient for survival. In fact, the scarf she was wearing now had come from Inge, her co-worker in the little shop in Hildesheim where the two of them made beautiful coats for stylish wives of wealthy men. They had worked together on the second floor above the shop owned and run by a widower. More than once he had indicated a personal

Maria

interest in Mia but each time she had politely refused his advances. Her heart was set on a farther horizon and she knew she would stay in Hildesheim only until she could find a way to America.

The memory of racks of coats made her mind return to an image from two years ago, of a five-year-old little girl for whom she had sewn a wool coat and matching hat from scraps at the shop. Two years ago now seemed like a snippet of time as she recalled the tiny face with eyes identical to her own.

Karin had been born in March of '49, the first of only two times Mia had been able to slip in and out of what had become East Germany. The second time had been in 1954, just two years ago, when Mia had gone back to Werda to try and convince Ella to come to Hildesheim and bring her little girl. Of course, it wouldn't be easy. The Russians, who now occupied what had been her country, shot anyone caught trying to "escape." However, there was always the hope that, if they were careful and lucky, they could reach freedom.

The border guards weren't the only issue. The real problem was her stubborn daughter.

Mia did not want to involve all the people of the underground network who would risk their lives to help someone who did not want to be helped. Ella was willing to entertain the thought of joining her mother only when she was having another fight with Karl. They were married when Karin was barely two years old and Karl's first wife, a war bride from Norway, got fed up with his drinking and abuse and left him to return home with her son. Now, despite that same abuse, Ella clung to the hope that she could change him and make their marriage work.

Mia could feel her rage rising in her throat again as she remembered the last time she had seen Ella and Karin.

María

"Your best chance for a good life, and a future for your child, is to get away from Karl and out of this hell-hole of a place!" she had screamed as loud as she dared. One had to be careful about what the neighbors heard. You never knew who would get some satisfaction from turning you into the authorities for plotting against the state.

"I can't leave him," Ella wailed for the hundredth time. "He's all I've got!"

"You have a child who needs you and you have a career. I know you'll have to go back to school to get another teaching license in the West, but that's better than staying here and spending the rest of your life being miserable."

"But I love him," came the inevitable tearful retort.

It was during that visit that things changed for Mia. Something in her daughter's petulant pout made her realize the futility of arguing. Ella was not ready for change.

Seeing no hope of bringing her daughter and granddaughter to Hildesheim, she returned to her sewing job and started in earnest to look for ways to escape alone, if that's how it must be, to America. That thought became her new passion, her obsession. All her spare time was spent in plotting ways to get there.

Then one day, Marina gave her the solution. Knowing that it might mean the loss of her closest companion, Marina had given Mia a slip of newspaper. On it was printed in bold letters, "Wanted, German woman to cook, clean, and keep house for professor. North Dakota, United States." The ad went on to say that the professor would pay for passage and that there would be room and board as well as an allowance.

The correspondence back and forth had taken months, but eventually the arrangements had been made. Professor Josef Keller had sent her a photograph of himself and his three teenage children, in front of a two-story wooden house with a sizable front lawn with hedges and a flower bed. He had written that in back of the house was an even bigger expanse of lawn with a garage and a field of corn and other vegetables beyond that.

There were two boys and a girl. The images were too small to see exactly what they looked like. From what she could tell though, they looked like most of the kids she knew in her own country, except they were better fed and clothed. Professor Keller was another matter entirely. He stood slightly to the side of his children with his hands clasped behind his back. Although he wore a shirt unbuttoned at the neck and no tie, his erect posture hinted at a dignified air in spite of the casual setting. Mia couldn't tell if he was smiling or not, but it didn't matter. The whole scene—the house, the children, and, especially, the man—was like a dream. After a life in crowded fourth floor tenements, often shared with far too many people, it would be easy to spend time in that house—a real house with a yard and a garden— and cook and clean and have a "normal" life. She was sure.

It had taken most of a year to get the proper documentation and approval, but, finally, she was on board the ship. He had booked passage for her in a small cabin she shared with another woman on the bottom deck.

The breeze grew chilly and Mia turned to re-enter the heavy double doors leading into a lobby area. The door to her left, led to one of the many tiny coffee shops. She entered and found a small, round table in front of a row of large windows. She sat down on one of two cane chairs and glanced through the window to the deck where she had stood moments before.

A young man approached the same spot where she had stood. Her startled gasp drew the eyes of the couple at another table, but she didn't care. The sight of him froze every fiber of her body. It was like looking at Kurt in another time and place. It was wrong, all wrong, and yet so wonderful at the same time. He hadn't aged at all and his familiar slouch was a reminder that twisted her stomach into knots.

Turning her head reluctantly, she quickly ordered a hot chocolate from the smiling waitress at her side. It took only a moment to make her order but it was long enough to change her world for the second time in the past few minutes. When she glanced back, he was gone. Had it been just her imagination? She didn't know—but the feeling in her heart was real. Had it been a sign that she was, indeed, making the right move? Whether or not it was, that's how Mia chose to see it.

The Atlantic waters were calm for most of the two-weeks crossing although two days of brisk winds whipped the dark sea into small, white-topped peaks that lent an air of excitement to the passage. There was plenty of time to eat leisurely meals, visit with new friends, and dance to one of the many bands playing every night. There were even staged performances, one of them a magician Mia particularly liked. If there was some innocent flirting between them, what harm could there be? This was just a transitional part of her life.

Her favorite times, though, were the hours she lay on padded lounges on one of the upper decks. Here she passed the time reading and thinking about her life that had, thus far, been so different from what she had dreamed of in her youth. After Kurt's death, she had given up the idea of marrying. No one had ever again come close to making her feel the way he did, and what they offered her was a shadow compared to the life she and Kurt had planned together.

Once, when Ella was eight years old, someone came close to tempting her. Heinz had loved her deeply and would have been kind to her little girl. However, in the end, even Heinz could not persuade her to give up her independence. Mia couldn't envision herself spending the rest of her life in a dingy apartment, having more babies, and taking care of a man who came home smelling of sweat and coal from the mines in which he labored daily.

Coal mines and the textile factory employed nearly all the adults in Werda in those days. Thankfully, children were no longer allowed to work there and conditions had improved, but they were still places that broke bones and spirits and left families deadened to the joys of life.

Even though Werda had grown into a sprawling, busy town, the wars and general poverty had stripped it of any gentility it once had. Mia had come to hate it after Kurt's death. She had escaped Werda by going to Hildesheim in West Germany after the war ended, but even Hildesheim could not offer the new life she longed for.

The professor was her big chance. It had taken much longer than she had hoped, but at forty-five she still had a lot of life left and she intended to live it well.

Visions of her future drifted in bits and pieces across her mind when a scraping sound interrupted her musings. A woman about her own age, whom she had met two nights ago at one of the bars with live music and a tiny dance floor, sat on the edge of the lounge next to hers.

"Hi, Mia," she said. "Want some company?"

Mia didn't, but felt obliged to say, "Sure. Have a seat. I was just thinking."

"I'm not disturbing you, am I?"

"No."

Anne and her sister had joined the ship at its stop in Plymouth, England, where it took on passengers and extra cargo and supplies. She spoke German with a strong English accent, having worked as a nurse in Berlin for a number of years. She had even studied for a while at the university there hoping to eventually become a doctor, but family obligations forced her to return home and abandon her dream. Still, Mia envied her. At least she had an education and interesting work—and, she was nice. Possibly a bit too friendly, but nice.

"What are you thinking about?" Anne asked while arranging herself on the chaise.

"Oh, nothing in particular. Just what it will be like to live in North Dakota. I know it will be cold most of the year. I'm not sure how that will work out because I really prefer a hot, sunny climate. But mostly I'm thinking about the family I'll be working for. I have no idea what they're like."

"It sounds like you're having second thoughts."

"Not at all. This is what I've been dreaming about for years and years and I wouldn't miss the opportunity for anything."

"Then why do you look so worried?"

Mia wearied of answering Anne's all-too-personal questions but didn't know how to disengage herself from the conversation without offending the woman. Besides, she would not have to see Anne ever again after their crossing so it didn't matter what she said.

"It's just that I always wanted to live in a nice house with a big yard but I never dreamed I would be a servant there. I always thought that if it ever happened, I would be the mistress of the house with servants of my own."

She felt embarrassed as soon as the words had escaped her mouth. Turning away from Anne, she hoped to hide the flush that was spreading across her neck and face.

Maria

Anne paused a few minutes before saying, "It sounds to me like you're scared, and honestly, Mia, you have every right to be."

Mia turned to her in wonder. With just those few words, Anne had succeeded in naming her problem and putting her at ease at the same time. Seeing the relief on Mia's face, Anne continued.

"After all, you're going to a place you've never been to, to work for people you've never met, and to a country where you don't even speak the language. That is a major leap of faith. You must be very brave to do such a risky thing. Or maybe you just want a better life so bad that you'll do anything to get it. I know how it feels. I've done it myself, you know."

No, Mia didn't know, but now she wanted to find out. How could this stranger know her so well in such a short time when her own family didn't know what to make of her decision.

"How can you possibly know how it feels?' she asked.

"Remember, I told you I had lived in Germany a few years after the war?"

Mia nodded.

"Well, I had fallen in love with a German soldier who had been brought to the hospital ward where I was working, close to the end of the war. He was hurt pretty badly. He'd taken shrapnel in his belly and leg from a mine that exploded near him. I took care of him for months and got to know him pretty well. I knew that falling in love with the enemy was just about the last thing I should do, but Tomas was wonderful. Not at all like we were told to expect. In fact, he was gentle and bright and loved to read. Often, when I was dressing his wounds, he'd tell me all about what he'd read that day. He would be so enthusiastic about plots and settings. He would act out the charac-ters for me. After a while, the time I spent with him was the best time of my day and, when the war was over and he was released from the hospital, he asked me to come with him back to Berlin."

Mia's expression registered her astonishment. Her eyes filled with tears as Anne continued.

"At first, it was really hard. The people, even his family, considered me an enemy and couldn't understand why he had brought me into their lives. He wanted to get married right away but I made him wait because I wasn't sure that we could make it under those circumstances. I studied German and when I spoke well enough to attend classes, I took my entrance exams and started medical training. After a year or so, we married and by that time most of his family accepted me and some even liked me. At any rate, they were kind enough and Tomas and I were happier than I had ever been in my whole life."

"So what happened to change all that?"

"What happened is a bullet through his head."

Mia gasped but Anne continued, almost in a rush to get the rest of the story told.

"He and a few other men had gone hunting and he was shot accidentally. At least they all said it was an accident. After all these years, I'm still not sure. There were a few people that never forgave him for bringing me home with him. I really can't say for sure if they hated him enough to kill him for it. After that, I couldn't stay. I went back home and picked up my life where I had left it off. But it has never been the same and I don't think I'll ever be that happy again."

For a long time the two women sat in silence. Finally, Anne spoke again. "Have you ever been in love, Mia?"

"Where to begin? I guess the simple answer is 'yes'. But it's a long story and so sad that I haven't talked about it for years."

Maria

"We've got time if you want to tell me."

Mia did. She wanted not only to tell her story but to have this unlikely new friend understand what had happened. So she started at the beginning. When she first met Kurt and first felt the warmth that would grow into a blazing fire of love and passion. She talked on and on about his strong body and handsome face, his generosity and wonderful sense of humor. She talked about the plans they had for a house of their own on the family holdings but not too near his parents' home. She talked about their dreams of children and the business he would someday inherit. She talked about that early spring day when he asked her to marry him and she said "yes" and got pregnant. She told Anne about the accident that had taken his life that very same day.

"And you've never married?"

"No. I never found anyone I wanted to live with that much."

"What about your baby?"

"Ella is twenty-seven-years-old now and has a little girl of her own. She's been difficult in some ways. Very bright, like her father, but she lives in a world of her own. She finished her teacher's training at the university and seems, if you don't look too closely, to be happy. I know she has problems with that man she married but she's too frightened to face reality and too stubborn to admit she made a mistake. I even tried to convince her to come with me and bring the child. At least they would have a chance for a decent future. I could have arranged for them to get out of East Germany. There are a few well-placed people I know who would have helped. She wouldn't hear of it and I finally gave up and decided to go alone."

"It sounds like this is your time to fulfill some of your own dreams. Who knows? You might even marry this man who's sent for you all the way across the Atlantic. And if it's not him, there might be some other American who will sweep you off your feet."

Anne's positive attitude was infectious and Mia couldn't help but smile. Besides, Anne was right. Who knew what would be possible in this new world she was going to?

Chapter 9

The remainder of the voyage was uneventful, made up of days of eating and lounging on deck and nights of drinking and dancing until nearly dawn. Mia and Anne had become inseparable, and Mia gave herself permission to enjoy every moment to the fullest. After all, once the trip was over, her night of Cinderella at the ball would come to an end, and she would have to adapt to her new role as scullery maid in the big old house in North Dakota.

There were no words to describe her arrival at Ellis Island. Docks teeming with people of all descriptions, more languages than Mia ever thought existed, and clothing so outlandish that, at times, Mia thought she was in another world and not just another country. Best of all was the immense Statue of Liberty that overshadowed the skyline each time she glanced in that magnificent lady's direction. A tearful good-bye to Anne and promises to write each other had been the bittersweet end of one life and the beginning of what she hoped would be a better one.

Mia loved the bustle of New York. The energy generated by so many people on the move was like a drug in her veins. Even the language was not too much of a problem. Many people from the various ships spoke German and clearly marked signs led her in the general direction of the train station from which she would depart for North Dakota.

Maria

Most of the time she allowed the crowd to carry her along. It was easy enough to melt into the teeming mass with her one suitcase of the most essential or beloved items that she brought from her previous life. Thinking of the tapestry she had taken from Dresden during the bombing raid made her clutch the battered suitcase more tightly to her side.

Mia's heart beat faster as she was jostled by bodies and sounds completely unfamiliar to her. Even the smells assailing her nose hinted at lives she could barely imagine. Despite shoving and shouting, Mia heard the familiar sounds of her German language somewhere up ahead and made her way toward a couple she had seen on board. When she reached them, they were able to point the way she had to go to board her train.

With no time to lose, Mia shoved her way through the crowd. Her old, worn shoes gave little support on the rough beams of the boardwalk leading to the platform she needed to find. Exhausted, and what seemed like hours later, she leaned against a lamp post to catch her breath as her train rounded the last curve. It whistled and steamed to a stop barely two feet from where Mia stood.

Excitement faught with exhaustion as she hauled herself and her suitcase up the last steep step.

She spent many of the hours on the cross country train to Grand Forks sleeping. The rhythmic clank of steel wheels on rails lulled her mind and softened the curves of her body into a comfortable slouch as her mind drifted from one imaginary scene to another.

"What would he be like? Would his children like her?"

"Grand Forks," said the huge sign over the station's double doors. Mia, more nervous than she thought she would be, glanced anxiously through the dirty window of her car as the train pulled to a jerking halt next to the platform. Several people were gathered near the doors of the station but she could not recognize the face she had memorized from the picture Dr. Keller had sent. Descending from the steep stairs clutching her suitcase, Mia felt her panic fully blossom for the first time since she started her journey. Everyone who had waited for the train to unload its human cargo seemed to have found who they were looking for. People were hugging and kissing and hefting small children into waiting arms. He had written that he would be here. What if she had made a mistake and had taken the wrong train at the wrong time? What if she had made a mistake in even daring to come to this distant country to build a new life? What if he had changed his mind and would not be here to meet her? So many "ifs" chased each other through her head that she didn't see the man inside the building looking at her through the window.

When he finally walked through the station's double doors and stopped in front of her, she smiled her relief. The corners of his mouth twitched in what might have been the beginning of a smile and he said, in German, "My name is Herr Professor Keller. You can call me, 'Herr Professor.'"

That was all. Not, "Hello" or "How was your trip?" Just that she was to address him by his title. Well, it would be easy enough to be distant and polite as long as he was fair in his expectations of her. She would work hard and she would save her money for the two years she had agreed to be in Herr Professor's employ in exchange for him paying her way half way around the world. Then, if things did not work as well as she hoped, she would move on to something else.

His children had not come with him to welcome her and he did not find it necessary to explain their absence. Instead of the family Mia had expected, she found herself alone with only this quiet man sitting next to her behind the wheel of the biggest car she had ever been in. In fact, she had not been in many cars at all but this was clearly an exceptional one. A two-toned green Chrysler with what looked, from the back, like fins on either side, it had huge wheels and black tires with a wide white stripe extending outward from the rim. Inside, the long seat and back were covered with a thick clear plastic, fitted to hug the contours perfectly. It was spotless, as was the dash and the rest of the interior. Only the slightest film of dust covered the long hood and she imagined it was because there were so many unpaved roads. She wondered if he washed the car every day.

She attempted conversation several times, but he was either uninterested in talking to her or preoccupied with maneuvering his shiny green tank around tight corners and along meandering roads. His refusal to answer her polite questions irritated Mia and she came to the conclusion that this man might be a professor but he was no gentleman. Sometime later, though, she noticed that he clutched the steering wheel rather tightly and concentrated intently on every move the car, or the traffic around them, made. When he finally pulled into a driveway and turned the ignition to "off", he sat back with an audible sigh. Mia decided he was either a bad or nervous driver, or both.

He seemed much more at ease and smiled as he got out of the car and came around to open the door for her. While she got out, he removed her suitcase from the trunk and led the way to the front door of the wood frame house she recognized from the picture he had sent so long ago. It was a pretty house, painted pale yellow with white trim around the doors and windows. Five steps led up to the front porch.She didn't have time to see much of the yard except for the two patches of flowers under the front windows. Even before they reached the top step, the door flew open and a tall, young man rushed at them shouting in German, "Dad, I'm late for practice! Can you give me a ride?"

"Slow down, son. I want you to meet Maria, our new housekeeper."

Maria

"I don't have time. I told you I'm already late. So, will you take me or not?"

"No, I will not take you. I did not make you late. And, yes, you have the time to say hello to our new housekeeper."

Knowing he was not going to get his way, the young man turned to Mia and grinned in a lopsided, charming way as he stretched out his hand and said, "Pleased to meet you, Ma'am. My name is Joe."

"Actually, I'm Mia. I'm pleased to meet you, too," Mia said as they shook vigorously.

He was more polite and charming than his father although Mia clearly saw the resemblance between the two. The graying, older man had undoubtedly once had the same kind of dark good looks his son had inherited.

"According to the birth certificate you sent, your name is Maria," said Josef Keller, senior. "Is that correct or not?"

"It's my given name but I've never been called anything but Mia," she replied.

"If your name is Maria then that's what I will call you."

Startled, Mia was unable to think of anything to say.

Coming to her rescue, Joe said, "Mia is fine with me and, Mia, would you mind if Dad took me to the gym? I'm almost late for orchestra practice, and this is a big one, we're performing at the university tomorrow."

"Of course, I don't mind at all. In fact, if you show me to my room, it will give me a chance to unpack and wash up a little."

Herr Professor turned cold blue eyes on her before reminding his son, "I told you I will not take you. That's final."

Maria

Shrugging, Joe grinned at Mia and turned to leave saying, "Gotta run. See you later. By the way, what's for dinner?"

By the time fall came around the trees looked like red paint was exploding from each limb. Brown twigs and yellow leaves had replaced green on shrubs and lawns and Mia was exhausted. She had worked hard most of her life but never under so much pressure. Herr Professor wasn't even the worst of it. She expected to cook and clean and wait on him. What she hadn't expected was that his three children would be so demanding. Elizabeth, the oldest, was seldom home, but Joe and Gary treated her like both their mother and their servant. Between polishing floors, shoes, silverware and windows, between washing, ironing, cooking and shopping Mia realized that her dream of living in a large house had more flaws than she'd ever imagined.

News from Ella wasn't good either. Each new letter was more depressing and desperate than the last. Just last week, Ella had written, "He's moved out for good. I'm glad it's finally over. Now I can concentrate on my job and Karin." Mia had hoped that this meant her Ella had finally reached a level of maturity and peace with herself.

Then, this morning, another letter had arrived from her daughter. Sitting on the wicker couch on the screened-in porch at the back of the house, Mia read, "I miss him so much I can hardly imagine how I'll make it another month, much less a lifetime without him. Karl will never be a good husband but he loves his daughter and is good to her. She loves him, too, and keeps asking why he isn't here anymore. I don't know what to tell her. I can't be strong for her sake when I can't even be strong for myself. It would help if Karin would stop mentioning him and give me some peace, but she doesn't seem to understand that I am hurting, too. I've sacrificed myself for her, trying to give her everything on a teacher's salary that she could possibly need. I am tired and I need a vacation—but, even though school is closed for another month, I can't afford to go anywhere. Besides, where would I go where I won't think of him every moment?"

Mia rocked on the loveseat, the letter in her hand resting on her lap. Her mind explored options and dreams.

She had come to America to start a new life, one that she had imagined was possible if she was patient, worked hard, and saved her money. Now her plans included a little house of her own with a yard filled with flowers and enough leisure time to enjoy them. Her favorite fantasy was a setting in southern California where the sky was sunny and blue all year round and she could stroll on the beaches she had seen pictured in a magazine that had a whole article devoted to a town called Santa Monica. She knew that it would take time and much more money than she had been able to save so far. She had even tried to figure out how she could arrange for Ella and Karin to join her. She wanted them to have a chance to make more of their lives than they could in Werda. Mia had always known that Ella's marriage would fail and that her bright but indecisive daughter would need Mia's strength and guidance to help her build a new future. However, it was Karin who needed Mia's help the most. The girl had potential but no chance to realize it if she couldn't get away from the deadening environment that was already stifling her. Besides, if she were honest about it, Mia had to admit that Ella was too self-absorbed to give Karin the guidance she required. In fact, Ella probably needed the child's initiative and energy to keep her own mind from succumbing to the depression that now threatened to overwhelm her. Mia knew she was the only one who could intervene and give her granddaughter a chance.

Maria

To that end, Mia had maintained her connections with the people in the underground who would make escape from East Germany possible for Ella and Karin when the time came. However, it was time itself that was the biggest problem. She would need several more years to save enough money to pay for their escape and a year of room and board in a safe house. It would take permission and proper documentation from various agencies for their emigration. All of that meant planning with no guarantee that her plan would work. Would the United States accept her as a sponsor for the two of them? Would Ella learn English and find a job to help out? She was a teacher now. Would she be willing to do some other work in exchange for freedom and a new life? Where would they live if the professor didn't accept them in his house? Ella was unpredictable and could change her mind even if she agreed to the plan. With a sigh, Mia made a mental note that none of this wishful thinking included the little house in Santa Monica.

With a groan, Mia got up from the loveseat and made her way to her room. Just two months ago, Beth, the professor's daughter, had married an engineer from Ohio. When his daughter moved, he suggested she take Beth's room as her own. It was much more convenient and larger than the tiny bedroom above the kitchen she had occupied for nearly a year. Narrow, steep stairs led to the two small rooms under the roof. They both had steep, sloping walls and were separated by a tiny bathroom. The two rooms were like mirror images of each other and she liked the privacy of what seemed like her own apartment. Still, the stairs were a problem after a hard days' work and difficult to negotiate on winter mornings when she didn't turn on the lights to avoid waking everyone. She cherished the thirty or so minutes in the early morning quiet with a cup of coffee and the newspaper she read and refolded so the professor wouldn't notice he was not the first to get the news.

Maria

Reading the paper and watching some TV shows like, "I love Lucy" was how she learned to speak English. At first, the professor gave her lists of vocabulary words to memorize. Later, he had her read the morning news and helped her translate.

On Sundays she had extra time for herself because she did not have to make breakfast until the family came home from church at noon. Mia went through the kitchen and turned right at the far end into the hall which led to the two downstairs bedrooms, hers with a window facing the back yard, and the professor's larger room with two windows facing the front yard and street. In a shoebox on the shelf of her petite closet, Mia kept her savings wrapped in tissue under a small stack of letters from Ella and the few photographs she had brought from Germany.

Without Beth, it was only the professor with Joe and Gary who would be coming home in an hour or so. On Sundays, she always cooked fried chicken with mashed potatoes, gravy, and either corn or peas, depending on the time of year. It had to be on the table promptly at twelve but she had plenty of time before she had to start breading the mountain of chicken legs, breasts, and wings. Just thinking of all that meat made her think about how little her family in Werda had to eat. The food she cooked here every week would support her own family for a month or more. There was more meat at one Sunday dinner than they sometimes saw in a whole year.

She spread the bills and coins on a corner of her bed and separated the bills into little piles of the same denominations. Between her salary of $120 per month and the small change she had managed to put aside from her household allowance, Mia had saved just over a thousand dollars, not enough to send for Ella and Karin. Too often she had added to the household budget from the coins that fell out of the professor's pockets and then slipped between the seat cushions where he always sat. At this rate, it would take at least three or four more years to save enough to start the process of getting her daughter and granddaughter on their way to America. Too long. Much too long. Mia felt it in her bones, a feeling of urgency she couldn't put into words.

Although she had never done it before, she knew she would have to talk to the professor and ask his advice. Before he had sent for her, he had researched all the options and requirements involved in sending for someone from the eastern block of Europe and, even though she did not want to let him know what her plans for the future were, she knew now that she would need his help. Perhaps he would even be willing to give her a loan, a sort of advance on her salary. Maybe one of his colleagues at the university would be interested in sponsoring or hiring Ella the way she herself had been.

Although there was some urgency, Mia would have to choose her timing carefully. If he was preoccupied, the professor would resent her interrupting him. If he was in a bad mood, he would dismiss her without listening. Sunday afternoons, especially if Joe and Gary were not home, would be best. Often, they brought home friends for lunch. Her fried chicken was becoming the envy of many households in town. Still, it was summer and "the boys" often had plans away from home on these warm, sunny afternoons. She would wait for the right day and time and trust she would not have to wait too long.

As it turned out, she didn't have to wait long at all. That same day, during lunch they were sharing with three other young men from Joe's university varsity band, Gary asked if he could bring his girlfriend for dinner the following weekend. Mia let her glance fall to her plate. After several moments, when she was sure she had everyone's attention, she asked, "What date is next Saturday?"

With a frown, Joe said it would be the twenty-eighth, "Why?"

"Well, because it's nearly the end of the month and I'm already nearly out of money for groceries," Mia said. "I'd like to fix something nice but I won't be able to get it until the week after next."

The stunned silence was interrupted by the professor noisily clearing his throat before he said, "How much more do you need, Maria?"

"At least ten dollars every week."

Herr Professor stared at her over the rim of his glasses while Mia continued to nibble on the crispy crust of a thigh she held between her fingers. When it became clear she was not going to say anything more, he grunted once and said with a forced cheerfulness in his voice, "Well, good then!"

"Thank you, Herr Professor," Mia said almost casually. "How about next Saturday, Gary? That is, if your father will let me have the extra I need for this week already."

Mia glanced at the man sitting at the head of the table and arched one of her brows. He managed to nod. She turned to Gary then and said, "Would a nice roast with potatoes and corn on the cob be all right, dear?" Gary nodded, his mouth full of chicken.

Joe's blue eyes were open wide and his mouth hung slackly as he stared at Mia in admiration. Almost softly, still staring, he said, "That was beautiful."

Two weeks later on another Sunday, Mia cut some of the flowers from rose bushes, huge and gnarled, on the side of the house, and arranged them in a beautiful crystal vase she found months before in a box under the eaves of the upstairs bedrooms. Both rooms upstairs were now used for storage but Mia had decided she was going to clean every corner of the house for what, in America, was called, "spring cleaning." She had found many similar treasures buried in the midst of mountains of junk that had been piled out of sight for decades. In one box, she found wonderful watercolor pictures still framed in beautiful handcrafted frames. When she asked, Herr Professor told her that Joe's mother had painted them in the early years of their marriage.

"They're beautiful," she told him and he had agreed. However, he refused to hang them and insisted she put them back in storage.

In another box, she found an entire set of porcelain dishes. The setting for twelve had been wrapped in tissue and newspaper. Herr Professor told her they were too good to be used when his children were young and even now that they were older, he didn't see any need to use good china for every day.

"In that case, wouldn't it be a good idea to give them to Beth? Her mother would probably want her to have them," Mia suggested.

"Actually, Beth's mother did not buy them. Joe's mother did," Herr Professor said. Mia was stunned. She had assumed all three children had the same mother. Her curiosity increased with each bit of history she unearthed under those eaves.

It was a box of photographs in beautiful silver frames that finally answered some of her questions. Both bedrooms and the bathroom sparkled by the time she found a small door hidden behind a chest she had moved. Only a hook secured the three-foot-square door which, when opened, revealed a small space someone had used to squeeze a cardboard box filled with framed photos. At first, Mia had taken the box into her bedroom where she tucked it beneath her bed. For over a week, she had removed each frame and polished the silver and glass until everything shone. Many of the photos had been taken in front of the yellow house when it was still white.

Beth, Joe, and Gary were depicted at various ages with their father and mothers. What interested Mia was that each child was held in the arms of a different woman. She could not be mistaken because each of the three women were decidedly different in coloring and stature. Although the photographs were in shades of grey, it was clear that Beth's mother was a tall woman with light, probably blonde, hair wound in a thick braid on top of her head. She wore a stern expression which even her frilly blouse and long flowing skirt did little to soften. Baby Joe, on the other hand, was held by a petite young woman with short, curly dark hair so much like his own. Gary, the youngest, was pictured with his older brother and sister and a woman nearly as round as she was tall. Her smiling face suggested a happiness neither of the other women seemed to have.

When Mia finally brought the box into the living room and placed it on the coffee table in front of her boss, he made no move to touch it. His stare was fixed on the box for a long time before he looked at Mia who had sat down on the stuffed chair across from him.

"Please tell me about these women," she asked.

"Why do you need to know?"

"I guess I don't need to know, but I'd like to. I live in this house and I take care of this family. It would be nice to know some of its history."

"I've been married three times," he said and waited for Mia to respond to this confession. Most people, in his experience, had stiffened or gasped when they found out about his many marriages. Mia remained silent while she waited for his next words.

"They all died. Nora, Beth's mother, came from Sweden the year before I met her. She was a beautiful woman when I met her and all she wanted was to have a family and be a good wife and mother. She got sick while she was pregnant with Beth and everyone thought it was the pregnancy. However, even after the baby was born, she didn't get better. She kept getting worse until she died when Beth was three years old. She was a diabetic and I think when she got sick her body wasn't strong enough to recover.

"Joe's mother, Jenny, was one of my students. She studied violin and might have been a good artist if she had had more discipline. She was full of life and had all kinds of plans to travel and perform all over the world. I don't know if she would have accomplished her goal. Actually, it's doubtful—but she was a wonderful young woman who helped me forget about Nora's death. Unfortunately, she never adapted well to being a housewife and mother. Her depressions became worse and she relied more and more on what she called her "special tea." Actually, it was laudanum. I should have watched her more closely. I know that now. One day I came home and found her unconscious on the bedroom floor. There was nothing the doctor could do to revive her. It was very sad. Such a waste of a young, vibrant life.

"Gary's mother, Elizabeth, was a lovely woman. She was kind, gentle, and a wonderful cook. My daughter's name is Elizabeth, too, you know, and she resented having yet another stepmother. That's why she insisted on being called Beth. Sadly, Elizabeth died shortly after childbirth in a tragic accident."

Mia didn't know what to say. She waited for him to continue, but apparently he was finished. Eventually, she asked, "So, you raised your three children all by yourself?"

"No," he said.

He had help from friends and had hired help during the years when the children were small and he had to work too many hours to take care of them himself. Until Gary was twelve years old, he had someone come in five days a week to cook and clean and take care of the children.

Maria

After that, he and the children took care of each other and the house. They did all right until a few years ago when Beth went off to Ohio to study. In truth, she had carried the brunt of the household chores. Joe and Gary, without their sister's constant coaxing, became too involved with their classes and music to be of much help. Their father had as little time and inclination. That's why he decided to send for her. He wanted someone from his own hometown along the Mosel River, but he was not sorry he had chosen Mia.

It was during the evening of that same day, after Mia had bathed and was sitting up in her bed reading a book about a young peasant woman in love with her master's son, that she heard a soft knock on her door.

"Just a minute," she said, slipping out of bed to get the robe from the back of the chair next to her dresser. Before she could slip it on, her door opened and Herr Professor let himself into her room. Startled, she turned to face him.

"Excuse me," he said.

Coming nearer, he reached for her hand. Mia didn't know what to say or do so she pulled away and sat down on the chair that still held her robe. Herr Professor sat down on the edge of her bed. Neither of them said a word. Mia simply stared at him until he got up again and turned to leave. Before reaching the door, he turned once more and faced her but, try as he might, the words he wanted to say wouldn't come. Instead, he turned away and left the room.

The following day, another letter from Ella arrived. In it she explained that she was thinking of letting Karl move back home. He had spent nearly every weekend with her and had begged to be allowed to come back permanently. Ella had written, "He knows how wrong it was of him to cheat on me again and he swears it's the last time he will ever hurt me. I know he means it, Mom."

Maria

That evening Mia decided to speak to Herr Professor and ask his advice. They were sitting on the couch in the living room watching "Gunsmoke." It was a television western set in the wild west of the previous century. Mia loved it.

When the last credits rolled, she said, "Herr Professor, I'd like to talk to you about my daughter." He looked at her with curiosity and then got up to turn off the television.

"What's the problem?"

"Well, you know that Ella is going through a divorce." He nodded and waited for her to continue. "I'm afraid she's going to change her mind again and allow her drunken, abusive husband to move back in again. That would be a disaster for her and for Karin. I want to help them get out of East Germany and, in fact, I want them to come here."

"Why would it be such a bad idea for her to reconcile with her husband?

"Karl is never going to change. He's a drunk and he's mean when he drinks. He's also never going to stop running around on her. More than once he's beaten her and Karin. Eventually, he'll hurt them seriously. Ella isn't strong enough to resist him and Karin needs a chance to grow up. Their only hope is to get so far away that Karl can't get to them. I know Karin loves her father but someday, if they stay there, she'll wonder why I never tried to help."

"Do you want them to live here?"

Herr Professor's blue eyes focused on Mia as he asked this. Mia knew that this one question hid much more than the simple words he spoke. She looked him squarely in the face as she said, "Yes."

"I suppose they can live in the two upstairs rooms and help you out with chores. But there are certain things Ella would have to agree to. She would have to learn English while she waits for permission to move to this country. After she gets here, she will have to find a job and go back to school. She's a teacher now but her education won't be acceptable here. She has a university degree that she started under Hitler's regime and ended under communist occupation. Work she completed under either of those governments won't be honored. Do you think she'll be willing to do that?"

"I don't know. I haven't asked her because I haven't wanted to suggest something I can't promise her will happen. She's capable and I can help her get to West Germany, but what she'll be willing to do once she gets here, I just don't know. I don't even know if she'll be willing to leave Karl for good.

"Well, let's assume she's willing and she gets to West Germany. How are you planning on getting her here?"

He was being so calm and reasonable. It was a relief to be able to talk about her plans. Already, some of the anxiety was dissipating and Mia felt the muscles of her shoulders soften. She hadn't realized how tightly wound she was.

"Well, I thought I'd try to sponsor her. I'm not a citizen yet, but I can apply to start the process so that by the time she can get here, I can be legally responsible. I know I'll also need a bank account so I can prove I can take care of them and I've already started saving, and...."

"Maria, I don't know if you're aware of it, but it will take several years to get your citizenship. Then there's the issue of enough money. You'll need to prove you can support them."

Mia felt her shoulders tighten again. Her eyes closed as her body slouched into the cushions of the couch. Slowly, his hand reached across the space separating them and curled around her fingers.

Maria

"Look at me," he said.

Mia once again raised her eyes to his. This time they glistened with her tears.

"Now, now. That's not necessary. Let's think this through. I'm sure we'll find an answer. Let's say I'd be willing to sponsor her. And, let's say she's willing to meet the conditions I mentioned already. Where will you get the money to pay for all of this?"

Suddenly, hope was flooding her body again and in a rush of words, Mia asked, "You'd be willing to do that? You would really sponsor them and let them live here? Would you let me borrow the money, too? I could pay you back every month. I don't need much and when Ella finds work she can repay you as well. Herr professor, would you really help us?"

Chapter 10

The following year was one of the busiest Mia could remember. It was 1957 and everything was going according to plan. She was now in complete charge of the household and had even gotten a raise. Every penny was going into the shoebox in her closet and she found more and more change between the cushions of the couch where the professor liked to sit.

Herr Professor had asked her to start going to church with him and his sons and she had obliged him. At first she was going every Sunday morning but, when she started to miss her hours of solitude, she cut back on church and now attended only once or twice a month. She knew he would have liked her to go more often but he never complained. She was meeting people, and had even made several friends. The best thing to come out of it though was the bridge group she now played with every week. Wednesday evenings they met at one of the women's houses and Herr Professor had agreed that she could have her turn at home, too. In fact, he seemed pleased to welcome the women, before he retreated to the study, when they came.

As expected, Ella changed her mind about coming to America a number of times—including on the very day of her departure. Then, at the last possible moment, she and Karin boarded the midnight train that took them to a secret destination in the Harz Mountains in West Germany. She wrote to her mother that she could sense it as she crossed the unmarked border between East and West Germany and that she wept inconsolably.

They spent the next year in hiding while papers were forged giving them temporary identities and a place to live until they could get permission to enter the United States as refugees. It was far from easy and Ella wrote often to say that the family that hid them in their basement, while kind, could never make her feel safe.

The house was a new one, built on the outskirts of Goslar, one of the most charming medieval towns in Germany left undamaged by the war. The tall fence surrounding the back yard with its flower and vegetable gardens protected more than the owner's privacy, it hid Ella and Karin's whereabouts to casual observers. Karin had to attend school and Ella found work in a shop selling expensive clothes. They used fake names and phony histories provided by the underground that had made escape from East Germany possible. Not many people were fooled, though. The mother and daughter newly arrived in the old town were too poor and shabby to fit in. Daily reminders that their presence was not appreciated became the norm.

In one letter Ella wrote to her mother that a group of boys in Karin's school had surrounded her daughter during a lunch break and spat on her while she cried and cowered until a teacher came to her rescue. In another, Ella explained how the owner of the shop in which she worked had made passes at her and that it had frightened her. She was afraid she would have to accommodate him in return for his silence.

With each new letter, Mia read a growing fear between the lines. Fear of being found out. Fear of being deported back to East Germany. Fear of another move. Fear of the loneliness that threatened to overwhelm her daughter's life.

All she could do was send back comforting words and glowing descriptions of life in America. She promised a new and better life—a life filled with plenty of food and classes at a nearby university. She promised Ella the comfort of a family and a career that would surpass the one Ella had given up. All Ella needed to do was continue her English classes and keep up her courage for a few more months.

During that year of planning and waiting, Mia had more excitement and happiness than she could remember since she was a young woman in love with Kurt. Herr Professor became increasingly attentive until it became clear to everyone that he considered Mia an essential part of his household and perhaps much more. He began to invite her to accompany him to some of the university functions. When he sensed her reluctance, he showed the sensitivity to buy her several new dresses and a new pair of shoes with a matching purse. Although she was shy and reluctant at first, she soon came to appreciate the respect with which she was treated. In particular, she liked it when Herr Professor introduced her as his special friend instead of his housekeeper.

She still refused anything more than a polite kiss on her cheek and his arm to steady her through crowds in the shopping district she loved to visit on Saturday afternoons. Until Thanksgiving Day in November of 1957.

It was the second Thanksgiving meal Mia had prepared and it was spectacular. The turkey, tender and golden brown, steamed on a huge platter of the dinner service that would someday go to Beth but which Mia had convinced Herr Professor to use on special occasions in the meantime.

"Why let such beauty waste in a carton under the eaves?" she had asked. Much to her surprise, this time he agreed with her logic.

A mountain of mashed potatoes whipped into creamy buttery peaks filled a huge bowl. Giblet gravy, thick and fragrant, filled a gravy boat with matching ladle. Golden ears of corn piled atop another platter lent their aroma to the table and made a lovely contrast to the dark red cranberry mold in its own copper bowl. Best of all, though, was the stuffing Mia had created by combining several of her favorite recipes. She'd made it with wild rice, dried apricots, prunes, almonds and more herbs than anyone would be able to guess.

Herr Professor's whole family would be there. Even Beth was coming from Ohio with her husband and baby son. Both Joe and Gary had invited girlfriends as well as two exchange students from Joe's biology class. The formal dining room was crowded but Mia couldn't imagine a more wonderful way to celebrate and say "thank you" for her new life.

As everyone passed their plates to Herr Professor and he stood at the head of the table delicately carving the bird, Mia couldn't help but think of her own family. She knew that there would be two more beloved faces at the table next Thanksgiving and that thought had kept Mia smiling throughout her preparations.

A quick picture of her mother flashed into her mind. How Hanni would have been astonished to see this feast. There had never been, even at a family wedding for all the people in Werda, a feast to rival this one. She roused herself and began to help the shyer guests pile food on their plates. Only the keenest observer would have caught the stray tear before it was wiped away by the corner of her apron.

Herr Professor was nothing if not observant. After plum tart with ice cream had been polished off, he surprised everyone by announcing that Beth and the other two young women would clean off the table and do the dishes.

"Mia has worked for days to make this the best Thanksgiving this family has had in years. She deserves a rest and a bit of wine to relax."

Maria

This announcement had the effect of a bomb being dropped in their midst. Josef Keller had never invited anyone to relax and no one could remember the last time he had shared his wine. Stunned and silenced, his children and guests began to scramble from their seats carrying dishes and shoving each other out of the way. Beth was the one to come back after the table was cleared and laid a clean cloth on its polished surface. She returned a minute later with two crystal glasses and sat one in front of the professor and another near Mia. Joe followed with a bottle of deep burgundy that he had already uncorked. He poured a slight amount into his father's glass. Herr Professor looked at it, raised the glass to his nose, sniffed, sipped, and declared it adequate. A female voice in the kitchen giggled and Joe turned with a conspiratorial grin in their direction. After his father's nod of approval, Joe poured wine for Mia and filled his father's glass before disappearing into the kitchen, noisy with the sounds of dishes being washed and laughter.

Herr Professor got up and closed the kitchen door before returning to his seat and looking at Mia. Her gaze was cast down onto her lap where her thumbs twirled furiously around each other. Herr Professor cleared his throat before reaching around the table and taking her hands into his own. Only a tremendous effort of will and a deep breath kept Mia from yanking them back.

"Look at me," he said.

Mia raised her eyes but kept her head down.

"Marry me, Maria." His voice reached her as though he were talking through a fog. It took almost a minute before what he said registered.

It wasn't that she was completely surprised. She had had an inkling of what was coming but had censored her thoughts and hopes with a fierce vigilance. She had no intention of reliving the kind of pain she had felt when Kurt had asked for her hand and gotten himself killed only hours later. Now it was different. For one thing, she was older. In her mid-forties, in fact—an age where few women found love again and even fewer married.

Misinterpreting her silence as reluctance, Herr Professor launched into a lecture about his virtues and why he thought she should accept his proposal. He listed his assets and status in the community. He told her, "I own this house and an apartment building in the center of town. I also have the farm which is doing quite well. My work is well respected and I am being considered for the dean's position that should be coming up next fall."

When Mia remained silent, he began to speak of his dream of moving to California following Joe's and Gary's graduation.

"I've been reading about a place called Santa Monica. You always said you liked the coast so I thought you might like it there. We could sell some of the properties here and buy a house where you can be happy."

At the mention of Santa Monica, Mia's head jerked up and she met his eyes. She could hardly believe what she was hearing. Was he serious about making her dreams come true? Could she possibly be that lucky? She was just his housekeeper. Did he want her just for the sake of convenience? A permanent servant legally bound to him by marriage vows? In all the time she had known him, Herr Professor had never expressed more than admiration for her. "How does he really feel about me?" she wondered.

As though he could read her thoughts, Herr Professor sighed and gripped her hand a little harder. "Mia, I love you."

With that, Mia could no longer restrain herself and she jumped up to embrace the startled man. When she sat down on his lap, rested her head on his shoulder and let her tears flow down his neck, he cleared his throat again and said, "Does that mean you accept?"

"Yes, Herr Professor. I accept."

"Then I suppose you may call me "Josef," but only in private, you understand."

"Yes Josef, I understand."

Chapter 11

M aria and Josef were married in 1958 in a church two blocks from their home. There were four big churches in Grand Forks that Mia knew of— one on each corner of the main crossing. She could never quite keep straight what the differences were—but Josef knew. They were married in the one Josef had helped to build when he was a young man and had first come here from the wine country of his German home on the shores of the Mosel river. The church had been his bedrock during the hard times. There he had married and buried his wives, christened his children. When, during the Second World War, he had been exiled to Canada, it was his friends from the church who welcomed him back after two years. The university, with some shame and embarrassment, reinstated him.

"You know we couldn't take a chance, professor. The authorities wouldn't allow us to have a German teaching our young men and women." the dean had said. He had never revealed who, exactly, the authorities were. Those terrible years were over and even their memory was fading with each year that passed. Now he could focus on the future.

Mia still got a letter from Ella at least once a week. In each one, she told her Mother how hard it was to live with strangers, how much she missed her father and her friends, and how difficult it was to raise a daughter who wanted to be left alone to escape into her books. Ella also hated the English language class she had to attend. However, Josef had insisted on her getting a start on this important part of her transition to a new life saying to Mia, "Remember your first year here, my dear. Remember how hard it was to meet people. It will help Ella get comfortable more quickly if she speaks our language. Besides, she'll need it when she starts classes at the university."

Aside from this one requirement, Josef asked for nothing. He had sent the money to make their escape possible, even though it was a dangerous and risky business at best. So many people had to be bribed and paid. There were many who could still betray them if they knew Ella and Karin's whereabouts and get them deported back to Werda. An old friend of Mia's had sent her a newspaper clipping that included Ella and Karin's names on a "black list". Virtually anyone could turn them in. Ella, although it was hard, had to keep a low profile.

In her previous life, Ella was well respected. She had managed to get her teaching degree and become an esteemed member of the community. She had also managed to marry the handsome pilot who, even though fast becoming the town drunk, was nevertheless pursued by most of the eligible and not so eligible women in town. In Werda, Ella had all the attention she could want—first for having a good job and marrying the popular bachelor, and then for suffering so much at the hands of a husband who refused to settle down. It was a lot to give up. Sometimes Mia was surprised that Ella had actually left. She speculated that her daughter was willing to take a chance on the life Mia offered because her life in Werda would be changing drastically even if she stayed.

Mia knew it was going to be hard work for Ella. She would have to go to school again, get a job and pay back the professor all the money he had loaned her. It wouldn't be easy. Sometimes, underneath the joy she felt about their reunion, she sensed unease when she considered her daughter's lack of maturity and independence.

However, despite her worries about Ella and Karin, it was a wonderful time for Mia. She was learning all about her husband's business ventures and had proven to be an astute student. As part of the agreement to marry him, Mia had insisted that Josef execute a will that insured she would inherit half of what he owned in the event of his death. She also insisted he add her name to some of his investments. Her argument that, "We've been through one war already and lost everything and you never know what might still happen," had convinced him that it was important to secure her future. She knew what they owned, she knew what their investments were, and she had learned to keep all the books. In fact, she had relieved him of all those bothersome issues and left him free to dream and live in his academic world. The arrangement made both of them very happy.

Ella and Karin were due to arrive in May. Right after Christmas, Mia started cleaning and rearranging furniture. She even bought a few things to make life easier for "the girls" as she had come to think of them. They would have the two bedrooms upstairs with their own bath. Joe and Gary each had a bedroom downstairs in the walk-out basement. It had a pool table and its own television surrounded by several overstuffed chairs. Mia and Josef lived primarily on the main floor.

For Mia, the time between Christmas of '58 and May of '59 was a time of nearly perfect joy. She had a big house with a big yard, a husband she could be proud of, and a large family that would be made complete when Ella and Karin joined them. Josef would retire in a couple of years and they would move to California. In the meantime, Ella would get her career on track again and perhaps even find a good man for herself. After all, Karin needed a decent father and Ella would always need someone to help her manage life.

During quiet evenings, after the dinner dishes were done and they had watched one of the westerns they both loved, Mia would read the paper from that morning while Josef read one of his educational journals or books. She noticed ads that had been placed by people seeking contact with other singles. When she asked Josef about them, he laughed and told her, "Those are from desperate old maids and kooks."

Still, she read them every night and started to see patterns.

"It might not be a bad idea for Ella to answer some of these. I mean, it can't hurt."

Josef wasn't interested until she pointed out an ad from an attorney they both knew who had lost his wife the previous year.

"You might have something there, after all," he conceded.

After that, Mia made reading the personals a daily habit and added a fantasy of Ella marrying a lawyer to her already rich imaginary life. If everything went according to her plan, Ella would have her U.S. teaching degree and a job within a year-and-a-half and would be married shortly thereafter. Karin would do brilliantly in school and have a regular, middle-class life— complete with a mother and father and a room of her own in one of those nice new houses on the west side of town.

Armed with these visions of the future, Mia spent her days keeping house, keeping the ledgers updated, and regularly adding a few coins to her growing stash in the shoebox. What she hadn't told anyone was that she had taken a few hundred dollars of her savings two years ago and invested them in some stocks she read about in one of the professor's journals. They had done very well and, within a few months of this initial purchase, Mia was teaching herself about the stock market. Maybe it was beginner's luck or maybe she had a keen sense for investments, but either way, Mia started making what she called "real" money by the time spring of '59 rolled around. She still hadn't told Josef about her "fun" venture. It wasn't that she didn't want him to know, she couldn't figure out how to tell him. He invested in land and bonds and things he could see and touch and didn't approve of the market.

"Too risky," he'd say. She would nod and smile. If he took that for agreement, it was just as well.

The day came when they picked Ella and Karin up from the train station outside Grand Forks. Everything in the house was spick and span. Joe and Gary had been instructed to stay home that afternoon to greet their new "sister" and her little girl. The boys had even washed the car and filled it with gas.

Josef had taken his shower and was wearing his best blue suit with the white shirt Mia had ironed into starchy stiffness. Mia herself wore a bright dress printed with bold flowers. She knew it was what Josef called "too loud," especially with the extra pounds she had put on since their marriage. Nevertheless, she loved the dress and it made her feel happy.

Riding in the car next to him, Mia remembered how she felt when he first picked her up from the same train station almost four years ago. She had lost some of her youthful enthusiasm for adventure and settled into a more secure and sedate life as a wife and mother. However, she didn't regret the loss. In fact, she was more content than she had been in many years.

As they rounded the corner and the station came into view, they heard the whistle of the train still about five minutes outside town. Their timing was perfect. It was always perfect. Josef made sure of that.

Maria

Waiting on the landing was pure agony for Mia. Josef stood beside her, his hands clasped behind his back, rocking back and forth from his heels to his toes. In contrast, next to him, she paced a step this way, then that, twisting her handkerchief into a tight roll before shaking it out again.

At last, the huge metal hulk of the approaching locomotive lumbered into sight. Huffing and puffing, it slid into place and came to a screeching stop in front of them. Steam roiled around them and, for a moment, Mia felt like she was suspended in clouds. Then she felt Josef's tug on her arm as he guided her along the platform and closer to the passenger cars. She saw a young, slender woman step onto the last metal stair before lowering herself to the station platform. The suitcase she was carrying nearly dragged her to the ground. Behind her came a girl Mia immediately recognized as Karin. She had grown so much!

"There they are! There they are!" she kept repeating as if Josef hadn't heard her the first time.

Grabbing his arm, she pulled him along as she waved frantically while rushing toward the pair and yelled again, "There they are!"

The only noise Mia heard above the pounding of her heart was the train's locomotive, now behind her, belching. She stopped just feet in front of them, waiting as the crowd began to disperse. Ella's shoulders drooped from more than the weight of her suitcase. In fact, now that Mia had a closer look, everything about Ella was drooping. The young woman had grown thin to the point of being gaunt. Her dress hung on her like a hand-me-down from a much larger woman. Circles under her eyes were a dark contrast to the pale skin stretched over high cheekbones. Hair, in a style she was sure Ella had intended to be smart and bouncy, hung in tight frizzy clumps. Ella looked like a breeze could have blown her over.

Maria

Next to her, Karin stood with the typical boniness of a ten-year-old. Compared to her mother, though, she looked strong and healthy. Her hair was braided on either side of her head and hung down onto the chest already showing some promise of breasts. She had out-grown the hand-knitted skirt and sweater Mia had sent her two years ago, but she wore them with pride. When she smiled, the ill-fitting clothes were forgotten.

Stretching her arms wide, Mia invited her girls into her ample embrace. As she held them to her chest, the three did a kind of skip-ping, rocking, swaying dance until she released her grip and held them both at arm's length to look at them again. Within moments, Ella threw herself into her mother's arms once more and started sob-bing. The people still on the platform turned their heads and looked to see what the problem was. Mia pushed Ella back and told her to stop crying.

"That's enough now. You're home and you're safe. There's noth-ing to cry about. A little dinner and a good night's sleep is what you need."

Ella nodded and blew her nose into the handkerchief Josef had handed her. Mia introduced her daughter to her husband and was relieved when he held both of Ella's hands and then put his arms around her and let her cry on his shoulder.

Karin was still standing quietly beside them and Mia now looked at the girl and said, "Liebchen, you can't imagine how glad I am to see you here."

"I'm glad to see you, too, Omi."

Suddenly, the child rushed to her and flung her arms around the soft middle of Mia's body. As Mia returned the hug and felt the strong warmth of her granddaughter's embrace, she smiled until she thought her face would break.

Maria

It surprised her, then, to get an uneasy feeling when she glanced in the direction of her daughter who was still clinging to Josef's chest and crying with long, loud sobs. He, in turn, supported her with one arm around her waist and the other around her shoulders. Mia didn't know why, but it made her uncomfortable to see them like this.

PART III

ELLA

Chapter 1

Her eyes wandered across the ceiling cracks that for years had meandered across the faded plaster. Like a spider's web, they meandered, joined, diverged and rejoined. She didn't like spiders much. In fact, Ella didn't like scuttling things at all. There was no way she could think about them without her heart pounding and her armpits getting wet. She tried it now and, sure enough, after a few seconds, the palpitations in her chest started and she felt the dampness under her arms. Her breath came in tight, little gasps. She sustained the image long enough to feel truly afraid before focusing once more on the ceiling.

She was sick again. It seemed to her that she was always sick or on the verge of getting sick. The worst of it was that everyone thought of her as frail and sickly—and frail was the last thing Ella wanted to be known as. Her mind created fabulous images of herself from things she had seen when the circus came to her remote region of Saxony. In fact, she often imagined herself performing feats of great daring, accompanied by astonished gasps and applause.

And always, always, the audience would rise to their feet and applauded louder than they had for any other performers, "Is it true that she's only six? It's impossible! How can someone so young be so skilled?"

Ella

Naturally, these were fantasies she kept to herself because she didn't want to lose their impact by sharing them with others. Besides, it was impossible to describe how strong and free it made her feel when she thought about flying through the air to the sound of a drum beating out its thunder.

There were so many things she kept to herself! Some were too beautiful to share. Others were just too naughty. She glanced across the room at her Grandmother. Oma didn't know, for instance, that in her mind, Ella called her Hanni, the name the grownups called her. Sometimes she called her by her real-grown name, the name she had been christened, Johanna. And sometimes, especially when she was angry with her for being gone so often, she called her mother Mia or the name her mother hated, Maria.

In real life, Hanni was Oma and Mia was Mommy because Ella was too young to use personal names. It was not proper and Ella thought of herself as a very polite and proper girl.

After a few more minutes finishing the laundry, Oma ladled two helpings of runny wheat broth into a ceramic bowl and brought it, along with a large spoon, to Ella's bedside. Depositing the bowl and spoon on a little table next to her bed, Oma ran rough fingers along Ella's cheek and held the back of her work-worn hands against her forehead.

"Still a little warm," she murmured before planting a soft kiss on her damp cheek.

"I brought you something to settle your stomach. It even has a bit of honey in it just for you."

Ella pushed herself up and scooted backwards to rest her back against the wall. There was an assortment of people in her young life. At six years old, Ella knew she was lucky to have so many aunts and uncles who doted on her. Then there were all her cousins who could sometimes be fun to play with but who, for the most part, bored her to tears. But, without a doubt, Mommy and Oma were the two most important people.

Oma was the kindest person Ella knew. No matter how tired the old woman was, she always had enough energy and time for a big hug, a treat from the pantry, and sometimes even a story. Oma knew all the good fairy tales. She had a real knack for weaving bits of her own story into the fabric of timeless tales of love and betrayal, honor, despair and so much more. Snuggled under heaps of blankets on cold winter evenings Ella listened spellbound to yarns Oma told while her long knitting needles clicked in syncopated rhythm to the rise and fall of her voice. When she was really inspired, Oma would twist the plot to insert a little girl who had an uncanny resemblance to Ella. Ella loved these moments with the old woman.

Mommy was another story. Ella, if asked, would not have been able to tell what she felt about her mother. It was not so much that she didn't feel anything but more that she felt so many different things. Mia could be warm and tender—like when she would swing Ella out of the zinc tub, her skin still steaming from the hot water, and wrap her in one of their huge towels to hug her dry. Or she could be very funny. Sometimes Mommy imitated relatives or the people she worked with and she would have everyone roaring with laughter. Mommy could be impatient and mean too. Really mean. Like when she would tell Ella to do something for her and Ella didn't move fast enough. A quick shove had sent Ella careening more than once.

Most of the time it was easier to lie low until she could tell what mood Mommy was in. Then they would enjoy a nice easygoing companionship, or, with a quick slip out the door, Ella disappeared to safer quarters with friends and neighbors. Luckily, there was always someone wanting to play in the meadow past the vegetable gardens or the park just a few blocks away.

Ella

When she couldn't escape Mia's bad moods, it was easiest to take a book and lie on her bed to read. Mommy never seemed to mind when Ella had a "headache" and took herself out of the way.

Tomorrow she would definitely have to be well again. It was Friday today and she had been in bed two days already. Tomorrow would be Saturday, her birthday, and school would be out by noon. She wanted to see her friends and was almost certain that her mother had invited a few of them for a surprise party. She noticed that Mommy had been bringing home extra food—a jar of preserves, a tin of dried fruits, for at least two weeks now. It was almost Christmas, so the food could be for the annual family dinner, but Ella was pretty sure there was enough for a birthday party too.

She climbed out of bed, slipped her house shoes on her feet and began to walk toward the kitchen sink where Oma was wringing out the last of their neighbor's wash. Her movements were fluid and strong so she knew the fever must have gone away. She loved feeling well again—and she liked the feeling of control her body gave her. She stopped behind Oma and flung her arms around the old woman's waist. Reaching behind her and encircling Ella with still wet hands, Oma hugged the little girl to her back and did a little jig that made Ella explode with laughter.

"Feeling better, my precious?" asked the old woman.

"Yes, thank you. Your soup helped a lot, especially the honey."

"Well, in that case I guess you'd better have some more."

With that Oma spooned another helping into a clean bowl and set it on the kitchen table while Ella scooted onto one of the chairs.

"Can I go to school tomorrow, Oma?"

"That will be up to your mother to decide," Hanni said turning back to the sink. With experienced flicks of her hands she shook each item of newly washed linen and laid it across the back of a chair or hung it on the clothesline that was fastened to hooks in opposing walls.

As if on cue, they heard Mia's footsteps climbing the stairs to their apartment. A few moments later, the door flung open and Mia rushed into the small living room. Her knitted cap was pulled down over her ears and a long coat with upturned collar protected her neck from the cold. Snowflakes covered her head and shoulders and flew in a white cloud around Mia as she shrugged out of the coat and hung it, along with the cap, on a hook near the door. Turning to her mother and Ella, she smiled.

"How was your day, sweetie and did you get the things we talked about?" asked Hanni.

"It was OK and yes," replied Mia as a knowing look passed between her and the older woman. She crossed the room to put her arms around Ella as the little girl gave a sigh. Hanni's shoulders relaxed beneath her dark dress.

"How are you feeling today?" Mia asked her daughter as she turned the little girl's face upwards and looked into her eyes.

"I feel much better, thank you. Oma made me hot tea with honey in it so I don't even have a sore throat anymore. Can I go to school tomorrow?"

Another knowing look passed between Hanni and Mia and Ella felt her face flush and her heart beat faster.

"We'll see how you feel in the morning. It would be a shame to miss another day," Mia said as another knowing smile passed between her and the old woman.

Chapter 2

The next morning dawned sunny and bright, the air's brilliance enhanced by a layer of snow that had fallen during the night. Ella's room was just as bright, as if a light had been turned on by mistake. The frail shoulders protruding from the top of her blankets were all but hidden by hair—pale brown, wispy and fine. Her delicate face was covered by almost translucent white skin and contrasted sharply with eyelids so discolored from her frequent illnesses and sleepless nights that they seemed painted. It wasn't until the lids began to flutter and open that the dull blue faded beside the extraordinary brilliance of Ella's blue eyes. They were startling now as they shone in the early morning sun and awareness crept into their depths.

"It's my birthday!" the little girl exclaimed in a whisper as she slipped tiny, cold feet onto the rug next to her bed. A soft, white nightgown slid down the bare skin of her thighs and lower legs until it stopped just short of her ankles. With cold and trembling hands, Ella stooped down and retrieved the bedpan from under the bed. Hiking her gown around her tiny waist, she squatted on the porcelain pot. The rim was cold and made her flesh quiver. It was not until her bottom had warmed the rim that Ella could relax enough to release a stream of urine that ran noisily into the ancient pot.

Ella could barely contain her excitement. It was 1936 and she had just turned seven years old.

Ella

Hanni lay on a narrow bed across the room, her soft, muffled snores made visible in the chilly air. In the third, slightly larger bed in the corner, Mia laid under a mound of feathers captured inside ticking that had once belonged to a distant relative. She did not snore but her even breathing was loud enough to give meaning to the rising and falling mound of quilted covers.

Ella had dreamed of this day for months and planned in exact detail how everything would look and feel on her special day. She had been clear about what she wanted for her birthday. She had made sure that her mother knew she wanted a new dress just like the one Annamarie, her cousin, had gotten last summer. It had been a big hit and Ella was sure that she would look even better in the flounces and smocking that had captured her imagination. The only difference was the color. In her mind's eye, Ella saw her own dress in a delicate blue fabric that brought out the color of her eyes.

If she got her gift soon, she would wear her new dress to school and dazzle everyone. There would be a birthday song sung in her honor and, at lunch, Miss Ottenburg, her teacher, would give everyone special treats to celebrate. Ella wasn't sure if anyone would bring her a present to school. But, they would all come to the surprise party Mommy had planned and then there would be plenty of goodies to eat and at least a few presents to open.

The more she thought about it the more excited she became—and the more annoyed that her mother and grandmother were still asleep. They should all be up and celebrating already. There should be oatmeal with some honey and a glass of milk instead of the regular dry piece of bread and weak tea Oma always made from herbs she picked in her garden.

A soft snort and stirring from across the room made her spirits rise. Oma was waking up. With a squeal, Ella rose, spinning from her squatting position on the bedpan and hopped across the cold floor toward her Oma's bed. Jumping in next to the old woman and snuggling into the warmth of her arms beneath the down blanket, Ella smiled into Hanni's eyes that were so much like her own.

"You know what day this is, Oma?" she asked.

"Yes, it's Saturday. I wonder if you're well enough to go to school. I guess we'd better wake your mom and ask what she wants you to do."

"No, no, no! I mean, it's a special day. Don't you remember?"

"Well, yes. I suppose it's special that Mrs. Werner is coming home from the hospital today. A few of us are going over to make sure she has everything she needs for the new baby."

"No, that's not what I mean!" shouted Ella louder than she had intended. She also had not meant to sound so whiney.

Oma's eyes clouded just a bit before her face opened up and a huge grin revealed the empty spaces that had become more prominent in her mouth during the last few years. Her eyes twinkled like gems as she cradled Ella in her arms and said, "Happy birthday, my darling, my precious, my sweet."

By this time, Mia sat up in bed and smiled sleepily at her mother and daughter. There was no way to keep the girl home another day, even if it was a bit risky to send her to school in such cold weather. She hadn't had a chance to fully recover from the last bout of flu. However, Mia had enough experience with her seemingly fragile daughter to know that underneath the delicate exterior was a solid core of willpower.

Mia opened her arms and invited Ella into them with a smile. The girl scrambled from her grandmother's bed and ran across the room to her mother to be swallowed up in hugs and kisses.

Ella

"Happy birthday, my precious".

Mia cradled the child and looked into the blue depths of her eyes, so like the girl's father's. Most of the family thought Ella resembled Hanni, but Mia saw only Kurt in her daughter's face. At the thought of Kurt, a shudder ran along her spine, but she covered her emotions by hugging Ella even more tightly. Her own green eyes had filled with tears and at Ella's wondering stare she simply said, "I'm just so happy that my little angel is growing into such a beautiful young lady."

Hearing the sound of logs being put into the pot-bellied stove and a match being struck, Ella asked, "What's for breakfast?"

"How about some nice warm oatmeal with a bit of honey to sweeten our girl's morning?" answered Oma between breaths that fanned the flames reluctantly taking shape inside their stove.

"Yes, yes, yes!" shrieked Ella while running across the room to hug the bent back of her grandmother.

"So, am I going to school?" asked Ella between slurping spoonfuls of sweetened oats cooked in milk instead of the usual water. Her feet were kicking at the air under her chair.

"If you think you can manage it, I suppose it's alright," Mia said with a smile in her voice.

Ella's legs swung even faster and higher and her mouth never stopped grinning, even to swallow her delicious breakfast. Would she get her beautiful blue dress before or after school, she wondered. After school, her mother said she could have the party they had planned and her best friends would be there to watch her open her presents. It might be better to wait until then to wear it, much as she wanted to feel the silkiness between her fingers right away. Mia announced she had to leave early so she could stop at the shop and check her inventory before closing for the holidays. Christmas was the one time of the year no one worked and it was only a few days away. Smiling, Mia bent to kiss the top of her daughter's head. She put her shawl around Ella's neck and added a hat, gloves, and coat.

"Oma will take you to school today".

Waving at the two of them from the doorway, Mia left quickly, closing the door behind her without mentioning a present.

The walk to school was freezing cold. Bright sunlight bounced off the icy crust on at least a foot of snow. They walked between three—and even four-feet high snow drifts created where someone had shoveled a sidewalk clean or the wind had driven snow against buildings and fences. It would be beautiful, Ella thought, if she could only ignore the biting cold on her face and her dripping nose. Mitten-covered hands kept wiping at it but did nothing to stop the flow. Thank goodness school was only a few blocks from her house and Oma hurried, eager to get back home and into the warm kitchen.

The morning was nothing if not magical. "Happy Birthday" was sung to her before even the first class hour had begun and everyone teased her in a playful way that only friends would dare. Even Miss Ottenburg seemed less harsh and demanding than usual. Best of all, her best friend had brought her a present, a pair of gloves with all the fingers knitted on them. Now she could look more stylish than ever!

By the time she got home, her mother was waiting for her with two of the ten friends that had been invited to celebrate Ella's special day. Mia was busy decorating the birthday Kuchen with little sprinkles of sugar. The cake was a flat affair. Dough had been rolled out onto a rectangular cooking sheet that had a short lip all around. The fruit preserves Mia and Hanni had been able to hoard throughout the long fall and winter now dotted the cake. Ella detected raisins, plums, apples, and what might be cherries. Dancing into the kitchen,

Ella

she was delighted to see that she was right—there were even walnuts sprinkled on top. It was a feast for the eyes!

She saw that Anna and Hilde, her school chums, were appropriately appreciative. She joined them at the table in the center of the room as Oma placed a precious glass of milk in front of her. The chatter began when Oma turned back to the stove where she was preparing Eintopf, a soup made from vegetables and sometimes, meat. Most often no meat made it into the pot, but today Ella smelled the aroma of chicken. This would indeed be a celebration to remember.

One by one, her friends crowded into the room filling every nook with laughter. Coats, boots, mittens and hats were stacked on the floor in one corner and the assortment of chairs and stools were pulled toward the table. A few years earlier, Ella and her friends had discovered the joy of gossip. Satisfied grins and whispers were interspersed with giggles by girls who were perfecting this ancient source of amusement. Even the noise elicited by her neighbor's banging on his piano added to the merriment. Nothing, except her new dress, which Ella was more certain than ever to get, could make her happier.

It was at least an hour before they were all finished with their meal and the extraordinary birthday cake. Everyone was full. The noisy jabber and screeching laughter were subdued when her mother clapped her hands and asked Ella to close her eyes. It was the custom for all gifts to be placed in front of the lucky birthday girl who could, after much tittering and muffled exclamations, open them and feast them on her bounty.

When Ella moved her hands from her face, she saw an assortment of gifts piled on the table. On top of the heap was a knitted hat matching the gloves her best friend had given her earlier in the day. Like most of the others, no pretty paper or ribbons adorned the gift. Those were luxuries few people could afford. Squealing with delight, Ella reached across and hugged her friend.

Ella

Next came a porcelain plate. This was a gift from Theresa whose father worked in the porcelain factory for which their town was becoming famous. On its inner surface was a picture of a beautiful lady. She was clearly a princess, if the clothes, all ruffles and lace, were any indication. Behind her, in the distance, was a castle on a hill green with lawns and lovely trees. Ella hugged this treasure to her chest and blew kisses across the table to Theresa who smiled shyly with delight.

A scarf, another hat, and then a book about a poor orphan girl who sold matches on a street corner in the dead of winter. There she was discovered by a kind man and his wife who, childless themselves, took her home and raised her. Everyone knew this story and had heard it a thousand times. Still, it was nice to have the book.

Someone else had brought an apple pie that Ella was glad she would not have to share. Marie had given her a picture she had drawn of Max and Moritz, the naughty cartoon boys who were a favorite of children for generations. The drawing was quite good and Ella was pleased. Then came a small thing wrapped in brown paper and tied with twine. It was from Kristel, the parson's daughter. When Ella removed the twine and unfolded the paper, a lovely, tiny silver cross was revealed. Everyone ooh-ed and ahh-ed when she held the delicate jewelry up by its thin leather cord. It glimmered in the sunshine that slanted across the children and cut a swath over the table. Ella slipped the cord over her head and let her fingers trace appreciatively over the delicate curves of her new necklace.

The last two gifts were a poem written just for her by her other best friend, Sylvia, and a pair of knitted stockings from the girl who lived next door. She and her parents had recently moved into the building and it was her father who kept banging out that dreadful music on their old keyboard. They were extremely poor, Ella knew, so the cotton stockings were a treasure they could ill afford to give away. Ella smiled her gratitude and was rewarded by a brilliant smile in return. She made a mental note to give special thanks and a hug to her new friend.

Finally Ella was handed a lumpy package wrapped in sackcloth and tied together by twine that could almost be called rope. Everyone fell silent as she reached for the much-anticipated gift. She smiled at her mother and grandmother standing expectantly in the doorframe leading to their hallway. Oma's eyes sparkled and Mia wore a bright smile. With trembling hands, Ella carefully untied the string. It would be used again and again as long as it held up. When she had placed it in the middle of the table and arranged the wrapped package neatly and at right angles in front of her, she unfolded the two paper ends and straightened them out before easing the two remaining sides away from the treasure inside.

A delighted gasp went up from every mouth around the table as the handsome dress was revealed. A delicate white collar trimmed in lace topped a dark brown velvet bodice that was embroidered in rich tones down to the soft wool skirt shirred to the velvet top. Where brown wool and velvet met, a wide ribbon covered the seam and the two ends crossed in the back to create a bow. Pearly buttons ran down the back from the collar to the waist. It was magnificent! And it was all wrong! As appreciative hands reached from all around her to caress the rich folds of her new dress, Ella's eyes filled with tears and she looked accusingly at the two women framed by ancient wooden doorposts. Mia's eyes became distant searing coals that burned into Ellas' before she turned away and disappeared into the room beyond. Hanni's eyes were already turned down and shadowed by her brows. Barely visible were the corners of her lips that had begun to tremble.

The circle of girls had become animated again and each of them took Ella's silence as amazement at the beautiful dress she barely

Ella

touched. Everyone knew how talented Hanni was with a needle and thread. All in all, they declared Ella's birthday a huge success and departed shortly to spread the news of her good fortune.

Chapter 3

Five years later, in 1941, the world had changed dramatically and so had Ella. Germany was at war again, creating chaos and confusion throughout Europe, and Ella had started her period, an event that created its own turmoil and trauma. To further complicate her life, she felt the first stirrings of love.

It was an early spring morning when she heard the sound of airplanes droning toward her village. The familiar terror stirred her heart and doubled its beating. For the past year, her life had been turned upside down. The airplanes were just the tip of the iceberg, though. For Ella, the beginning had come with the disappearance of two classmates nearly a year ago. It was because they were Jewish, she had been told—but they had been Jewish ever since she had known them and it had never been a problem before.

When she had first asked what this meant she was told to lower her voice. Some things had become unsafe to discuss openly. Later, when the rest of the family had gone to bed, Hanni told her that some Jewish people had apparently been causing a lot of problems. She wasn't quite sure what kind of problems but it had something to do with taking jobs from hardworking Germans.

Ella thought about this for a few days before she asked her grandmother to explain. All Hanni could say was that none of the Jews in their town were making trouble so it must be others, maybe in larger cities. It was a shame innocent people had to suffer for what someone else did—but there was nothing to be done. Unfair things had happened often enough to their own family and neighbors. It was the way of the world. As unsatisfactory as this explanation was, Ella could not ask anyone else for more clarification. She had been warned not to discuss adult issues with anyone outside the family.

"You never know who you're really talking to," had become one of her mother's mantras.

She didn't have to be warned too often. Although she couldn't put it into words, she could sense the difference everywhere. The atmosphere in her school, her neighborhood, in fact, her whole town, was one of fear. Of course, no one talked about it.

The other measurable change was that many of the young men had also left. The Jews had left silently, escorted in the early dawn by rifle-bearing guards to a hamlet past the river that separated family garden plots from the meadow. The other young men, the German boys from local farms or sons of factory workers and small shop owners, had left noisily, their heads lifted high with national pride and dreams of personal glory.

One of them was Karl. He had flown in his Messerschmitt over their town with half a dozen other planes one early October morning. Like always, before they knew whose planes were thundering across their skies, Ella and her friends, on their way to school, had run into the stone alcove of a nearby house, their hushed voices speculating. They had heard the thunder overhead and watched as the formation of iron birds winged its way toward them. Someone shouted from an upstairs window that they were "ours." Relief flooded through Ella and her friends as they slumped against each other and rolled their eyes in exaggerated but very real relief.

Ella

They could hear the change in the engines as the planes dropped lower and slowed for their landing in the meadow. Sputtering could be heard in the distance. It mingled with the sound of people rushing downstairs and mothers hurrying children into sweaters and down the street in the direction of the newly arrived group of young pilots. Of course, Ella and her companions joined the crowd and made their way to the edge of the meadow in time to see a dozen or so airmen climb from open cockpits. She couldn't tell the difference between pilots and navigators—but it didn't matter because only one of them stood out.

Karl was at least six inches taller than all the rest. As the group of young men ambled in the direction of the growing throng of spectators they unzipped flight jackets and pulled leather hats off their heads. His was the most captivating. He swung his jacket over one shoulder and grinned at the young man next to him. They both burst out in laughter and Ella's heart nearly stopped as she watched his head rear back and his mouth open to reveal perfectly straight, white teeth.

Nearing the crowd, his gaze casually scanned the waiting townsfolk, coming to rest for a moment on her face before he continued his search. Too late, Ella became aware of her mouth hanging open. His gaze had moved on before she had a chance to close it. By the time she had recovered her composure enough to look at him again, he was hurrying toward a stout, middle-aged woman. She rushed into his arms, her features an older, more feminine version of his own.

Kristel, Ella's friend, leaned over to whisper in her ear, "That's Karl and that's his mother, Elizabet Lehmann—the one who owns the Lehmann Brewery on Heiligen Weg. Isn't he gorgeous?" Indeed he was. In fact, his straight, dark hair and almost olive skin gave him an exotic look that was multiplied tenfold by his easy charm and the dashing uniform he wore so well.

Ella

The last airplane engine had stopped roaring and the propellers had come to rest. The gathered people had started to disperse and were slowly walking back toward town, some accompanied by one or two of the airmen. Karl was already half way across the field by the time Ella roused herself from the dreamlike state that still held her in its grip.

"Let's go, Ella!" shouted her friend. "We're already late for our first class."

Ella spent all of that day in a trance. Her teachers thought she wasn't quite well and, for the most part, left her alone. On her way home she went the long way around, taking a gravelly footpath that meandered through a grove of ancient birch trees and beyond the small pond she and her friends sometimes used as a swimming hole. The path turned almost back on itself but in a slight westerly direction and came out behind the meadow where Karl and his friends had landed. Nothing was left except the tracks in the trampled grass where the planes had been. Ella didn't know what she had expected to find, but she felt strangely let down. The rest of the way home she brooded about whom Karl had visited in Werda and where he was headed next.

When she got home, her mother stood in front of the sink peeling potatoes. The kitchen was warm and smelled like onions and soap. Washed linens hung on clotheslines strung across one corner of the room. By the time Ella put her books on the little table next to the couch, Mia scraped the peeled and cut potatoes from a board and into a pot of boiling water and onions.

"Ella," she called to her daughter, "put some salt, pepper, and parsley in there," pointing at the stove with a knife. "We can eat in fifteen minutes. And go wash your hands."

When they were seated at the table and about to start their meal, sirens started to wail with an urgent, undulating shriek. Oma, Mia and Ella rushed to the door, grabbing sweaters as they went. Joining the other tenants, they hurried down six half flights of stairs each one more crowded with frantic tenants than the last. Everyone was able to push and shove their way into the cellar that had been converted into a makeshift bomb shelter. Actually, not much converting had been done. There wasn't enough room to make many changes. Small windows, facing the inner courtyard of the old apartment buildings, had been painted black. Chairs had been added and stacked in corners where there was room. Most of the space was still, as always, taken up with bins of coal and vegetables, mostly potatoes, which had to be stored in cool, dry places.

As they entered, everybody took a chair and placed it where they had become accustomed to sitting and waiting out the air raids that increased in frequency as the war progressed. It seemed that nearly every day they found themselves huddled together in the musty gloom. Sometimes it was twice or even three times a day. No one could predict when the sirens would raise their alarm again and although each of them wondered, they never speculated out loud. It was an unspoken taboo. The children, who had not at first understood, now seldom made even the slightest sounds.

Later, after they had returned to their kitchen and cold soup, Ella asked, "Who is Karl Lehmann, Oma?"

Her grandmother glanced at Mia before answering.

"He is Elizabet's son. You know, the woman who has the brewery outside town. She has two more boys, Gottfried and Hans. They're all in the armed service. I think maybe Karl is in the air force and the other two are in the army. But I'm not sure. We don't have much to do with that family."

"And that should be the end of it, Ella," her mother added.

Ella

"Why?"

"Because I said so!" her mother shouted before looking at her own mother and then adding more gently, "Because they're trouble. They've always been trouble. Ever since they got here from God knows where."

Ella wanted to ask more questions but her mother's eyes told her there would be no further explanations—and there was no arguing with her mother's eyes.

The next three years or so became a routine of school, helping out with chores at home, and gymnastics, for which Ella with her slight but strong body became quite well known. The chores Ella did reluctantly, even belligerently. It was boring work like scrubbing floors, trying to make a dinner with almost no food and helping Oma with the endless laundry she still did for those few families who could afford to pay. It made Ella feel small and dirty somehow. As though she labored invisibly for powerful forces she could serve but never equal.

School and gymnastics were altogether different. There she shone like a star, a brilliant light in the midst of mediocrity. She excelled in all her classes and although she had to work for most of her A's, the work was not too hard. Her favorite was gym, a subject she and her classmates took very seriously. It was considered essential to be physically fit and, for Ella, it was a chance to perform in front of a crowd. There was nothing she liked better than showing everyone how she could tumble, twist and turn on a mat, on parallel bars, on rings-in fact, anywhere. Practices were rehearsals for major events. Sports competitions were one of the few entertainments left. They became like mini-wars in the midst of the war they were all trying not to think about.

She also liked her history, culture, and politics classes. They had changed over the past two years and were now all taught by the same young instructor who never tired of ranting about the glories of ancient Germania and the magnificent new Reich they were in the process of building. Ella liked him. The schoolwork was easy and the young teacher definitely interesting. It amused her to watch his easy assurance fail and his fluid monologues sputter when she looked at him as if enraptured by his words. The giggles that erupted around her every time she managed to unnerve the young scholar delighted her. He was sent by government authorities to instruct them in the whys and wherefores of the new world order. This daily ritual did little to enhance the seriousness of the academic setting and the passionately offered lessons. However, Ella never tired of the feeling it gave her when she managed to make him sweat.

Still, she had to be careful. It was no laughing matter if her game turned sour and the young teacher turned her in for obstructing his work. His lessons were considered important for a well-rounded curriculum and absolutely essential for passing the week-long entrance exam for university admission. In fact, no one could graduate without a complete knowledge of Hitler's life, his ideas, and the magnificent role her country would play in the future of the world.

One morning, the earnest young teacher was explaining the highlights of illustrious leaders from Germany's glorious past that eventually led to their supreme commander. Herr Hitler was the greatest leader of the greatest Reich the world would ever know. As he explained the highlights of each historic figure, he wrote their names on the blackboard, one below the other in the sequence of their reigns.

Ella

When he came to the last, the greatest of them all, he wrote Hitler's name in capital letters to highlight that man's supreme contributions.

Ella, her pretty mouth puckered in an appealing pout, raised her hand. Proud of his performance and delivery of this morning's lesson, Herr Konrad pointed to Ella and nodded his head.

Sweetly, Ella asked, "Honorable Herr Konrad, if Herr Hitler is of the utmost importance in the history of our great nation, why have you put his name at the bottom of the list?"

At her words, the young man became visibly shaken. A profound silence lasted several seconds before the first giggle could be heard from the back of the room. Soon, the infectious sound spread until loud laughter escaped from every mouth except that of the young man clutching the podium in front of the class. His face had drained of all color. He did not move when the bell rang and chairs scraped the old wooden floors. Papers were shuffled and stuffed into leather satchels. Even as his students filed out of the classroom, some still giggling, the young teacher did not move. Ella was the last to leave and smiled triumphantly in his direction before following her friends. She did not see the young man's eyes follow her departing back or the expression of fear and horror in them.

The following morning the young man was not there. Another, much older and sterner, one had taken his place. No one dared to ask why.

Chapter 4

Mia repeatedly refused to tell Ella where she went when she left for two or three days at a time. Even Oma wouldn't let on what she knew. Sometimes Mia came home exhausted and sat at their table with a hot mug of brown, bitter liquid that passed for coffee these days. When even that was not available, she might sip on a steaming cup of hot water looking at her reflection through the swirling vapors in the darkened window. At those times, Ella knew she was not to interrupt her mother and retired quietly to the little desk her uncle Willi had made her two years before.

At other times, Mia stormed through the door with a smile on her face and, usually, a brown paper package hidden under her coat. A couple of sausages, a loaf of fresh bread, and sometimes even a bar of chocolate were the treats she smilingly shared. Mia never revealed how she came to have those treasures. When pressed, she alluded to special requests for her sewing talents by one or another of the few wealthy patrons she still had in Dresden. Sometimes she let on that one of her friends happened to have enough to share. Most often, though, Mia simply said, "What you don't know can't hurt you."

She was probably right. It would have been better not to know what had happened last summer—the summer of '44. It was probably the worst time of Ella's 15-year life.

Ella

The attack on her town by Russian soldiers was the most frightening thing Ella had ever experienced. Not since raiders had rushed down the hills that lay to the east, nearly fifty years ago, killing most of Hanni's family and neighbors, had anyone in Werda felt such devastation. Shrieking mothers and wives ran into and out of each other's arms frantically seeking comfort from the pain of the inevitable slaughter of their helpless men. Only later, after all the boys and old men lay dead in bloody bundles on the meadow stained dark with their blood, did the women, who had no more strength to scream out their agony, stop wailing and sit in stupefied heaps near the beloved corpses. Some, clutching their dead children and fathers, rocked back and forth, moaning. Others lay or sat with the dead, too stunned to make either movement or sound.

Ella had been there from the beginning. From when they first heard the rumble of armored vehicles descend upon their defenceless homes to the moment when the last boy fell, his face ripped open by the bullets his pleading and cries could not stop. Almost all the young men were gone, serving in Germany's war machine on some front. Emil had been one of the few who were not allowed to join the army due to his emphysema. Ella had known him all her life. He had lived in the apartment below hers for as long as she could remember. They had played together when they were children and, more recently, had had long discussions about becoming teachers. Emil loved children. He had two younger siblings and was often seen reading to them and playing games that the children his own age would not play with him anymore. It didn't matter to Emil what they thought, he went right on reading and playing with the youngsters. Now, nothing would ever matter to Emil again. He died clutching his grandfather's shoulders, shielding the old man's chest. They had fallen in a tangle of limbs when the bullets struck and hurtled their bodies into the air before crashing them to the ground.

She couldn't remember how she got home, how her legs, weak with shock, had made their way back to the familiar front doors and

Ella

up the ancient stone stairs to her apartment. She couldn't remember how long she had been sitting on the stool in front of the broken mirror, staring at the empty eyes that looked back at her. It must have been a long time, though, because it was getting dark outside when Hanni could be heard climbing laboriously up the long flights of stairs.

"Why, Oma?" asked the young woman with the sunken eyes and pale skin.

"Because it is God's will," came the soft reply from the old woman clothed in a black shawl stained with blood and wet with tears.

"How can this be God's will?" the young woman screamed at the image of her grandmother in the mirror.

"God had nothing to do with this and if He did, then He is a terrible God without kindness or mercy."

"Hush, child!" warned the old woman. "Someone will hear you."

"Let them," Ella answered even more shrilly. "I don't care about them or anyone else anymore."

With a tired motion of her arm and a shake of her head, Hanni removed her shawl. Dropping it on the chair next to the door, she walked toward her granddaughter who was still staring at both their reflections in the mirror. When she had crossed the room, she stood behind Ella and put her hands on the young woman's shoulders. They looked at each other in the mirror before Hanni said, "You have to care. That's what this is about, you know. To care even when it hurts. To have the strength and courage to keep caring even when your mind and body want nothing more than to turn away from the pain."

The silence stretched between them until Hanni turned away and sat heavily on the bed near Ella's stool. Both their eyes filled with

Ella

tears and they hung their heads. As Hanni's sobs grew louder, Ella raised her eyes to the mirror again. When her own sobs started, she could not tell if it was because of what she was feeling or because her own image in the mirror looked so pathetic.

Mia had been out of town scouting surrounding villages and farms for black-market food at the time of the murders and did not return until a week had passed and the dead had been buried. Atrocities had been committed during some of her other absences but nothing had ever been as hurtful and damaging as these murders. Ella and Hanni were both sitting at the table eating boiled potatoes, their usual supper. There hadn't been any other vegetables for months already and meat was totally out of the question. To make matters even worse, the men who had farmed the few acres still under cultivation were dead now and so were the ones who had managed to offer luxuries on the black market for anyone who could afford the exorbitant prices.

Without a word, Mia took off her sweater and threw it on a nearby chair. She walked over to Ella and sat down next to her and pulled her daughter's head onto her shoulder.

"I'm so sorry," she whispered into her Ella's ear while stroking the fine, light brown hair.

"I'm so sorry," she said again as Ella straightened and wiped at tears that had started to fall once more.

Hanni, across the table, spooned potato soup past trembling lips.

"You know it's going to be over soon. We can't hold out much longer. Our boys are fighting and dying in droves. And when I say "boys," I mean boys. Some of them are no more than ten or eleven years old, if that."

"That won't help all the ones who already died," said Ella. "I've known most of them all of my life and they never did anything wrong."

Ella

At least not anything that they should be killed for. Hell! They were my friends!"

"Don't swear, Ella. Of course they didn't do anything to get themselves killed, except they were born in the wrong time and the wrong place. But right now that isn't the worst of our problems. The worst is that the living don't have anything to eat. Eventually the winter will be here again and we need coats and better shoes. We have to think of the future and that means I have to leave again and see about working permanently in the city. Otherwise, there is no way we can survive."

"I want to go with you," said Ella in a desperate voice.

It was awful for Mia to see her daughter's sunken eyes and her tiny figure too skinny to be pretty anymore.

"I'm sorry, sweetie. I can't take you. I'll be looking for work and then, hopefully, working day and night to have enough to send back home. I won't be able to take care of you. You and Oma need to stay here and carry on the best you can."

"But, Mommy, I don't want to stay here anymore. There's nothing left here to stay for."

"Yes, there is. You have your grandmother." Besides, you have less than a year left to finish your schooling before you take exams. You must not let anything get in the way of that. Once you finish your degree and qualify to teach, you can go anywhere you want."

Ella knew there was no point arguing with her mother. In her heart of hearts she even knew that Mia was right. There was no point in doing anything until she was a teacher. Then she would have some choices. She already knew she would never choose to stay here. That would be like a living death. Anything but that.

Two days later, Mia prepared to say her good-byes and leave again. It was an uneasy farewell because Allied forces were reported to be seen everywhere. At night, Ella and Hanni sometimes saw bursts of flames and bombers speeding toward Dresden. Thus far, the city had been left relatively unharmed. There was no point in attacking a city that housed only women, children, and the wounded—but Ella felt uneasy anyway. Mia tried to be cheerful and Oma tried not to cry but it was clear to all that Mia's plan was risky.

Ella walked her mother to the train station. It was a large building that promised adventure as you walked through its huge front doors swinging on ancient metal hinges. They were kept quiet and mobile by grease, regularly applied by a caretaker who looked old enough to have built the doors himself. When Ella first stepped into the large reception area, pillared in columns and tiled in alternating dark and light squares, she felt a sense of ancient continuity. Past wealth and glory met present poverty and defeat here. She felt stone columns and floors come alive and whisper to her of great events that had taken place within these walls.

After buying her one-way ticket to the city, Mia swung around to find her daughter looking at her with sad eyes. Without ever saying a word, and without probably meaning to, Ella broke her heart. Mia looked at her daughter and thought back to the time that she had been Ella's age. She had been this young and this naive when she and Kurt had made love, when she had conceived their child. From that moment on, Ella had been a part of her life and Kurt had not. It was almost as if, when he left her, he left a part of himself behind. Ella had come to represent the love Mia and Kurt had once shared, a love that she could never replace. Now, another parting and another piece of her heart was being left behind.

When it was time to say good-bye, Mia hugged her daughter and wished, for the millionth time, that it was Kurt she held in her arms. Even now, it was guilt for this secret thought that made Mia's legs carry her swiftly to the daughter waiting with outstretched arms. As the train pulled away from the platform, she even managed a bit of a smile for her child who waved frantically on the other side of the dirty window.

Chugging ever faster, the departing train whipped Ella's hair and skirt into billowing clouds on the lonely, ancient platform.

Two days later the unthinkable happened. Dresden was bombed. It was such a barrage of firepower that the city burned for days. Anyone who could not get out within the first few hours did not survive.

Chapter 5

For Ella, the waiting seemed a timeless, emotionless vacuum that might have gone on for days or weeks or months. In reality, it was only a week since the bombing and since she had last had word of her mother. Life went on in the crazy way that had become normal. It had evolved into an incomprehensible sequence of familiar, meaningless tasks. Somehow, she went to school and attended classes that held no interest or meaning anymore. After coming home, she helped Hanni with tasks that were only slightly less meaningful than the classes she had just left. At night, Ella went to bed too early, stayed awake too long, and slept too fitfully to get any rejuvinating sleep. Her mother was missing and, perhaps for the first time that she could remember, Ella missed her mother.

"Oma! I can't stand the waiting! Why haven't we heard anything yet?" Ella shouted one night when the whole of the world seemed dark and hopeless. When the old woman didn't answer, Ella feared that she had died in her sleep. Gingerly, fearfully, she tiptoed to Hanni's bedside. But, just as she reached out to touch what she feared would be a corpse, she heard her grandmother's stifled sobs. Quietly, she returned to her own bed.

It rained for days. And with the rain came black soot and ash from Dresden, that once-beautiful city where Ella had run and played near their great river. Now, the remains of lives that had once flourished were being blown far and wide, stripped of their identities. With no one to mark their passing, they were washed down streets and gutters, finding their final rest in soggy, unmarked graves.

"Oma, where is she?!!" Ella asked for the hundredth time

And for the hundredth time, Hanni thought of the many dead whose only remaining power was to elicit tears from those still living. The thought made Hanni choke back her own tears and the terse response she was about to make. Instead, she stopped and really looked at her granddaughter.

The girl (or young woman, Hanni nowadays could never make up her mind about that) looked hysterical with eyes darting left and right. They seemed to search for someone or something without a reasoning mind to guide their direction. They reminded Hanni of the eyes of a wild animal caught in a trap with nowhere to run. The blue eyes looked intense and at the same time far away—as though Ella were not registering much she saw. She was sitting on her familiar stool next to the small desk. Her body, tense and leaning forward, looking like she was searching for something it had lost. Even her nostrils were flared. It made the skin on her nose stretch across the bony bridge in startling white pallor—and she was so thin! Even through the dress, Hanni could see the outline of Ella's shoulder blades and the bones of her spine making little ridges down her back.

"You look hungry, sweetie. Let me heat up some of the potato soup from last night for you."

"You know very well that I don't want to eat. All I want is my mother. Why do you think you can make me feel better by feeding me that same, tasteless mush?"

"I just want to do something to help and there's nothing else I can do. You're so skinny that I think maybe some food will make you feel a little better."

Ella

"Well, that slop certainly won't do it," said Ella waving dismissively at the pan sitting on top of the pot-bellied stove.

They didn't have enough wood or coal to heat the regular cooking stove so their heat had to be coaxed from the ancient metal stove in the corner of the living room. It was black with claw feet to support its round middle. The top of it was a series of interlocking rings that could be lifted off to create an opening of various sizes so that wood could be shoved down into its cavity. In the middle of its belly, there was a metal door on heavy hinges with a coiled lever that, if you were fast enough, could be raised to open the door without burning your fingers. It was wide enough for a small load of coal to be shoved inside. This was always a messy task and Ella felt guilty when she saw her grandmother prepare the soup for their supper.

That same evening, a full moon shone through the yellowed lace curtains. The small window, a two-foot square, had been built high on the wall five feet from the sagging wooden floor. Ella, if she turned her head toward her left shoulder and looked up, could see the brightly lit sky. Earlier in the evening, she had eaten the watery potato soup Oma had heated for them both. She hadn't been hungry but felt obliged to make her grandmother feel better after being cross with her earlier. Ella knew it wasn't anybody's fault that they had not heard a word about her mother. She couldn't help but worry and when she was under stress she always snapped at the nearest person. She sighed remembering Oma's hurt look and the smile that replaced it when she gobbled down her simple meal. It was easy to make her grandmother happy. She wished her mother were more like that. Thinking that of her mother made her feel guilty again. Angrily, she turned to Oma and asked if she could go to the school dance that night.

"It's the weekend and there's nothing else to do. Besides, all my friends will be there and all the teachers, as well."

Ella

Oma looked at her disapprovingly and said, "You know your mother said, "not 'till you're sixteen". That won't be for nearly a year."

"Oma, who knows where my mother is or if she'll ever come home again, so it's really up to you."

As soon as the words left her mouth, Ella regretted them. Her grandmother's stricken look reminded her that Mia wasn't just her mother but Oma's daughter, as well.

"Oh, I'm so sorry, Oma. I didn't mean to hurt your feelings. It's just that I feel so bad and worried and seeing my friends will cheer me up. You know how much better it makes you feel when you can talk to your friends. Well, I'm the same way."

"It's still not what your mother wants you to do and I don't want to go against her wishes. Besides, as awful as it might sound to you, there is no reason to change the rules."

"What do you mean no reason to change the rules? Nothing is normal anymore and rules don't count when they don't mean anything. Who know what will happen in the next six months? There may not even be a school building standing in the next six months." Then, more sweetly "Oma, all my friends will be there….. please."

Hanni sighed in resignation. Her shoulders slumped and she waved a hand from Ella toward the door as if shooing her out. Then she walked to the table and sat heavily in the nearest chair before balling her hands into fists and covering her mouth with them. Ella couldn't tell if her grandmother was holding back angry words or just tired and using her fists to prop up her head.

"Oh, thank you! Thank you!" she squealed with delight.

She hugged her grandmother's shoulders before rushing to the small sink on the back wall and dipping her hands into the cool water

Ella

they kept in a bucket next to it. She rubbed her face clean and dried it with one of the rough towels that hung on a hook beside the sink. She then inspected her face in the mirror and decided to comb her hair and roll the upper half of it into a bun on top of her head. Only a few weeks ago, she and Silvia had practiced for days styling their hair in this new fashion. So much had happened since then, but arranging her hair made Ella feel things were almost normal again.

By the time she had rearranged her hair several more times, changed dresses twice, pinched her cheeks to make them red, and kissed the top of Oma's bent head, Ella whirled out the door feeling almost happy. This would be her first evening out without an adult chaperone. It was exciting and a little scary. Ella's heart pounded in her chest as she jumped down the stairs three or even four at a time. When she reached the front door leading to the cobbled stones of the sidewalk, she was out of breath. Leaning heavily against the stone archway, Ella breathed deeply several times before heading in the direction of her school.

It wasn't a long walk and the familiar path through the park with its huge oaks and meandering gravel walkways eased some of Ella's tension. She felt bad for defying Oma. Surely she, Ella, had every right to make her own choices. She knew that her grandmother was simply following the rules. Silly, backward, old-fashioned rules her mother insisted on. These thoughts made Ella begin to feel uneasy again. This time because she was thinking unkindly about her mother, her mother who might be, even now, dead. She was grateful when Sylvia and Marlis called her name and waved from the direction of the small lake that, in summer, was home to a large family of swans. She backtracked part of the way and waited for them at one of the crossings. They hurried toward her and, when they came near, told her in excited voices that some of the pilots had come home again and were expected at the dance.

Ella

As they rounded the last corner, the school came into view. It was dusk and it struck Ella that the building she had come to know so well for so many years had never looked as beautiful. Tonight, she saw it with new eyes.

The failing light brought great stone walls into frieze-like relief and portions where teachers still toiled in meetings or other school-work shone like beacons in the fading twilight. It was a huge edifice, four, and in some places five, stories tall. It had been built over three generations ago by people who had dreams of an education for their children. Of course, it hadn't started out quite so big—the building had grown with their dreams. Now it housed three schools in various wings. Everything from kindergarten to pre-university classes were offered. It had playgrounds in the back for the younger children and benches for eating lunches when the weather allowed. In green alcoves stood half a dozen statues placed there by various organizations to honor heroes who had fought and died for this land. Most recently, a statue of Hitler had been commissioned by a local party representative and placed in a conspicuous position right next to the imposing entrance. Seeing it like this gave Ella a feeling of pride and satisfaction that everything was right in the world or would be again soon.

In back of the main building and a little to the left, was the newest addition. Looking at it made Ella's heart skip a beat. The gymnasium dwarfed the older parts of the main building on that side. With a rounded dome to give it the height needed for equipment inside, it measured at least eighty feet long on each side. The cinderblock walls, much newer than the old school building next to it, sparkled in what was left of tonight's twilight. To Ella, it looked beautiful, like a promise of shiny things to come.

It was to that building that the girls were headed and the nearer they got to it, the more excited they became. Their giggles turned to outright laughter as they shared their plans for the evening. Silvia

Ella

in particular was intent on dancing the night away and with no one less than Werner, the doctor's son who had been sent home from the front lines due to an injury to his right arm. A stray bullet had ripped through a wooden makeshift barricade and shattered his elbow making him useless on the front. He was at least a year and a half older than Silvia and she had had her eye on him for as long as they all could remember.

Ella could not imagine how she would spend the evening but hoped she would have the chance to dance at least once. She had been here often enough for sports events but this was different. In fact, it was so different from anything she had done here before that, when she stood in the open doorway, her jaw dropped in surprise. The parallel bars she knew so intimately had been pushed against one wall along with the gymnastic floor mats and the "horse" on which she had often twisted and leaped. The six long ropes that usually hung from the ceiling had been tied together and elevated along with the parallel rings on which she had won three blue medals. Instead of equipment or bleachers, chairs lined the sides of the auditorium. Mothers served juice in glasses they normally used at lunch. Best of all, across from the entrance and against the far wall, a platform had been set up on which eight musicians were tuning and setting up instruments. Spotlights lit the impromtu stage.

A large crowd milled about and included most of the girls in her class. A few of the kids were younger than she, but not many. There were parents mingling in the crowd as well and Ella got a pang of jealousy thinking how nice it must be to have your parents attend such a function. She did notice, though, that all of them were mothers. The war had taken the fathers. Everyone pretended not to notice the lack of boys at the dance. In fact, this was a party to celebrate life in spite of the war, in spite of the losses and deaths it had caused.

Minna, one of the girls one class younger than Ella's, rushed over to meet them after they had stepped inside.

Ella

"Can you imagine," she shouted above the noise. "I'm so angry with my mom. She insisted on coming along tonight and that's about the last thing I need".

"But isn't that kind of nice?" Ella asked.

"Are you kidding!" Minna nearly shouted. "Who needs a parent snooping around when this is supposed to be our dance?"

Ella had to agree it could put a cramp in someone's style and after that silently thanked her lucky stars for her good fortune.

After the band, mostly older girls and some women, started to play, the lights were dimmed and Ella found herself in the middle of a group of girls whispering instructions to each other. Directions were given as to who was to ask whom for a dance and who was to be avoided. It was an interesting game, but, in reality, any girl would have danced with any of the few boys who were there. Mostly, girls danced with other girls for lack of suitable partners. For Ella, that part was a huge disappointment. Nonetheless, she liked the music and wriggled her hips to the beat of the drums played by one of the local farm girls.

The truth was that Ella had felt exhilarated and lonely at the same time. She didn't understand it but she desperately wanted to have a good time and, at the same time, she wanted to go home. Oma was there probably feeling terrible because she had defied her and gone off without her approval. Ella knew the wave of her hand had been more frustration than consent. However, as soon as she had this thought, Ella wanted more than ever to stay right where she was.

While thinking, Ella had unconsciously moved further into the shadows of the great hall. She was alone, if you didn't count all the hubbub going on around her. Her girlfriends were still huddled in a tight knit group or dancing with each other. When the last song of the set came to an end and more lights were turned on for the first inter-mission, the double doors opened.

Ella

Karl led a pack of six or seven young men into the gym. Ella couldn't tell how many because she could not take her eyes off Karl. She was glad she was alone so that she could watch him without being noticed or teased. It would be too embarrassing to get caught gaping—but she just couldn't help it.

Karl moved with the grace of a natural born dancer through the crowd that had already formed around him and his friends. With each step, more people from the dance floor joined him. She wanted to do the same, but didn't dare to get any nearer. She was content to keep her distance and just watch.

Now he was making his way toward one of the small tables set up for the adults supervising tonight's activities. When he reached the first of the four chairs around it he stopped and pulled it away from the table with his booted foot. Swinging his right leg over the low back of the chair, he sat down and leaned his elbows on the tabletop and propped his chin on interlocking fingers. Ella, standing in the shadows to his right, could now see his profile clearly. An easy smile played across his lips as he looked up and nodded his thanks to the young woman who placed an open bottle of beer in front of him.

As his friends and admirers gathered around him and pulled empty chairs near his table, Ella's line of vision was broken and she moved further against the wall and even further into shadow. The floor mats that had been piled there were stacked in clusters of four or five and now made an excellent step that raised her above the heads of the crowd.

He sat easily in his chair and in the glow of admiration his presence generated. He was like a magnet for young and old alike and both the women and old men looked at him as though a god had entered their midst. He spoke with them all. With equal ease, he kissed the top of baby Heinrich's head as he lay sleeping in his mother's arms and then winked and flirted with the mother who had turned crimson from the attention. Ella then saw him turn to old Fritz who had pulled up a chair next to Karl and waited for the young man to notice him. With an easy smile, he turned to the old farmer and took one of the gnarled hands into his own in a firm but friendly grip.

"How are you doing, Herr Eckerd?" asked Karl.

"Better, now you're here. What I want to know is how is it going on the front and how come you're here when we've heard that you fly boys are needed more than ever on the eastern line of resistance?" came the reply in a booming voice.

"Well, the truth is, Herr Eckerd, a general alert has been issued and a lot of troops on the ground and in the air are being moved to strengthen our defenses. We'll be headed back up north tomorrow and I suspect we'll run into resistance on the way."

A general intake of breath could be heard from the group that was gathered around the welcome visitors. This was not the good news they had hoped for. It meant that more fighting could be expected and more of them would lose their lives or those of loved ones.

"But how are we holding up against the pressure?" farmer Eckerd pressed.

"We're doing the best we can. But, you have to remember that we're in kind of a vice with enemy squeezing us from both the east and the west. And now that Americans are fighting alongside the Brits and the French, it's that much harder. We've had to weaken our stand in the north and the west to move troops to the eastern front and that's been a terrible drain. But, I assure you Herr Eckerd, we're doing the best we can and we have the very finest fighting machine ever seen anywhere, anytime. Every one of our men is worth a dozen of theirs any day, so we can't help but recover from this setback in Dresden. It's only a matter of time. Isn't that right, Franz?" he asked turning to one of the friends he had brought.

Ella

Franz, in turn, looked at the pilot next to him. They both mumbled something under their breaths and nodded without ever meeting anyone's eyes.

No one was fooled by Karl's show of bravado, but everyone was grateful for the reassurance the hollow words brought. Some hope was better than none at all, and wasn't that what they were doing by even having this dance? It was a show of resistance and pretence that everything was normal or would be again very soon. No one said what was really on their minds—that this was the beginning of the end. An end most expected sooner rather than later. For tonight, it felt good to play music and dance as though there was no tomorrow to worry about.

Lights were being dimmed once more and band members had taken up their positions while tuning their instruments. Girls giggled in small groups that formed around the welcome guests. Ella moved even further into the shadows.

Karl got up from his chair and turned to his right as though heading for the platform where the musicians were playing an old folk song with a haunting melody and familiar beat. It was a waltz, a favorite. Some girls' eyes followed his movements and some were cast down in disappointment. Each of them secretly hoped he would ask them for this dance. Instead, it looked like he was going to the other side of the hall.

After he had taken several steps past where Ella stood in shadow, Karl turned around and, in two quick steps, stood in front of her. He reached out a hand and lifted her chin so her eyes had no choice but to meet his own as he whispered, "Dance?"

Ella was too stunned to answer and, instead, let herself get pulled into the crowd on the dance floor. Her eyes focused on her feet but she could not see where she was stepping. Nor could she keep her balance without Karl's guidance as dancers jostled her on all sides.

Ella

She could barely breathe and, when he stopped and took her into his embrace, she thought she would slip through his arms and then through the floorboards. Neither of those things happened. Instead, she felt the strength of his arms around her waist and the beat of his heart against her cheek. His feet followed the rhythm of the music perfectly and just as perfectly they guided hers in imitation. Now, Ella seemed to glide and swirl in a cloud of warmth and sound and dimmed light. Her breath came in small gasps and her skin felt clammy and on fire at the same time. As the music neared its end and the last bars played a protracted crescendo, Karl gripped her waist even tighter and, with his right hand, pulled her more forcefully against his chest while he stretched the length of his body along and on top of hers. Ella was bent almost double and her long hair brushed the heels of her shoes. The music ended. Slowly, Karl brought her upright again and bowed politely.

"Wait for me at the door later and I'll take you home," he said before turning and walking away.

Ella had no idea how she spent the time until the dance ended. Her friends asked her how it felt to be held in Karl's arms and she had no answer for them. She couldn't describe the sensation with words that only trivialized her feelings. They swarmed, they swooped, they giggled and, eventually, they left her alone—and that is how she stayed the rest of the evening. He never made another attempt to seek her out.

At ten o'clock, the lights were turned up once more and the musicians began packing their instruments into well-worn cases. The babble of voices could be heard over the scraping of chairs as these and folding tables were removed into a storage room at the back of the gymnasium. Ella made her way to the double doors that stood open and leaned against the wall in the deepest part of the shadows. She had not bothered to find her friends or to say good-bye to any of the parent and teacher helpers who were still working inside to clean

Ella

up and put the gym in order. In fact, after her dance with Karl and the brief exchange with her curious friends following it, Ella had not spoken a word to anyone.

After most of the students and adults left and only a few remained to lock up, Ella turned to leave for home, convinced Karl had forgotten about her. She couldn't blame him. She was a child compared to him. He was at least ten years her senior. He had probably danced with her out of pity, seeing her slouch in the shadows against the wall. Thinking about it made her flush with embarrassment and she rubbed her hand across her brow to hide her eyes even though no one could see her face in the dark.

Then, she heard his voice. He reached for her arm and said, "Thanks for waiting. I couldn't get away any earlier."

That was all he said to her all the way to the corner and down the street that led to her home. It didn't occur to her until much later that he seemed to know where they were going even though she had not told him where she lived. For Ella, their silence was welcome. She was too embarrassed to speak and didn't know what to say to him anyway. So they walked quietly, their footsteps matched in the warm evening air.

When they came to her front door, Ella was surprised to see lights in the upper story of the apartment house. They shone from her apartment and should have been turned off long ago in deference to the "black-out" orders that had become second nature to all of them.

Voices rose from the open windows of her living room, another sign that something was not as it should be. Ella could not think about that right now. She stood in the alcove that hid the front door of her building and Karl stood one step below her on the sidewalk. She was glad that he could not see her clearly because her face was still flushed. Her chest rose and fell with exaggerated depth and little sighs escaped her parted lips.

Ella

As she was about to say, "Good-bye," his lips closed over hers and his body, now in the alcove with her, pressed against her chest. She couldn't move, in fact, she could hardly breathe. Small moans escaped from her throat and she felt her body sag against him. She had no idea how long they stood there locked in each other's embrace before he released her mouth and his hold on her waist. When he did, she stiffened and tried to pull away. There was little room to move and all she managed was enough space to breathe more freely.

At this, Karl turned away from her and stepped down and out of the alcove pulling her along. On the sidewalk, below a row of windows long darkened for the night, Ella leaned her back against the wall and Karl stood in front of her with one hand thrown up against the wall above Ella's head. He leaned easily, supporting his weight and lowering his head to look deeply into her eyes. His dark hair fell in thick strands from his forehead and partly across his eyes. Their color was indistinguishable in the dark but Ella knew they were green, the same color as the meadow just after summer when the grass had lost some of its brilliance but had gained deeper shades of autumn hues. His high cheekbones created the illusion of hollows in his cheeks and deepened the angles of his chiseled chin. His mouth was soft and luscious with full lips that were slightly swollen from the kiss they had just shared. Now they were curved in a smile as he watched confusion play across the features of her face.

Just then, her mother's voice reached them. "Who are you with, Ella and what are you doing?"

Startled, Ella pushed Karl further from her and stepped forward to turn and look up at the open window just below the roofline. She saw her mother's silhouette leaning out of the window frame and, from its stance, Ella knew her mother was tense.

"Mom! What are you doing home? I was so worried about you. We all were. We didn't know what happened to you. Are you alright?"

Ella

"Of course I'm alright. What I want to know is what are you doing down there?"

"I was just saying good-night. I went to the school dance with some friends, you know, Silvia and Marlis and…" One of the windows of an apartment below their own opened and someone shouted, "What's all this racket? People are trying to sleep here!"

Ignoring their neighbor, Mia shouted again, "Who is that with you?"

"Nobody," said Ella more quietly. "A friend who walked me home."

"I know who that is and it's not Silvia," said Mia retreating from the window.

"I'm sorry," said Ella softly, turning toward Karl again.

"It's okay." He took her into his arms once more and leaned down to kiss her again.

Just as Ella thought she would die with delight, she heard a noise above them. Then there was a thud and suddenly, cold water hit the top of their heads, drenching them both. Pulling apart and gasping for breath, Ella and Karl cried out in shock. Not knowing what else to do, Ella turned and ran into the building slamming the front door closed behind her. She didn't hear her mother yelling from her window to Karl to leave her daughter alone or he would get a lot worse than a bucket of water.

By the time Ella ran up the flights of stairs to their apartment, Mia had opened the front door, waiting for her.

"How could you!" shouted Ella in a rage when she saw her mother with hands balled into fists on both hips.

"How could I?" Mia grabbed Ella's hair and pulled her into the front room of their apartment.

Ella

"How dare you ask me that when you weren't even supposed to be out tonight and you disobeyed not only me but your grandmother, too."

Shaking with fury and soaked with water, Ella glared at her mother. "Everything was fine till you came home! I wish you hadn't!"

With that, Ella turned and walked across the room toward the bathroom with all the dignity she could muster. She felt her mother's shocked stare follow her and heard the beginning of sobs from her grandmother who dropped onto the sofa like a rag doll.

Ella didn't care what they thought as she slammed the bathroom door behind her and locked it. It was only when she turned around and saw the reflection of her face in the mirror that tears began to well up in her eyes. She had never seen herself look so disheveled. Her hair was a mess and her mouth was already swelling from the pressure of Karl's kiss. In fact, it looked bruised and, with tears now falling down her cheeks, the picture of desolation was complete.

Chapter 6

After the end of the war, Mia found a permanent job in what was now called "the West." She was gone for nearly three years. By now, in 1948, Ella was eighteen years old and working as a teacher in the school where she had started her education and first met Karl.

She was pregnant. She hadn't seen a doctor but she knew it just the same. Karl knew it too, but he'd chosen to believe that the child wasn't his. He came home after the war, still triumphant with a Norwegian war bride and his conviction that Hitler would rise again. Her grandmother suspected it but was careful not to mention anything.

One cool, dark evening after their usual supper of boiled potatoes, Ella finally said, "I don't know how this happened, Oma." With an almost imperceptible rise of her eyebrow, Hanni asked the required question, "What, Sweetheart?"

"Oh, you'll never forgive me." Hanni didn't answer. She sat on the worn couch and leaned deeper into its soft cushions, waiting. "I made a big mistake and now I'm going to have to suffer for it the rest of my life."

As the silence stretched on, Ella realized she would have to say the words she was finding so difficult to utter. She was grateful her mother wasn't here—but even with Oma, it was one of the hardest sentences she had to say.

Ella

"Well, there was a night last June when I came home real late. Remember? The truth is that I saw Karl that night. I know I wasn't supposed to see him anymore but I just couldn't help it. And to make matters worse, Silvia was supposed to stay with us but she didn't. She left even though she had promised to stay. And then there were the other guys, you know, friends of his. They all had girlfriends. And everyone was having such a good time. I just don't know how it happened."

"How what happened?"

"Well, if you must hear me say it, I think I'm going to have a baby."

"There's only one way that can happen".

Ella's face crumbled at those words. Hanni was so cold. Not quite condemning but also not sympathetic. Ella didn't know what she had expected but it wasn't this resigned, matter-of-fact response from the one person who had always shown the utmost tenderness. It didn't seem right or fair.

The sobs came easily. All Ella had to do was think about how she had worked so hard to get through school, how she had never had much of anything because they were so poor, how all she had really wanted was for Karl to love her the way she loved him and how her life was going to be ruined now because the one thing, the only thing she had ever been really proud of, her career, would be taken from her. Her life was over and she hadn't even had a chance to live it yet! Besides, it wasn't her fault that she was pregnant. Karl shouldn't have been so insistent. She had felt sorry for him. He was nearly ten years older than she. He knew that she couldn't say "no" to a war hero. In a way, what she had done was even her duty, wasn't it? She had satisfied him! But here she was, paying the price.

"Ella, when is the baby due?"

Ella

"Sometime in March, I think".

"We'll have time to get ready. You will have to write your mother and see if she can get some baby clothes and blankets. Maybe Werner from next door will make a small crib and if the neighbors don't mind....." Hanni stopped, interrupted by a wail from her granddaughter. She had thrown herself on the couch next to the old woman and was clutching a pillow to herself as though she was trying to push it through her stomach and out her back. The sobs came louder and faster with each breath Ella took.

"Ella, I don't know what you expect me to say, but this is no time to hide our heads in the sand. What's done is done. We have to take care of it the best we can. There is a lot to do before the baby comes".

"But it's just not fair", sobbed Ella even louder. "I didn't mean to do anything bad. Why do I have to be the one to suffer? Shouldn't Karl do something?

"I think he's already done it, dear".

Hanni got up from the couch and walked to the sink where dishes waited to be washed. She had been afraid something like this would happen. Ever since Ella became infatuated with the young pilot, Hanni had worried that her headstrong granddaughter would do something foolish. Although she loved Ella dearly, Hanni knew the girl could be swayed this way and that, whichever way the wind might blow. She seemed so strong and confident and yet she had a strange inability to make decisions or to stick to them once she had made them. It wasn't that Ella lacked intelligence. She had plenty of that. Instead, it was almost as though a piece of her was missing—something that would make Ella's strength real instead of the pretence Hanni knew it was most of the time. Worst of all, Ella seemed to believe the lies she told herself.

Ella

When she finished cleaning their tableware, Hanni put a pot filled with water on top of the stove and made sure there was enough firewood inside to heat it. She then got two earthenware mugs from one of the kitchen shelves and added dried, green leaves and some dried, yellow flowers to both mugs. The chamomile and peppermint would do them both good. Chamomile to sooth and calm them and peppermint for flavor. A teaspoonful of honey in each mug finished her preparations. While she waited for the water to boil, Hanni watched Ella still sobbing on the couch. She had exhausted herself and was crying more quietly into the pillow still clutched to her chest.

When the water was hot Hanni filled both mugs and walked back to the couch. Ella first shook her head before changing her mind and reaching for the tea.

After they were both comfortable, Hanni stroked Ella's hair and raised her face so she could look into her granddaughter's red-rimmed eyes. "Now, child, tell me what happened and what you expect to come of it."

"Like I told you, I got pregnant! And that's all there's to it".

"Ella, obviously, that's not all there is to it. Now be reasonable and let's discuss this so I can help you. Otherwise you're on your own and I don't think you're ready for that. Do you?"

"No", answered Ella through clenched teeth, her head sunk onto her chest. "It was pretty much like I told you. We all went out together but when we got ready to come home Karl said he wanted to show me something. So we left the others and he gave me a ride on his motorcycle to the little hut out on the edge of the woods. You know, the one that's been empty for years. They say a shoemaker lived there once." Ella looked at her grandmother who had drawn in her breath and was staring across the room as though she had seen a ghost. "What's the matter?" she asked, concern creeping into her voice.

Ella

"It's nothing, Ella. I know the place you're talking about but I haven't thought about it in years. How come Karl took you there of all places? It must be a mess after all these years."

"But that's the whole point, Oma. Karl's family bought that property when they built the brewery but never did anything with it. Then, when they knew he was coming home, his mom and dad and two brothers fixed it all up for him and…." Here Ella began to sob again and Hanni sat back and waited. With a catch in her voice, Ella continued.

"He took me there to show me the place. And it looked real nice. It was cozy even though there's not much furniture. God, I don't even know how to describe it to you. There was a back part that had a big table and a sink with a pump. He has a stove there that's bigger than ours. In the living room part there's a big fireplace. He said that his brothers had rebuilt it. There are some rugs and a couch and even curtains on the windows. And in one corner, they put a big bed with quilts and his featherbed. Oh, Oma!" Ella began to wail again.

"Hush, Sweety. It's going to be all right. We'll figure something out." Memories filled Hanni's mind while Ella pulled herself together before continuing her story. Hanni stroked Ella's hair as she tried to comprehend the irony of this coincidence. Vivid images of the times she had spent in the same cabin with a man she had once loved flowed through her mind. Ella didn't know that the "shoemaker" was Mia's father, her grandfather. There was no point in bringing up the past now. For a brief moment Hanni wondered if this was still more punishment for the indiscretion of the young woman she once was.

"Anyway, we were there and I imagined what it would be like to live there with him. Omi, you know I've loved him from the first time I saw him. He knows it too and that's why he brought me there. And at first I thought ….." At this point Ella's voice trailed off again.

Ella

"What did you think?"

"Well, after all the time we spent together I thought maybe he loved me too. I mean, we've never been together before, you know, like that." Here Ella looked meaningfully at her grandmother. Hanni nodded.

"He was always gone, you know. So, anyway, I thought that he felt the same way I did and that he took me there to ask me to marry him. But that wasn't it at all. He said that I was one of his best friends and he knew he could trust my judgment. And then…" Here Ella could not continue for sobbing. Inhuman choking spasms issued from her throat. Hanni could only sit and wait until they subsided enough for Ella to continue. "He told me that he was bringing his wife from Norway home and that they and their son would be staying in the cabin. Then he asked me if I thought it would be nice enough for them?" At this point, Ella fell silent and Hanni pulled her closer to hold her shaking shoulders.

"But then how did you get pregnant?" Hanni asked.

"When he told me he was married and had a little boy I started crying and he put his arms around me. We were near the bed so we sat down on it. Anyway, one thing led to another and before I knew it, well, you know. Oma, what am I going to do?"

"You are going to have a baby, that's what you're going to do. And remember, you are not alone in this. You have me and you have your mother. And the rest of the family, for that matter. We'll help you. We've always helped each other through the hard times and we'll do it again."

Chapter 7

Ella had never been happier. She was getting married. Her little girl, Karin, was five years old and even though her mother and grandmother had tried to talk her out of it, Ella had decided that Karin would be her flower girl. After all, Ella reasoned, she was marrying the child's father and it seemed right that the whole family should make an appearance. It was important to Ella that everyone see them together. After all the talk about her chasing Karl and ruining his marriage, she was not about to let an opportunity like this pass her by. They were wrong about her. She never chased anyone. She didn't have to. There were plenty of young men who wanted her time and attention. In fact, it was Karl who had made a nuisance of himself, coming to her home unannounced at all hours of the day and night. Most important of all, after she was born, he had never denied that Karin was his daughter. To tell the truth, he doted on her and never missed the chance to hold her and play with her. Even though he had been awkward at first, Karin couldn't wait to be with her daddy.

However, today was Ella's day. The day when all her dreams came true—the day she would begin her life as Frau Karl Berndt. Her mother had made her wedding dress from carefully saved scraps of exquisite fabrics. The silk and lace gown was offset with a collar trimmed in satin, which was repeated in the sash binding her waist.

Ella

The flowing, sweeping affair was crowned by a circlet of satin roses that anchored a lace veil to her head. It swept past her white boots and at least a yard and a half behind her to become, what Ella hoped would be, the envy of all who were scheduled to witness her matrimony.

It had been a long time coming, this day of hers. She had overcome obstacles no woman should have to confront. When she had first known that she would have a child, she had confided in her Oma. That sentimental old woman had cautioned her to be practical. She had told Ella, "Keep your job. Do not expect help from anyone except family. Most important of all, stay away from Karl!"

Ella had been shocked. She had expected tears of joy from her grandmother and comforting words about the difficulties. The last thing she expected was this practical advice that gave little regard to her feelings. If she had expected anyone to be practical, it would have been her mother.

That too had been a surprise. After Ella wrote her mother that she was pregnant, a long silence preceded the letter that told Ella in no uncertain terms how disappointed her mother was in her and how angry she was with Karl. The next time Mia had managed a visit, she ranted and raved about ingratitude, stupidity and a wasted life. "You are an embarrassment!" had stung Ella particularly hard. However, after all the harsh words had been said, Mia became excited about the child that would make her a grandmother. For the rest of that visit she had unpacked the old treadle sewing machine and made little sack-like garments gathered at the top to go around a small chest with two straps that would go over tiny shoulders. Little shirts with both short and long sleeves came next. In the evenings, for over a week, her mother and grandmother sat together knitting sweaters, caps and booties for the fall and winter when her baby would be crawling on cold floors. They seemed so content and chatted easily while Ella stewed and fretted and got more than a little jealous of all the attention her unborn child was getting while she was left alone to manage her feelings.

She had wanted very badly to get her mother's sympathy but all Mia would say is, "You've made your own bed and now you have to lie in it. It's not like you didn't know what you were doing either." When Ella started to protest, Mia said, "You are old enough to know better than to sleep with someone else's husband. You won't get any sympathy from me and, in fact, I think you should be grateful that we're helping. At least you're not alone to raise it."

Ella left it at that and only sulked openly when the two older women seemed too content and outright happy with their endless little preparations. It was clear that the two people she depended on the most to understand and support her when anxiety threatened to overwhelm her couldn't get past their own happiness to be of much use.

Today, though, it was different. All the attention was on her and she was determined to make a good showing. It was still early. The ceremony would not be until four o'clock that afternoon and she had worked her fingers to the bone to make everything perfect.

Last night, Eva and Silvia picked up the flowers old Frau Schweige had promised her. They were a wedding present from the yard in back of the old woman's house.

Frau Schweige was a widow and her husband, the previous pastor, had been a friend to all the families under his compassionate spiritual care. After his death, his widow was invited to stay in the small house at the edge of town they had lived in over forty years. There she continued to grow the most beautiful flowers for many miles around. No one ever succeeded in achieving the profusion of colors and variety Frau Schweige coaxed out of her garden. Ella was delighted when the old woman made her offer and she and her friends gathered the treasures in huge bundles to put them into a wooden cart they took turns pulling to the church. This morning, Eva and Silvia were hard at work arranging the flowers on the altar where she and Karl would stand when they said their vows.

Her wedding dress was laid out on her bed with the appropriate accoutrements—white silk stockings her mother had paid a fortune for years ago in a specialty shop in Dresden. A lace garter with extra soft rubber tips that snapped the stockings in place as well as panties and a bra of soft white cotton Silvia's mother had made her from precious fabric bought ages ago. There was also the new pair of shoes her mother had bought in an exclusive store near the opera house in Berlin that catered to only the wealthiest patrons. Best of all were the jewels Oma gave her—a fine-linked gold chain from which hung a teardrop shaped red stone and a matching pair of earrings. They were the most beautiful gifts Ella had ever received. They lay next to the other treasures that would make her day perfect. Ella had asked where her grandmother had gotten such exquisite jewelry but Oma only mumbled something about not asking silly questions and someone making shoes. It made no sense to Ella, so she ignored it. There were more important things to attend to.

Mia's gift to Ella and Karl was her presence and most of the food and decorations. She took nearly two weeks of vacation from her job and managed to get back to what was now called "East Germany" via her elaborate and secret underground railroad. She showed up with gifts for everyone, especially Karin.

The pastor, not her family's Catholic priest but Karl's Lutheran minister, agreed to perform the ceremony that would make her Karl's wife. His reluctance was overcome when Ella joined the Lutheran church that her family had avoided for generations. Oma was especially put off by her decision to switch faiths, but Ella didn't care. It was her life and, if this is what it took to make her relationship with

Karl permanent, then that is what she was going to do. Besides, she had never been religious and the switch made very little difference to her. She went to church once a year, at Christmas, and whether that was in one church or another didn't much matter. She had spent too many years in school attending classes designed by either Nazis or communists to care about her religious roots.

Mia had also left the Catholic Church. It was during the war when the church demanded tithes whether or not people had jobs, whether they were hungry and homeless or whether they managed to make ends meet. Few families did much better than that and those that did had position as well as money. They usually avoided tithing altogether. In her case, she had been without both work and money for herself or Ella when Ella was a small child. She went to the pastor to ask for help and instead was told she would be excommunicated if she did not catch up on her delinquent contributions. Before leaving him, Mia withdrew her membership and told the priest in no uncertain terms what she thought about him and his religion. She had not set foot in a church since.

So, thankfully, Mia made no objections to the Lutheran wedding. What was important to Mia was that Karin would have a normal family life with a mother and father and a decent home. To her, it was regrettable that Karl would assume the responsibilities of head of household, especially since a number of much more suitable men had offered to do the same since Karin's birth. However, even Mia had to admit that Ella seemed happier than she ever had and that Karl appeared to genuinely care for his little girl. One could hope for the best, she concluded.

Ella took a long bath in water scented with herbs Oma had picked and tied into a small linen sack. It floated in the steaming water. Ella dropped soap shavings into the water as well and they created a layer of bubbles that hid her body and surrounded her neck in unspeakable luxury. It was warm and wonderful and eased some of the tension in her shoulders and back. She closed her eyes and imagined again the ceremony that would make her a married woman. The church would be beautiful with afternoon sunlight illuminating the stained glass windows and throwing bits of color throughout the church's interior. Everyone would be dressed in their finest clothes and they would sit politely in the pews her friends were decorating.

There would be all the teachers from both the middle and high schools. Some of the administrators would also attend, but mostly because Karl had been appointed to some obscure post within the newly formed police system. No one was sure how he had managed that, but no one wanted to offend a man they could not quite place. Besides, one of Karl's brothers, Hans, was an attorney with excellent connections. In other words, it was worth most people's while to attend the wedding of someone who had access to so much political power. This meant that Ella had to invite many more people than she had at first intended. In retrospect, though, she was happy with the arrangements. A wedding well attended by the right people would go far in laying to rest some of the ugly rumors about her behavior with Karl when he was still married to Inge. She had seen it happen before. Being accepted by the right people made a person acceptable to everyone.

Her smile deepened at these thoughts and she sank lower into the warm soapy water. She raised her arms and watched bubbles slide the length of her arms into the hollow where they met her shoulders and from there around the outside of her breasts and back into the tub. She stroked her hands and felt the smoothness of her skin and took special care to linger on the finger that would soon be encircled by the gold band marking her forever as Karl's wife.

With a sigh, Ella grasped the sides of the tub and raised her chest higher in the water so she could let her head drop back and into the warm suds. Swishing it from side to side, she felt her hair, wet and heavy, brush against her back. It was a delicious sensation and Ella relished every moment. It reminded her of the way her hair brushed her shoulders when Karl ran his hand through its wavy strands and let it gently fall.

She recalled the first time they had made love in his family's cabin near the edge of the woods. Her skin had tingled and glowed with each caress of Karl's hands on her cheeks and neck and shoulders. The memory of the way he had reached around her waist and pulled her to him to brush her lips with his made her gasp and she looked around the kitchen quickly to make sure she was still alone.

Sliding deeper into the water, she continued her reverie. Of course, at first she knew pain. Finding out Karl was already married, discovering that she would have a baby, having Karl visit her and Karin only to leave them again for his family. However, over the course of two years, they became closer. She asked his advice when work issues troubled her and involved him with decisions about their daughter. In time, they began to have dinner together regularly, usually Friday evenings.

She never asked what Inge thought of this arrangement. She didn't care. She also didn't care when people started saying Karl had two families. When he came more and more often, even during the week, to spend time with his little girl, Ella made sure she was alone with him from time to time. Eventually, he spent as much time with her as he did at home. When Inge finally announced she would leave him and take herself and their son back to Norway, the town gossips pointed their fingers at her. They also made sure she heard about the other women Karl was supposedly seeing. Ella didn't believe a word of it. When Inge left, Karl swore he loved her and would be faithful to her if she would only consent to be his wife. Ella didn't doubt him for a moment.

Chapter 8

The next morning dawned brightly. Sunbeams caught motes of dust in the bedroom where Ella and Karl slept like sweaty corpses flung onto crumpled sheets. The wedding had been everything Ella had dreamed about with guests from her school—even the principal—and from Karl's office in the police complex. There were uncles and aunts she hadn't seen in years! So many had come to make her day special. Even a few of her mother's friends, people Ella had never met, came all the way from Dresden. They were easy to spot, in their store-bought outfits and city hair styles—and all they talked about was how their city was being rebuilt. It was as if they thought that only Dresden had known the horrors of the war! Still, it was wonderful that they had travelled so far to be part of her day.

All of Karl's family had been there too! This was perhaps one of the best parts!

Ella smiled as she thought about how much better her wedding must have been compared with the one in Norway. After all, she was not a war bride, not some foreigner who had preyed on the affections of a boy far from home. Ella was a local girl who was married to a local hero. She was now a member of a strong family with powerful ties. It was just as it should be!

Ella nudged her husband. She wanted to relive the day with him! "Karl, my love, did you see how your mother looked at me last night?

Ella

Did you see the smile on her face when she looked at us at the head of the table? I think she's starting to like me—a lot."

Karl buried his head deeper under the blankets. His head pounded too much to even consider talking.

"Karl, come on. She wouldn't have put on such a wonderful party if she didn't love the fact that we were married. Think of that spread! I've never seen anything like it! I've never seen so many pastries—not just plum pie but more cheesecake than the town has ever seen. And that endless supply of beer from her brewery! Even your friends commented on it."

She smiled again as she thought of his friends. They had crowded around her wanting to kiss the bride and dance with her. She had been flattered at their attention and at how Karl had kept his arm protectively around her waist so that his friends could not take their attentions too far. She loved his possessiveness. All of it made her feel sheltered and safe and treasured. There had only been one time she felt uncomfortable—and she was sure it was because Karl had been drinking.

As the evening wore on, Karl's two brothers, Hans and Gottfried with their wives as well as his mother, Elizabeth, and her husband, Max, joined them at their table. Ella couldn't help but notice how Karl, being the oldest son, was already, more or less, the head of the family. His presence far outshown Max, his step-father, although he was married to Elizabet and the father of her two younger sons. Max never seemed to mind not being the center of attention and, especially last night, he gladly allowed his wife's oldest boy center stage.

Flanked by his mother and his new wife, Karl stood unsteadily, raised his glass high above his head and called for attention. The noisy room fell into hushed silence as all eyes turned to the handsome groom. Karl first looked at his mother and then at his wife while both women gazed at him adoringly.

Ella

His voice only slightly slurred, Karl said, "Ladies and gentlemen, I'd like to introduce to you my mother, Elizabet, without whose generous contributions of beer this party could never have happened".

Everyone cheered loudly and many banged beer steins on their tables and beat knives or forks against glasses that threatened to shatter. Ella, who had been prepared to stand next to her husband, sat in stony silence. The attention that should have been hers was deflected to her new mother-in-law and there was nothing she could do. Thank goodness Hans was still sober enough to see what had happened. He immediately raised his glass higher and, with a voice geared to carry over the din, looked at his older brother and said, "And now, a word about our newest member of the family".

Despite the huge amount of alcohol Karl had consumed, he took his brother's hint and loudly proclaimed, "And now, ladies and gentlemen, I would like to present to you the reason for this celebration, my wife, Ella".

A roar and cheer exploded. Hans poked a finger into Ella's hips and whispered out of the corner of his mouth, "Stand up!" Ella raised her eyes from her lap and looked gratefully at her new brother-in-law. His reassuring smile gave her courage as she stood. The crowd cheered even louder. Gottfried looked at her with a strangely speculative expression and then at Hans before winking at her now blushing face.

Chapter 9

The trains' wheels beat a metallic rhythm as Ella and Karin rushed to new lives. Karin was eight years old now. They were going from Berlin to the first stop in West Germany where they would be met by strangers and taken to Goslar, to a family that had agreed to keep them in hiding until they could make their way to America. That is, if they could get off the train and into the waiting car without being detected by special police who kept a sharp eye out for people trying exactly that kind of maneuver.

It had been three long years since Ella's marriage to Karl blossomed, died and dissolved. How odd that the marriage ceremony she so desperately wanted also marked the end of the good part of her relationship with him. Ella was exhausted. She felt as though she had been running uphill through thick mud as fast as she could. Her heart, what was left of it, kept pace with the wheels' rhythm that shattered the silence in their cabin.

Ella looked at her sleeping daughter stretched out on seats across from her. The girl's face was expressionless. She must have been exhausted too, because she fell into a deep sleep almost as soon as they boarded this train over two hours ago. They had left Werda before daylight and changed trains in the huge station in Berlin. The whole time, Ella was terrified her plan would somehow be found out. However, no one questioned the papers the frightened woman and her daughter handed to inspectors. At that point, there was still no reason to doubt their legitimacy. Karin looked so fragile and vulnerable that Ella, once again, wondered if their departure from their painful but familiar life was the right thing to do.

When her mother first wrote to her nearly two years ago from a place called Grand Forks, North Dakota, with the suggestion that she and Karin come there and start new lives, Ella set in motion the process of her divorce. A permanent move from so much pain had seemed like a perfect solution to the endless trauma Karl's behavior created in her life. He had cheated on her from the very beginning of their marriage and after only a few months had barely tried to conceal his sexual forays. After a year of watching helplessly while her marriage disintegrated, Ella filed for divorce—only to find out that Karl had no intention of letting her go. He was apparently perfectly comfortable in their sham of a marriage. After he was asked to resign from his job in law enforcement, he was hired as a teacher and had been sent to work in a town too far away to commute daily. Shortly after their wedding, he had moved to Goerlitz and came home only on week-ends.

The enforced separation from his family hardly troubled Karl. In fact, it served him well. He lived like a single man, coming and going as he pleased. On week-ends he would take the train "home" only to spend every minute with his mother and brothers and the endless stream of friends who could be counted on to share the brewery's draft. They, like him, had survived the war in body but not in spirit. Having once thought of themselves as world leaders, they now drowned their anger at a fate that had robbed them of their illusions and their pride.

Often he took his daughter with him, but seldom his wife. When she protested, Karl reminded her of the times, early in their marriage, when he had taken her along and how she had complained that he would never let her out of his sight. It was true that he had seemed to hover until she felt she could barely breathe. And yes, she had been unhappy, at times. She hadn't realized then that her complaints were the beginning of the rift that would end in divorce.

Looking out the window at the still dark landscape rushing past them, Ella reminded herself that it had only been a matter of time and, regardless of how she acted, Karl would eventually have strayed. Besides, the drunken rows had gotten worse with each passing weekend until she dreaded hearing his footsteps climbing the flights of stairs to their apartment. It was all she could do to keep from shouting at him every time he opened the door. Toward the end, she simply went to bed when she heard him approach and pretended to sleep. Her marriage was a hopeless failure and her mother was right about her needing a new start.

Ella hoped she and Karin could hide a whole year without being found out. The arrangements her mother made from the United States took over a year to finalize. There were the petitions to the bureau of internal affairs with dozens of interviews requesting and justifying a visit to "the West." Ella lied to her interrogators repeatedly and told them that her mother was in West Berlin, fatally ill—that she wanted to see her daughter one last time and had wealth she wanted to leave to her family in "the East." Month after month, Ella answered the same questions, terrified she would slip up on some minor detail. It would mean the end of her opportunity to be truly free and probably cost her her life. However, she hadn't slipped up. After nearly losing hope, she received permission for one week-end. She and her child got tickets for one Saturday with a return stub for 8:00 pm the following day. It was now 5:00 am Saturday morning and Ella was taking Karin on a trip from which they would, one way or another, never return.

In Goslar, a beautiful, ancient town in the Harz mountains, they would be met by strangers who Mia had already paid. There they would stay in hiding while they petitioned to be allowed to immigrate to America. If that was approved and they passed all the physical exams and mental evaluations, they would take a ship, the *Italia*, and cross the Atlantic, a voyage with so many stops that it would take over a month. Once in New York, they would board another train and go to North Dakota.

So many emotions fought for dominance in Ella's heart that she couldn't feel which one was the most urgent. Fear, hope, loneliness, anger and so many more kept her reeling in confusion and despair. Every once in a while she remembered how strong and focused she could be, but not very often. Lately, fatigue gripped her like a vice most of the time and sheer will and determination was all that kept her going.

Ella had hoped that the conflict within her would dissolve once she was on the train, but it hadn't. Only the fact that her mother had already made all of their arrangements kept her going. Each mile they left behind drained her of more energy and resolve. But, there was no going back. That would mean a life sentence for her and custody of Karin for Karl. She couldn't do that to her daughter. No, the time for choosing was past, only worry that the right choice had been made was possible now.

Ella's head began to drop until the rhythmic lull of the train speeding her to an unimaginable future stole the last of her resistance and her chin bounced lightly on her chest.

Karin stirred in her blankets until unfamiliar noises woke her from an exhausted sleep. When she first opened her eyes she was disoriented. Then she remembered! They were escaping! She was on her way to places and people she had never heard of. Behind her was everything and everyone she had ever known and loved. She would never see them again.

That was too hard to think about so she looked at her surroundings in the dim light of the cabin. Her mother sat in one of the corners of the bench opposite her own, her head nodding up and down, her lips slightly parted. Next to her, outside the window, a dark landscape sped by, lit by the suggestion of a silvery glow that promised dawn. She noticed that the dark, round silhouettes of trees rushing by the window had become interspersed with the unnatural shapes of shattered buildings. The shapes got closer and closer together until the trees disappeared completely. Now their jagged edges and peaks reached into the sky creating an endless mosaic of sharp corners and broken walls.

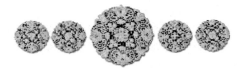

As the sun rose, the ruins contrasted sharply with the backdrop of a sky trying to turn blue. She glanced again at her mother sleeping opposite her when her eye caught a movement outside the window. She saw smoke and noticed some of the tall chimneys in the distance were alive with the curling vapours. The people in this town were beginning their day. Fathers and mothers were going to the factories. Children were going to school. For them, it was just another day. For them, life would continue as it had the day before. This wasn't true for her. For her, this new day meant a very uncertain beginning. Looking again at her mother's fragile body slouched in the corner, Karin knew only one thing for sure. She would have to be strong. She would have to do her best to make things better for this delicate woman. Mother wasn't well. Karin had grown tougher in these last years as she watched her mother crumble under Daddy's cruel indifference. Now, she didn't know if she could carry on without Oma to talk to.

She already missed her Oma. The thought of her made tears well up in Karin's eyes. "How can I ever live without you, Oma? You are the kindest, smartest person in the whole world. How can I live my life without you, without ever seeing you again?" Karin shut her eyes tightly. She didn't want her mother to see her crying when she woke up.

She stopped the tears, but she couldn't get rid of that clench in her heart. Oma was her one true friend, her one sure and safe love in a world of grownups battling for her affections. Somehow, although she didn't know how, she would have to manage without the strength and kindness of her Oma beside her. Now, she, alone, had to be strong.

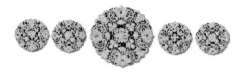

Their arrival in West Germany was all too much for Ella. When she and Karin first got there, it was as though they had arrived, cold and hungry, in the strangest world she could imagine.

The underground railroad had made arrangements for them to stay in seclusion with the Koenig family who risked their own safety to welcome and hide them. They showed them Goslar and where they would be shopping for necessities with the money Mia had sent.

Mother had provided well for them. Yet, despite this, Ella still lived in extraordinary fear. They could not be recognized! There was no place that was really safe! She began each day by searching the newspaper for news of their escape from the East, for possible pictures of herself and Karin. She imagined that, by now, Karl would have alerted his friends on the force to the fact that she'd stolen his daughter from him and asked them to make Karin's return a priority. A thousand times, especially in the night, when every sound seemed to wake her, Ella wished that she hadn't taken this insane risk.

Ella

Then, after two months, when the notice did appear, it was oddly freeing. There was only a brief mention on a page near the back of the paper, and their names were part of a long list of those who had escaped East Germany and were supposed to be in hiding in The West. Naturally, the article mentioned that the same people, herself and Karin included, were blacklisted and could expect no leniency from the East German government once they were apprehended and returned home. However, seeing all the names, and seeing hers intermixed with so many others gave her some sense of relief. It had been two months. She hadn't been recognized. Perhaps she could afford to let go of some of the panic inside her.

All that was before she met Emil, the man for whom she worked selling clothes in his upscale shop on one of the bustling streets of Goslar. They met at a party her host family sponsored and she had helped to put on. Ella, holding a tray of hors'dourves, had graciously offered Emil one of the tidbits. He was obviously attracted to Ella and detained her with questions about her life in Goslar. Perhaps her reluctance to reveal specifics intrigued him or her pretty face lingered in his thoughts. Whatever had been his original motivation, he soon became a regular in Ella's life. He took her to restaurants and events she had never dreamed of enjoying and even asked her to help him host a special sales promotion in his business.

After only a few weeks, Emil asked Ella if she would like to work in his designer showroom. Ella was delighted. She thought she would enjoy the work and was thrilled to get a raise so soon.

Now, she felt safe and even comfortable knowing that she had a future here, if she wanted it. Emil had made it clear that he wanted to be more than her employer. He had even told her how important he thought it was that she re-marry and that her new husband should adopt her little girl. He even went so far as to suggest that he would consider a girl like Karin as his own.

Ella

Whenever Emil took one of her hands into his own and gazed at her tenderly, she wanted to pull away and get on with her work. However, he was persistent and always misunderstood her reluctance as shyness. That was the problem in a nutshell.

Like yesterday afternoon, following a particularly hectic few hours, he came to the cash register where she was standing and turned her to face him and said, "You look tired little Ella. You work hard every day and you don't let me do enough for you in return."

"But you pay me a good wage—much better than anyone else gets for this kind of work".

"That may be true, Ella, but you know, I'd like to do much more for you."

There it was again, the promise of a bright and comfortable future as the wife of a respected businessman—a leader in the community, a gentle man who would do almost anything she asked of him.

Except the truth was that Ella could not stand the thought of Emil touching her. Even his presence near her made her uncomfortable. It wasn't that there was anything to fear. On the contrary, Emil was kindness itself and was always careful to be respectful. There simply was no chemistry for Ella. After so many years of turmoil and heartache with Karl, the stable comfort Emil offered seemed as foreign as the land to which she was moving.

When she wrote her mother about Emil, Mia urged her to consider carefully whether she might not want to stay right where she was instead of chasing after an unpredictable future in a distant land.

By then Ella had made up her mind. Her future would be in America. There was no way she could tolerate Emil's touch for longer than she had to. She even learned to push aside the feelings of guilt she felt about disappointing the man who had made her life so much easier. If he was satisfied to provide beautiful new coats for her and Karin and buy foods she could never afford on a working girl's salary, for the opportunity to spend a few evenings in her company, well that was his business. It wasn't like she was lying to him when she had told him that she would consider staying in Goslar. She had considered the idea and rejected it and would tell him her decision when it was closer to the time they would actually leave. She ignored the doubt that crept into her heart during those times when she looked at Karin, now happy in her new school and with the man she knew might become her new father. Rarely did she allow herself to wonder how her child would survive a future as a stranger in a foreign country. Karin was strong and somehow she would manage. It was she, Ella, who must take care to keep her spirits up and make sure no one took advantage of her.

So, she focused on the many tasks she needed to complete to continue her journey into another life. There was endless paperwork to be filled out and scores of appointments to keep with doctors and investigators determined to scrutinize every aspect of her life. Even with her mother's sponsorship and the backing of the professor her mother had married, getting through the maze of bureaucrats was an all-consuming task. Sometimes she swore that they all had only one goal in life and that was to trip her up and keep her from getting approval to immigrate. It was her job to be smarter than any of them—and she was smarter.

In the meantime, dinners with Emil were, if not exactly stimulating, at least not unpleasant. She knew that he secretly hoped she would not get approval to leave. If that happened, she might need to reconsider his offer one more time. Until that happened, if it ever did, Ella was determined to keep her own counsel and take only those steps that had to be taken.

Chapter 10

"I don't like it in here", said Karin, twisting her hand and trying to disengage it from the death grip Ella had on her wrist. For her part, Ella couldn't believe her daughter was making such a scene. Karin was usually so reserved, polite and proper. This behavior was out of character for the child. Didn't she know how hard it was on Ella whose nerves were strung too tightly already and about to snap? Karin was supposed to be the bedrock Ella could lean on for support during stressful times like this. Instead, her daughter was being irrational and, if she didn't stop her irritating behavior immediately, they might both be dismissed by the doctor who was watching them with curiosity through steel-rimmed glasses.

Earlier this morning Emil had driven them to a complex of barracks set up to finish processing the thousands of people who had petitioned to immigrate to the United States. There had already been months of filling out questionnaires, providing documentation of various kinds, submitting character references provided by anyone who would vouch for her legitimacy-including those who were paid for their effort—and numerous health assessments by scores of doctors.

Emil looked utterly dejected as he pulled up to the curb to let them out. In spite of that, Ella could not hide her elation as she jumped out of the car and nearly collided with Karin getting out of the back seat. This was the last hurdle. One last interview, with an American doctor, and a few more questions before they got their stamp of approval to book the next cruise ship leaving for America. They had passed all the tests leading up to this important moment and Ella could almost taste success.

That is, until Karin chose this, of all times, to act out. Ella had no idea what had gotten into the child except that she hung back when it was their turn to enter the examination room with its white, antiseptic walls and rows of gleaming silver steel instruments.

"I don't want to go in there!" whispered Karin in a desperate voice between gritted teeth. Twisting ever more desperately to get free of Ella's grip, the girl spun around with her arm choking her own neck at an odd angle. Ella didn't know what to do. She was past being embarrassed and was now trying to think of a way to slap Karin into submission and get her into the examination room. If the girl would only stand still enough for Ella to catch her eye, she could give her "the look." It might already be too late. The doctor had gotten up and was walking toward them. Two nurses heard the commotion and entered the room behind Ella's back. There was no way to get Karin straightened out and come in again for a new start.

The doctor, a tall young man with sandy blond hair and unusually white teeth, stopped short of Karin and bent down to look into her eyes. Slowly, he reached out and unfastened Ella's hand from the death-grip it had on the girl's twisted arm. His eyes never left Karin's face. The girl looked around and saw there was no escape through the door or the two small windows set high up on the far wall of the room. Resigned, she sighed and cast her eyes in the direction of the doctor's shoes.

"I so much excuse, please, you", managed Ella in near hysterical tones. She cursed herself for not studying English as much as she should have these last months! "She sorry."

Ella

In perfect German, the American doctor said, "It's all right Ma'am. Your girl is just scared. Isn't that right, little girl?" he continued, now looking directly at Karin. A curious look came over Karin's face but she made no effort to answer the doctor.

"Why don't we sit down over here while I go over your records and ask you a few simple questions." He led them in the direction of a table and chairs under the two windows. Silently, he pointed at them and indicated that they each should take a seat.

Ella, too angry with Karin and confused by this turn of events to know what to do, did as she was told.

The doctor, after checking his notes one last time, looked at Karin and, in a soft, gentle voice asked her slowly, in German, "What is your name?" The girl just stared at him. Clearing his throat, he said, "How old are you? Again, Karin made no effort to answer. A sharpness was visible around her eyes and her skin had drawn tight at the corners. Her eyes refused to focus. As the simple questions continued and Karin remained stubbornly uncooperative, Ella squirmed. Beads of sweat gathered in her armpits and between her breasts. In another moment, she felt the beads turn to rivulets and run down her sides and from her neck into the elastic of her bra. She had never felt so embarrassed, frightened and angry at the same time.

The questions that kept running through her mind was why her usually bright daughter could take this important moment to exert a stubborn streak that might well cost them the permission they needed to enter America. "I've sacrifice so much for this opportunity," she thought. "How can she spoil everything for us? How dare this little brat do this to me?"

The doctor laid down his tablet and pen and turned to the nurse with the words, "I guess that's all for this one".

Ella

Karin jumped from her perch on the examination table and turned brightly to her mother and said, "What kind of doctor is he when he can read my name on the chart and still doesn't know it? These people are either stupid or they're trying to insult us. Let's get out of here".

Ella nearly fainted. The stark, white walls of the examination room threatened to close in on her and, for a moment, darkness descended. The nurse, who had been standing near the door, reached out to Ella and steadied her.

Behind them, the doctor began to chuckle. Shaking his head, he said, "I guess I was wrong. The kid isn't retarded, just insulted. We can probably use someone with her spirit. Permission to enter the United States is granted." Signing the stack of forms he had retrieved, he turned his back toward the group still hovering near the door and picked up another stack of immigration applications.

Chapter 11

They were finally on board the *Italia*, a huge, luxury liner with more amenities than Ella ever imagined existed in the entire world. Right now, she needed as much distraction as this voyage would allow so she was relieved to note that the list included swimming pools, saunas, game rooms and much more. After all the stress of the past year and, especially the last several months, Ella could hardly wait to unwind. She was still upset with Karin because she had given her such a scare at the American doctor's office two weeks before. She hadn't been able to calm down much except when she let Emil buy her several glasses of wine with the dinners he insisted they share as a farewell. He was still hoping that she would change her mind about going or, at the very least, decide to come back after seeing that the country of her dreams was less than she imagined.

Looking over the railing and seeing the crowd milling about on the decks below, Ella finally felt good about her decision. This day, listening to a band playing on a lower deck, she resolutely faced her new beginning with gusto. The hard times were behind her, the good times ahead. No, Ella decided, she would never change her mind.

"Karin!" Ella called turning around and looking in the direction where she had last seen her daughter. Her voice had an edge. Trying to compose herself, Ella shouted again, "Karin, where are you!" The girl was nowhere in sight and Ella felt her cheeks flush with rage.

Ella

Karin was impossible lately. Disappearing into the milling throng was the last thing Ella expected from what used to be her thoughtful, gentle little girl. This new independence would have to be nipped in the bud and Ella resolved to apply more pressure to that end. After all, this was no time for the child to decide to leave her mother without companionship and support.

All the passengers were now on board and the last of their families and friends were being ushered toward gangplanks. It was almost time to shove off and Ella felt the swaying of the huge vessel beneath her feet as engines geared up to move it from the pier and take her into another world and another life.

She looked down at the dark, mesmerizing water and, lost in her thoughts, barely felt the jostling throng crowding the railing to wave a final farewell to loved ones on shore. Suddenly, the ship's horn roared behind her on the topmost deck and she jumped, nearly shoving the man who had taken a place close to hers onto the deck. Just in time, he grabbed the rail and twisted back around. Startled, Ella looked up to discover a handsome face with dark hair now disheveled from his near fall. He was at least a head taller than she and had an air of casual sophistication emphasized by his neatly tailored trousers and elegant jacket over a cashmere turtle neck sweater. When she began to stammer an apology, he smiled down at her while running his fingers through his hair.

"It's quite all right, I assure you. That noise can startle anyone who's not expecting it. Are you all right? You seem a bit shaken."

"I'm just fine, thank you. And, actually, I should have expected that blast. It's not the first time I've traveled on board a ship, you know," she lied. As soon as the words had left her mouth she regretted them. There was no good reason to pretend to be well traveled just because it was clear that he was much more experienced than she would ever be. As the silence lingered between them, his smile faded a little.

Ella

"Well, have a lovely trip. Perhaps we'll see each other again before it's over."

"Yes, I'd like that. I plan to do a lot of swimming. Maybe we can see each other at the pool".

"Actually, I don't care much for the pools on board. They're filled with salt water and I'd rather have a beach if I'm going to swim in that. Good-bye, then." At that, the young man turned and gracefully made his way through the crowd.

"Bye!" Ella called toward his retreating back hating the too interested tone in her voice. Turning back to the railing, she rehearsed over and over again the different possible conversations she might have had with the first interesting man she had seen in a long time.

Her musings were interrupted by another lurch as the ship pulled away from its berth and someone bumped against her side. For a moment she thought the man had come back to return the favor. Before she could feel the full measure of satisfaction, Ella recognized Karin. Frowning, she turned to the girl and was about to scold her for her carelessness when another blast from the horn interrupted her.

Unaware of her mother's mood, Karin threw her arms around Ella's waist and hugged her mother tightly. Ella looked down on the top of her daughter's head and, after the slightest hesitation, started stroking the shiny brown hair so much thicker than her own. After all, this was a turning point for both of them.

Chapter 12

The nightmare woke her just as her body was being flung against the wall. The ship was now in the full grip of a storm and there seemed little chance of it easing any time soon. Ella didn't know whether the nausea she felt was from being tossed around in bed or was a carry-over from her feelings in the dream.

She had dreamed that she was back in Werda during the long months when she had tried so desperately to recapture her husband's heart. She was at Karl's family brewery where the whole family gathered to celebrate Hans' birthday. There were at least 60 or 70 people, including countless children, scattered in bunches throughout the huge old building and the great room of the old farmhouse. It was a combination of living area, kitchen and sleeping nook where Elizabet, Karl's mother, and her husband preferred to sleep, reserving their bedroom upstairs for guests. In the middle of the room stood a long table around which many of the adults, including Karl, his brothers and his parents were gathered. Ella was sitting with them, between Karl and his brother Hans. Everyone was more than a little drunk, including herself, and the conversation had gotten louder and more animated with each round of bottles Elizabet had brought from her warehouse. Children could be heard running on wooden floors upstairs banging doors and shouting at each other. What struck Ella most was the feeling of life around her. She was nearly overcome with joy at the sensation of belonging to something so human and vibrant as this family. Karl's left hand rested possessively on her right thigh and—was it her imagination? Hans, sitting to her left, was stealing glances at her much more often than the conversation required. Martha, Hans' wife, sat across from her, the expression on her face unfathomable. She was looking from Hans to Ella and back again, all the while struggling to keep all traces of emotion off her face.

In her dream, it seemed to Ella that nothing could be better than the warm, sweaty air in this great room lit by kerosene lights and candles. The noise of voices and radio music was almost deafening while the clouds of cigarette smoke threatened to choke her any moment. She was in heaven.

Then, as if by magic, everything changed. The sounds and lights faded as though she had moved a great distance from the table and its occupants. She seemed disconnected somehow. Hans, Karl and Martha seemed to look through her instead of at her. No one could touch her or see her. No matter how hard she tried, Ella could not reach out to touch them. She had disappeared from their sight and sat, alone, in a world of her own.

Waking from this horrible reminder of what once had been—of what she had once been a part—left Ella shaken. She still felt the loss of Karl's family and the sense of security they had given. Even now, after all these months, the thought of them brought tears to her eyes.

She knew that there was no turning back any more. That thought, too, added tears to Ella's eyes. She felt the burden of all the things she could not change weigh down her body and crush her bones into the bunk mattress.

Remembering the dream made her sweat again and she wiped distractedly at her brow. Try as she might, the images would not leave until Ella clutched her blanket and forced her mind to go back to the time she was still trying to save her marriage. Karl had come home for the week-end as usual. This time instead of picking up his daughter to take her to his mother's house, he sat down in one of the overstuffed chairs Ella had recently bought and told her he wanted to talk to her. Obediently she had sat down across from him and listened while he told her that he would be filing for a divorce. When she burst into tears and, between sobs, begged him not to leave her, he only sighed and looked away. The humiliation of that last encounter made her weep as bitterly now as she had on that day.

She had clung to Karl's leg, wailing like a wounded animal, as he dragged her across the floor toward the door. She loved him and she hated him. Most of all she hated that she loved him, needed him, wanted him at any cost.

"I won't let you leave!" she had screamed at him.

"And just how do you think you're going to stop me? Let go of me or I swear I'm going to shut you up for good! I've had enough of your whining and nagging and twisting every god-damn thing into a major drama. I said, LET GO!"

Still lying on the floor on her stomach clutching his right leg, she turned her tear-streaked face upward to look into his furious one. In a final last jerk, Karl freed his leg from her clutches and stepped quickly closer to the door leading into the hall and freedom.

"At least tell me why we can't talk about this and figure out a way to fix it."

"Okay, Ella. Just one last time. Not that it'll do any good, but maybe you need to hear this again. It's not going to change anything between us, mind you, but you need to remember this. Get up off the floor and sit down.

"I can't move. Help me up, please."

Ella

Settling into the stuffed chair nearest the door, Karl said, "Get up yourself or, if you prefer, stay on the floor. It doesn't matter to me."

"Why are you being so cruel to me? I haven't done anything to you to deserve this."

"You asked me to explain again why I'm leaving. What did you not understand when I told you less than a week ago that if you make another public spectacle of yourself and humiliate me in front of my family and friends I will get the hell out of here?

"But I didn't try to humiliate you! It just hurt my feelings when you danced with that new teacher two times before you ever asked me to dance."

Ella pushed her hair behind her ears and pulled her knees to her chest. Still on the floor, she wrapped her arms around her legs and started rocking back and forth.

"That didn't entitle you to cut in and tell me that I've spent enough time with her and that it was time for me to dance with my wife."

"What's wrong with that?" Ella demanded. "Most men would be flattered if their wives cared enough about them to cut in".

"I don't know who you think you are, but the truth is that you are an embarrassment to me. You're not happy 'till you control every move I make and for that matter, everyone around you. If you can't be the center of attention every minute you just can't stand it. I thought I could ignore it and come home once in a while to be with you and Karin. But, you just won't let anything be good long enough to have a moment's peace. Well, I've had enough of it. When I return, it will only be to see Karin. "

"That won't be very often. You can't take that much time off from your whores!"

Karl smiled, got up from the chair and strode toward the door. With his hand on the doorknob he turned around and calmly said, "I'll come and get the rest of my things in the morning".

He closed the door behind him leaving Ella still rocking herself on the floor of the living room. She stopped wailing, too shocked and angry to make a sound.

The next months were a nightmare. Ella discovered that a divorce decree had been initiated without her knowledge over a year ago and had been processed and nearly finalized. All that was needed to dissolve her marriage was a judge's signature. That was easy enough to obtain and within three days of Karl getting the rest of his belongings from their apartment, he was a free man. If she had known he had already made his preparations so far in advance, she would never have let him back in the apartment to visit his daughter. Karin was the only hold she had left on him and the last thing she wanted was for him to enjoy her whenever he wanted.

After that, things had moved swiftly. Because Mia had been making arrangements over a year for their escape to Goslar and had already paid for their shelter with a family that was part of the underground escape route for East German people, the remaining wait was shorter than Ella anticipated. Only a few weeks after Karl moved out of their apartment, and before Karl's next scheduled visit, Ella and Karin found themselves on the train that would take them permanently away from what had always been home. Of course, none of it would have been possible without Hans' help from the very beginning. Her brother-in-law had listened to her plans without comment. He eventually brought her a document signed by the highest court authority giving them a twenty-four hour pass into West Germany.

Ella

Hans could have signed the pass himself, he had risen in the court system faster than anyone could have anticipated, but he must have felt it was wiser not to be connected to their escape. Because, of course, everyone knew they would never be seen again.

When the storm subsided, Ella continued to lie in the bunk. She took a long breath and snuggled deeper into the blankets. This was her time, a time of new beginnings, a time to leave behind the pains of the past. In an odd way, thinking of letting go of the feelings which had ruled her emotional world for years was unpleasant. After all, the pain—breathing through the pain, fighting the pain, holding on to the good beneath the pain—had kept her alive all these months. When everyone else let her down, only the pain remained. Without it, she wasn't sure who she would be.

Everyone betrayed her in some way or another. Oma had not protected her enough from Mia's outbursts and was almost eager to see her go even though she professed undying love and the wish to see her get a new start in life. Mia, her own mother, left her behind when she went to Dresden to work and again when she had sailed to America searching for adventure and a new life. Of course she was sending for her now—but that was after the fact, wasn't it? Then her beloved Karl had betrayed her and left her, and then even tried to blame her for their failed marriage—as if the whole thing had been her fault.

Worst of all, after all her suffering and hard work to build them a new future, Karin had nearly managed to get them rejected by American Immigration Authorities. It was unbearable to imagine what might have happened if Karin had been successful. She would have had to crawl back to Goslar and marry a man who bored her to tears. As always before, she would have to pay the price for someone else's selfishness.

Chapter 13

K arin was thrilled when her father came to pick her up on Sunday afternoon. He said he wanted to see her before taking the train to Gorlitz where he taught in the local high school and from where he made occasional truck runs into Russia with local produce in exchange for building supplies. He didn't like having to deal with a former enemy but life was what it was and sometimes choices were limited. So, he made the best of it and, when he was there, stayed with a nice family that had a son close to his own age and a daughter several years their junior. Thrown into the bargain was the fact that she was pretty and more than willing to entertain her brother's handsome friend in exchange for a bit of coffee or even a pair of nylons now and then.

Although neither of them knew it at the time, the day he spent with Karin after that final scene with her mother was to be their last together. It was a glorious day filled with bright colors and warm sunshine. They walked along the river bank, near their family garden plot and on to the meadow where other children were playing. They heard familiar sounds as they walked hand in hand—shouts from children playing and an occasional command from a parent warning a child to stay close. Hundreds of birds twittered in branches above their heads and all across the little valley. In the distance a train's whistle heralded its approach to their small town. "Do you want to run with your friends, Liebchen?", he'd asked.

Ella

Karin clung tighter to his hand. "No, Papa, I want to stay with you."

Karl took Karin's hand in both of his own. He led her to a bench on a slight rise overlooking the field where he had touched down his plane the night he visited a school dance where he met Ella.

Everything had changed since then. His country lost the war. He lost his career and youth—and now he was losing his family.

As he looked down at his little girl she raised her eyes and smiled the brilliant smile that always touched his heart. This time Karin's smile broke his heart.

"Sweetheart" he said. "You know I'll always be your daddy and I'll always love you".

"Of course".

"And even though things might change, promise me you'll always remember that".

A little concerned at the tone in his voice, Karin looked at her father and answered, "I'll remember."

Chapter 14

It was a fabulous voyage. Dancing nearly every night, endless entertainments during the day, food that the people at home could not even imagine and more attention from handsome young men than even Ella could dream of.

There was only one misfortune the entire trip. A storm, brewed to the north, overtook them in the middle of the Atlantic. Waves higher than any in recorded history towered above them only to crash mercilessly onto decks strung with ropes for handholds. None of the passengers were allowed to leave the safety of the inner ship and most were confined to their cabins, too seasick to wander far from their bunks.

The only moment of real panic Ella had the entire time was when Karin opened one of the doors leading to the deck outside the gameroom. A massive gust of wind burst into the room and sucked the little girl outside in a matter of seconds. Ella, paralyzed by fear, could see her hanging onto one of the rails while wave after wave washed over her and dragged her feet and legs into the unending swells. Luckily, a young sailor pulled himself, hand over hand, along the ropes crisscrossing the deck toward Karin. When he reached her, they both hung horizontally like clothes strung on a windblown line as the sailor inched them toward shelter one handgrip at a time. The cheer that went up from the other passengers when they reached the gameroom nearly split her eardrums!

Ella stayed with Karin for quite a while after that incident—until she was sure Karin was unhurt and had stopped crying. She helped her daughter change into dry cloths and patted her head gently, hardly giving a thought to how late she would be when she joined her new friends at one of the ship's café's.

The day they sailed by the Statue of Liberty was a cloudy one making visibility difficult. Nevertheless, Ella and Karin stood by the railing of the topmost deck and watched the green lady with upraised arm and torch glide slowly by.

Ella didn't know how she and Karin made it to the train station and then onto the right platform for their train to Grand Forks, North Dakota. She remembered a uniformed man talking to Karin and gesturing in the direction her daughter dragged her long before Ella was ready to give up her seat on the suitcase that had become her refuge from the surging throng. "Mommy, hurry!" the little girl shouted again and again. She was about to collapse from exhaustion when Karin pulled and then shoved her the last few steps toward the nearly departing train. They ran through steam billowing from massive engines and shoved their suitcase up the steps just before the last whistle. Someone gave her a push from behind and helped Karin up behind her right before the door closed and they were committed to the last leg of their journey.

As the train picked up speed, they stumbled several car lengths before finally finding an empty compartment. There, Ella could stretch out her tired legs. Karin made herself comfortable across the seats opposite hers. She was hungry but food would have to wait. Exhaustion drained her body of its last bit of strength before she closed her eyes and let the rhythm of the train lull her into slumber.

A day and a half later, Ella and Karin, rumpled and stiff from hours of sitting on hard seats, pulled to a stop in front of a sign that

Ella

said "Grand Forks."

"Ella! Ella!" came the shrill sound of her mother's voice. Excitement raised Mia's voice by several octaves. Time had not diminished her talent for projection and the combination threatened to break the eardrums of anyone unfortunate enough to be near her. The gentleman standing next to her never flinched, however, not even when she took her handbag and waved it frantically from side to side nearly hitting him. The purse, a formidable weapon in Mia's hands, was finally flung at the man's chest as she surged forward through the crowd toward her daughter and Karin.

"You're finally here. Really here. I almost can't believe it. My babies are here, Professor!"

The professor was looking directly at Ella and then Karin. His eyes moved from one and then to the other. First Ella, from head to swollen ankles. Then Karin, from green eyes that revealed nothing, to shoes that had become too tight nearly two years earlier. His eyes missed nothing and gave nothing away.

"Let's all go home and have something to eat. I fried chicken and peeled potatoes. All we have to do is boil them and cook some corn. You must be starving!" Mia shouted.

Ella looked down at Karin and put her arm protectively around her daughter's shoulders. The two stood immobile, like a statue cast in flesh, before walking in the direction Joseph and Maria had taken. Arm in arm they followed the older couple toward a parking lot. Neither of them had ever seen more than a handful of cars at a time and the sight of so many automobiles was nearly overwhelming. Karin looked up at her mother to make sure that she was not overcome by the sight. Ella seemed composed as she followed in the footsteps of her mother and new stepfather. Her eyes were fastened on his back as he strode purposefully toward a green Chrysler parked on the far side of the lot they were crossing. She noted how easily he carried their heavy suitcase, packed as it was with what remained of their lives.

As Mia and Ella chattered away on the ride from the train station, Karin tried to relax into the hard plastic cover fitted over the bench that was the back seat. She closed her eyes and thought once again of Oma and the last time she saw her.

Karin had been only 8 years old—now she was 9 and a half—when Oma woke her late one night and told her to get dressed. Tearfully, sitting with Oma in one of their overstuffed chairs, her Great Grandmother had told her that she and her mother were going to America. Karin had asked who was going with them. As she softly said the names, one after the other, of all the people she loved, starting with Oma herself, each shake of the old woman's head plunged Karin deeper into despair. It was true then, only Ella and Karin would be going. Later, Oma's white handkerchief waved dimly in the dead of night, getting smaller and smaller, as the train sped away from home. Karin glanced at the only companion she had left in life. Ella sat next to her, her beautiful profile etched darkly in the dim reflection of the compartment's night light. Like a premonition of the future, Karin's mother looked remote and the child knew she was now utterly alone.

Nevertheless, a great adventure was starting. They were going to America. What a splendid vision that name evoked! A place so grand that when Radio Free Europe mentioned it, everyone was in a panic to change the dial for fear of going to prison. It was a crime to be caught listening to descriptions of a life more beautiful than most could imagine. Karin was going there to live forever. A place where people were never hungry.

Before they could leave the shores of Europe and sail half way across the world, they would have to stay in hiding for at least a year in the Harz mountains of West Germany. There they would take examinations and get training enabling them to seek asylum in their new home. A lot of preparations had to be made and they not only had to be sound of body and mind but had to have a sponsor who would take responsibility for them physically and financially. Omi had taken care of that and she and the Professor would be taking them in. Ella had explained it all to her but it was still confusing.

The Harz mountains were beautiful and they had a year to wait in hiding before exit visas would be given. A year in hiding, hoping no word of their whereabouts would reach the authorities at home – those who would gladly see their return and inevitable imprisonment. Already, Karin's uncle, an increasingly prominent attorney in Berlin had been found dead in his office. Escape by members of well-known families could not be tolerated. Karin did not think about him or his four children very much. She loved them too much and had already learned that some pain is unbearable. Karin wished her mother would not cry so much. She also wished she were not so lonely.

Her father had been fond of telling her, "Head up, shoulders back and a smile on your face. That's right. You never know where or when the next marvelous surprise will find you." It was hard to smile and trust the future while sitting in this strange car in a strange land with people and a language so different from anything she had ever known. Loneliness threatened to overwhelm her as she lowered her gaze to her lap and, blinking, saw a tear fall onto the fabric of her skirt. As the wet spot spread to a dime-size stain, Karin looked up and into the rear-view mirror. The professor's blue eyes stared back at her. For a moment, panic gripped her heart and her mother's and grandmother's voices withdrew into the distance. When his eyes finally turned back to the road, Karin glanced at her mother, now smiling, and then out the window where houses with manicured lawns were speeding by. Desperately, she tried to remember her father's exact words when he told her he would always love her and exactly how he looked that last day she saw him so long ago.

Breathing deeply, she recalled how Oma's arms felt wrapped

Ella

around her shoulders. She remembered how Oma's love always made everything unloving feel far away. All of their lives had started with her...Johanna. Her deep-set eyes and courage to live beyond hope had made their family possible. Courage, inherited by her daughters and passed from one generation to the next, ensured survival. Slowly, the memories warmed the spot in Karin's stomach that the professor had frozen.

CPSIA information can be obtained
at www.ICGtesting.com
Printed in the USA
LVOW01s0856050216

473815LV00001B/5/P